*For Sophie
Thanks for bullying me into mafia.
Your full-on STANDALONE mafia book is coming ...
soon ... ish.
But seriously, thank you for all that you do.
You're the best*

Pucking Hate That I've Always Loved You

DL GALLIE

I vowed never to give in to my feelings for my sister's ex.
But now Miller Wentworth is back, and everything I've tried to
bury starts rising to the surface.
It doesn't matter how good he looks, how kind he is, or how
easily he connects with my son.
We can't happen—not with the secret I'm hiding.
But the closer they get, the harder it is to keep my distance.
I've always pucking loved him.
But if the past catches up to us, it could all fall apart before it
even begins.
I'm so pucking screwed.

1

EVIE

SITTING in the stands next to Mom, Dad, and Selene, they all cheer as the high school hockey team takes to the ice. Dad seems really interested in tonight's game, and my gut is telling me this game before the playoffs is going to be a big earner for him and his dealings.

For those wondering, my dad is a mafia boss but not just any mob boss, he's one of the Chicago Five. There are five families who preside and have control over the city: the Salvatores—us—the Gottis, the O'Brians, the Zilenskies, and last but not least, the Van der Kündts. Each of the families operate within a defined territory and each has its own hierarchical structure. The Salvatores are the least mafia-like of the five, but do not mess with my dad. Daniel Salvatore may look like a teddy bear, and he is when it comes to Sel, Mom, and me, but you mess with his family or daughters and he will end you before you take your next breath. As they say in the movies "you'll be sleeping with the fishes."

I'm home for my baby sister's eighteenth birthday this

weekend, and we're at the game tonight as a *family* because Selene's boyfriend, Miller Wentworth, is on the team. Like always, my eyes gravitate toward *him*. He's one of the star players on the team and rumor has it, he and Jameson "JJ" James are going to make it to the NHL one day. I don't know shit about hockey but I will admit, I love it when the players go down and get hurt. Not in a sadistic, I'm a psycho kind of way; but in an assessing, how can I help them kind of way. I'm currently at USC studying to be an orthopedic surgeon. In a few years, I will officially be Dr. Evie Salvatore, qualified orthopedic surgeon with a focus on sports-related injuries. It would be a dream to work with a professional sports team. I don't care if it's hockey, basketball, or baseball, I just want to be able to do what I love, fixing broken bones and ligaments.

My eyes focus back on Miller and my heart skips a beat. I know it's wrong to be ogling an eighteen-year-old boy, especially since he and my sister are dating, but that man is F I N E, fine. He can keep his skates under my bed, well, if he wasn't with my sister he could.

Speaking of Selene, something is up with her. I know I haven't been around much with school and whatnot, but she seems different. On edge, as if she's harboring a massive secret. You'd think with this weekend being all about her she'd be smiling and soaking up the attention, but if anything, she's closing in on herself.

Mom and Dad are throwing her a massive party, just like they did for me when I turned eighteen. The Selene I remember would be making it all about her, but the Selene sitting next to me doesn't seem excited at all. I make a mental note to check in on her more but, for now, I will hang with my family and drool over the boy I've secretly always loved.

It's not just the fact he's dating Selene that means he

and I can never be, it's the fact I'm seven years older than him. Seven years might not seem like much, but when he's a senior in high school and you're almost finished with college, that's just plain wrong. Do I like to read about age gaps in books? Hell fucking yes I do, but this is real life. Age gaps are frowned upon, especially when the woman is older. I'd be referred to as a cougar and I don't want that. I still remember the first time I saw him, a few months ago, when I came home for Daddy's fiftieth birthday ...

...Walking downstairs I make a beeline for the kitchen. This girl needs coffee and she needs coffee stat. My first cup of the day is always my favorite. Stepping into the kitchen, I smile when I see Martha preparing breakfast. "Martha," I singsong to our long-time maid.

"Evie girl, how are you?"

When I'm in reaching distance, she pulls me in for a hug and I wrap my arms around her. She may be the help but she's also family. "I missed your hugs," I tell her.

"I've missed your smiling face around here. The place just isn't the same without you here."

"Lies, you tell lies."

She turns away from me and grabs my mug and fills it up with my "bitch juice," as Selene likes to call it. Handing me my cup, she bops my nose and goes back to preparing breakfast.

"Everyone is outside since it's a sunny day. Can you let your father know it'll be about ten minutes?"

"Roger that." I salute her, before I swipe a chocolate croissant off the plate and quickly jump out of the way, avoiding a hand slap. She makes these especially for Selene, that girl would live on these if she could, so I have to get one now while I can.

She shakes her head and smiles sheepishly. "Don't let your sister see you took the first one."

"Sister schmister," I throw back at her. Blowing her a kiss, I take another bite of my chocolate croissant, moaning at the buttery flaky goodness mixed with chocolate, and head out to the patio to meet the family for breakfast.

Dad is on the phone, pacing back and forth. When he sees me, he smiles but then he gets back to his call. Looking around, it looks like no one else is out here so I head over to the loungers by the pool and drop down onto the chaise. Splashing in the pool garners my attention and when I turn my head, my eyes widen. My mouth pops open and I swear drool drips down my chin as I unabashedly stare at the Adonis emerging before me. Water sluices down a toned and tanned muscular body—hello, 'V' muscles, leading to what looks like an impressive dick hidden behind swim trunks. My eyes roam back up his stunning physique before they land on the face of an angel. An angel sent from heaven to tempt a woman like me. He runs his hands through his dirty-blond hair before shaking his head from side to side.

When he notices me staring—ogling—him, he grins at me. His smile is electric and that little smirk has my body coming alive in a way like never before. "Hey," he offers by way of greeting.

"Hhhhhey," I manage to stammer but before I can make more of a fool of myself, my sister joins us. She's wearing a skimpy bikini and from the look on Dad's face, he isn't impressed with her attire.

"Morning, boyfriend," she coos at the god before me, slipping her arm around his waist and snuggling into him.

"Morning, girlfriend," he replies with hearts in his eyes. She gazes up at him with a megawatt smile on her face, and that's when I register what each of them said. Boyfriend. Girlfriend.

Oh my God, I was just checking out my sister's boyfriend. My heart deflates for a brief moment but then I realize, he's very much younger than me, and taken.

Why are the hot ones always younger? Or taken?

My moment of wallowing is broken when Daddy bellows at Selene over her bikini choice.

... The sounds of the stadium erupting around me snaps me back to the present. When I look back to the ice, I realize Miller just scored and the first period is nearly over. *Shit*, I was daydreaming of Miller for a lot longer than I realized.

His eyes lift to the crowd and they find me, well, Selene, but I pretend the kiss he just blew is for me. If he was mine, I'd blow a kiss back and do that cheesy heart-shape thing with my fingers. Then after the game, I'd fuck him in the locker room because everyone deserves a locker room romp after scoring the first goal of the game.

Thankfully, people can't read minds because I would be hauled off to jail for the inappropriate thoughts I have in relation to that man. They can set my cell up next to my father's, a two-for-one Salvatore family deal. Me for inappropriate thoughts of a younger guy and him for his latest illegal deal.

Secretly I was hoping all these months later my feelings for him would dissipate, but like the first time I saw him, I'm still smitten. And like the first time I saw him, I will shove those feelings aside because I will not do that to my sister. Miller is hers, not mine.

2
MILLER

THIS WEEKEND HAS BEEN AMAZING. Last night we won our game, meaning we head to Scottsdale for the final varsity game of high school next week. To top that off, we're going in as the favorites to win. A win in my last year would be phenomenal. And tonight, we celebrate my gorgeous girlfriend Selene's eighteenth birthday.

I'm heading over to her place early to spend a little time with her before all her friends and family arrive. I'm also hoping we can get a quickie in. It's been too long since I've been balls deep inside of her.

Ringing the doorbell, I'm greeted by her mom, Sophie. "Mrs. Salvatore, you look beautiful."

"Save the charm for my daughter," she tells me, but I notice her cheeks darken a little. For an old chick, she's kinda hot.

"Do you know where I can find her?"

"She's in the library," Martha says, joining Sophie and me in the foyer. Her arms are full of decorations but she has a frazzled look on her face.

"When you get a moment, Mrs. Salvatore, can I run something by you?" Martha asks her boss.

"Sure," Sophie answers, smiling brightly at the maid who is more family than employee.

Without saying another word to me, the two women head off in the direction of the backyard, where a tent has been erected. No doubt, it will be in the midst of being transformed into something magical and totally OTT for Sel. Daniel and Sophie Salvatore never hold back when it comes to their daughters, but what would you expect from one of *the* families who reign over Chicago. It's so surreal that my girlfriend is the daughter of a mob boss, but after the warning he gave me when Sel and I became serious, I knew I was going to treat her like a princess.

"You hurt my baby girl and I will wipe you and your family from the history books. There will be no mention of the Wentworths, and anyone who dares utter your name, will follow suit. My daughters mean the world to me. They hurt, I hurt, and then you hurt."

"Sing out if you need anything," I offer but secretly I hope they don't because I want time with my girl. Thankfully, I'm not sure they even heard me.

Turning down the hallway on the left, I head toward the library. I should have guessed she'd be in there. If Selene isn't in the pool or her room, she's in the library. It's her favorite room in the house, and I'm sure it's because of the rolling ladder. Yep, she's obsessed with the rolling ladder. She tells me it's because of *Beauty and the Beast*. That's her favorite Disney tale. I cannot tell you how many times she's made me watch the movie, but it always put her in a good mood and then I benefited from her good mood.

Reaching the library, I hear hushed voices and when I peek into the large room, I find Selene is with Klaus Van der Kündt. That old fucker lives up to his last name, he really is a cunt. I refer to him as Van der Cunt and that always earns myself a smack in the stomach from Sel. According to her, that old fuck can do no wrong. He's always touching people, especially Selene, but whenever I bring it up with her, she just laughs at me and brushes it off. One time she even accused me of being jealous of the creepy old man. To an extent I am, because no one touches what's mine, but there's something about him that rubs me the wrong way.

The two of them seem to be in a heated discussion. Selene looks like she's on the verge of tears but at the same time, she looks ready to tear his throat out. My thoughts of them having a fight are confirmed when Selene slaps him across the face. The sound of her hand colliding with his cheek echoes around the room. As someone who has been on the receiving end of one of her slaps, I feel bad for the asshole. That is until he roughly grips her upper arms and pulls her into him. I see red at him manhandling her like that and that's when I step into the room. "Get your fucking hands off of her," I growl. Both of their heads snap toward me, but he doesn't let go. "Let. Her. Go," I snarl again, stepping farther into the room.

My blood is boiling as I march over to them but before I get halfway across the room, Selene pulls free of Van der Cunt and walks over to me. "Hey, baby," she sweetly purrs, as if I didn't just walk in on the two of them arguing.

"Don't 'hey, baby' me, what's going on? Are you okay? Van der Cunt had his hands on you."

"I'm fine, it was nothing," she protests, as he growls.

"It's Van der Kündt." He places emphasis on the ü sounding like oo, but the cUnt, can fuck off. I'll call him whatever I want.

Before I can tell her off for lying to me, she presses her lips to mine and passionately kisses me. Her tongue pushes into my mouth and she grinds her lithe body up against mine. My cock hardens between us as she continues to assault my tongue and press herself into me.

Van der Cunt growls from behind her. Opening my eyes, they gravitate toward him and he looks pissed. Selene doesn't seem to care he's here, she just continues to kiss and maul me. Wrapping her arms around my neck, she presses herself tighter against me. Being a man, I slide my hand around her back and up into her hair, gripping the strands tightly as I kiss her back. She breaks the kiss first and I miss her lips on mine. She glances over her shoulder and I swear she deflates when she realizes we're alone now. Before I can ask her what was going on when I walked in, she takes my hand in hers and drags me up to her bedroom.

The door slams shut behind us. She marches over to the bed, pushes me down onto the mattress, and straddles my thighs. "As much as I love where this is going, are you sure you're okay?"

"I'm fine," she snaps. She reaches for my belt and makes quick work of undoing it. She flips open my button, lowers the zipper, and frees my dick. She wraps her hand around it and squeezes. All thoughts of what I walked in on evaporate as she continues to pump my dick in her palm. Leaning down, she swirls her tongue over the tip before opening her lips and sucking me deep into her mouth.

The door to her bathroom slides open but Selene doesn't notice, she's focused on my dick and giving me the best blow job. She continues to suck me as I stare at her sister, Evie, in the Jack-and-Jill bathroom doorway. Her eyes dart from what Sel is doing and up to my face. When she notices me watching her, her eyes widen but she doesn't move ... or look away.

Selene cups my balls and presses on that magical spot that instantly has me coming down her throat. Grunting through my release, my eyes dart back to the bathroom doorway, but I find the space now empty. I'm upset she's no longer there and that thought confuses me.

Selene sits up and wipes at the corner of her mouth, smiling up at me. "What was that for?" She shrugs and reaches for her dress, inching the silky material up her thighs. "Sel, what are you doing?" Again, she shrugs and when her dress is bunched around her waist, I notice she isn't wearing any panties. "Where are your panties?"

"I seem to have lost them," she purrs. Slipping her hand between her thighs, she runs her fingertip along the lips of her slit. "I'm so wet," she whispers, as she continues to slide her finger up and down her weeping pussy. I may have just come down her throat, but my dick begins to harden once again at the erotic sight before me.

Gripping her hips, I flip her onto her back, causing her to squeal at the sudden movement. Situating myself between her thighs, I quickly pull my dick out and give it a stroke. My gaze flicks to the bathroom door again but it's still empty of her sister, and I find myself upset that she's not watching us anymore.

"Please," Selene begs when I take too long to thrust into her but I have to admit, I love it when she begs for my cock.

"Who am I to deny the birthday girl?"

Selene smiles at me and waggles her eyebrows. Gripping my dick, I lean forward and line it up with her pussy, ready to push in, when from the hallway her dad calls out, "Selene, sweetheart, your guests are starting to arrive."

"Shit," I hiss. Lifting myself up, I jump off Selene and the bed and I dive into the bathroom, sliding the door closed. Leaning against it, I close my eyes and breathe deeply. Getting caught fucking the birthday girl is not how I want tonight to start ... or for my life to end, but death while having sex, not a bad way to go out if you ask me.

Opening my eyes, I glance up and over into Selene's

sister's bedroom. She has her back to me and she's in nothing but a bra. One leg is raised on the edge of her bed, giving me an unobstructed view of her toned and taut ass. And her back is fucking sexy. *Who knew a back could be so sexy?*

As if sensing me, she looks over her shoulder. When she notices me staring back at her, her body stiffens and she gasps in shock, just as a bright pink vibrator falls to the floor. Now it's my turn for my eyes to widen. She spins around and quickly slides the door closed, giving me a brief glimpse of a bare pussy.

A knock from Selene's side has me jumping in my skin. "Just a sec," I call out. Putting my dick away, I take a deep breath and when I open the door, Selene is standing there with her dad. "Mr. S," I offer in greeting, but the man is scowling at me.

"What have I told the two of you about keeping the door closed?"

"The wind blew it shut," Selene answers.

"Mmmhmpf," he replies, not believing his daughter. "Let's head down and greet your guests."

"Let's," Selene excitedly replies. Taking my hand in hers, we exit her bedroom and when we step into the hallway, Evie is coming out of her bedroom.

"Holy shit," Sel exclaims, "you look fucking hot, Eves."

"Language," her dad growls from behind us. "But your sister is right, you look lovely, Princess." And I have to agree, Evie Salvatore is gorgeous and she looks fucking stunning tonight. She looked amazing moments ago but now in her black halter dress, which showcases her tits and legs, she's a walking wet dream.

Internally, I berate myself for thinking of my girlfriend's older sister like that, but me appreciating her sister is nothing compared to what happens later.

3
EVIE

MY MIND HAS BEEN a complete mess since the party started, well, actually, it was before that. What possessed me to do *that* with the bathroom door open, I will never know. For some messed up reason, seeing my sister and Miller in the throes of passion caused my insides to stir and another body part to tingle. It was wrong, so so wrong. I'm sick for getting aroused at seeing my sister blow her boyfriend but when he turned his attention to me, it was mesmerizing. Like a car accident, I couldn't look away. It was the hottest thing I've ever been a part of but when I think of the betrayal to my sister, I'm disgusted with myself. Then there's Miller, how could he do that to Selene?

Thankfully, I have a party to keep me and my dirty mind occupied, but fate is a bitch and throughout the evening, I notice Miller everywhere. And every time I see him, I'm reminded of what I saw in my sister's room.

And what he caught me doing just after.

And how much of a shitty sister I am, but one thing I have noticed, something is off with my sister.

You'd think after getting your rocks off like she did earlier, she'd be on cloud nine, but she seems aloof and distant. I noticed her demeanor sour as soon as Dani Van der Kündt arrived on the arm of her husband, glowing since she's pregnant, again. This will be daughter number four for them. Apparently, Mr. Van der Kündt is going to keep knocking her up until he gets a male heir. Wonder if I should inform him that according to studies—not that any of them have been factually proved—if you're stressed when conceiving, you're more likely to have a girl. They clearly need to relax but, then again, if I was married to Mr. Van der Kündt, I'd be stressed too. He's an egotistical sexist pig who needs to get with the twenty-first century and start treating women with respect. I get he's from the "women should be seen and not heard" generation but times have changed grandpa. How Dad is friends with him I will never know. I have a feeling it's one of those "keep your enemies close" types of friendship.

"I never would have picked you for a pink dildo kind of girl," a deep voice murmurs from beside me.

"And I never would have picked you to be a cheating asshat, but here we are," I throw back at him.

"How did I cheat?"

"You were looking at me while my sister was blowing you."

"And you were looking at me while your sister was blowing me."

"So?" I snap, anger building in my veins at the audacity of this man, no, boy. 'Cause that's what he is, an eighteen-year-old-Adonis boy.

"Admit it, Eves, you were wishing it was your lips wrapped around my dick. Then when you were in your bedroom with your vibrating pink friend, you were wishing it was my cock sliding in and out of your cun—"

Interrupting him, I slap him across the cheek. "You fucking prick," I whisper-hiss. Looking around, I'm thankful no one is witnessing this. If this got back to my sister, she'd be devastated.

"I knew you'd be a firecracker. I bet you're wild in the sack."

Raising my arm, I go to slap him again but he grips my wrist in his hand and pushes me up against the wall. His groin presses into me and, for a brief moment, I lose myself and push my hips into his semi-hard length but then reality slams back into me and I sneer, "Get the fuck off me."

He leans into me, his heated breath skating over my neck, and as much as this is nice, I can't do that to my sister … or any other female, I'm not a cheatee.

With all my might, I finally shove him away. Glaring at him, I step in close to him. Our noses are millimeters apart. "You may be hot with your scruff and washboard abs but you're dating my sister, show her, and me, some respect."

"Respect needs to be earned," he throws back at me. Taking a slight step back, I miss the closeness but from this angle and light, I can see flecks of gold in his eyes. "And from where I was just pressed up against you, you want me, little girl."

"Please," I scoff, "I'm no little girl, little boy. I'm also seven years older than you."

"Age is just a number," he arrogantly throws back at me.

"And Hell is just a sauna." Pushing him in the chest, I clench my teeth, and my fists. "Do better by my sister, Miller, or there'll be hell to pay."

Before he can reply, I step around him and with my head held high, and my panties soaked, I stalk away from him. Snagging a bottle of tequila from the bar, I head out of the tent and make my way inside the house.

Storming up to my room, I slam the door behind me and

flip the lock, before I do the same to the door to the joined bathroom. Sliding down the wall, I bring the bottle to my lips and drink, wincing at the burn, but I deserve it. After what I almost did earlier to thoughts of my sister's boyfriend and my altercation with him just now, it has me sick to the pit of my stomach. I'm the worst person to have ever lived. How will I ever look my sister in the eye again?

4

MILLER

EVER SINCE SELENE'S BIRTHDAY, things have been off with us, but at the same time, I haven't ever been laid this much. I'm guessing her sister didn't say anything to her about my bonehead moments because she's not punishing me. But then again, I *technically* didn't do anything wrong. Sure, I thought it was hot getting a blow job while staring her sister in the face. And fuck yes, it was hot catching her pleasing herself with her pink vibrator. And yes, I was a jerk confronting her at the party but I didn't do anything physically.

Even though Sel has been riding my cock at every chance, I'm still a horny fucker. My palm and I have become well acquainted in the last few weeks. What shocks me is, it's thoughts of Evie I whack off to, not Selene. What's with that?

"Are you fucking listening to me?" Selene snaps. We're at the mall looking for a prom dress. I don't know why I have to be here for this, isn't this one of those mother/daughter bonding things?

"I am, yes, and I still think the first one. You reminded me of a princess in that one."

"I don't want to look like a princess, I want to look like a vixen."

Pulling her into my arms, I gaze into her chocolate orbs. *I never realized how similar Evie's are to hers.* What the fuck, Miller? "Babe, you're a vixen in anything you wear but, to be honest, I just want to see what you have on underneath your dress." I waggle my eyebrows at her and it diffuses the situation immediately, sexual innuendo for the win.

"Why? So you can tear it off with your teeth?"

"You know me too well. What do you say we head over to the lingerie section and I can help you with that? I think that's a far better use of my time, and then you can go dress shopping with your mom and surprise me."

"You just wanna get me naked."

"Can you blame me?"

"Well, no, I can't, have you seen me?" she confidently replies, and that's one of the things I love most about Sel, her confidence.

"Let's go." Lacing her fingers with mine, I drag her through the dress section and over to the lingerie department. Flicking through the racks, I pull out a hot pink number and hand it to her. "Really, pink?"

"I think you'll look fucking hot in it … as will I with it between my teeth as I tear it off you."

Grabbing my hand, she drags me into a changing room, giggling. She pulls the curtain closed and pushes me down onto the chair in the corner. Leaning down, she presses her lips to mine quickly and then steps backward. She seductively begins to sway her hips side to side. One by one she pops open the buttons on her blouse. Wriggling her shoulders, she lets the material fall down her arms and flutter to the carpet below. Reaching behind her back, she unclasps her bra and just as she's about to bare her tits to me, the curtain flies open and the attendant is scowling at us.

"You, out," she commands, pointing at me.

Reluctantly, I stand up. With my eyes on the chick, I readjust my dick, blow a kiss to Sel, and exit the dressing room. Smirking to myself, I walk out of the lingerie department and head over to the sports department. Sel will know where to find me. Whenever I end up here with her and disappear, this is where I always go.

I'm flicking through the jerseys to see if they have any new ones when my phone pings with a text, opening the message, I smirk when I see it's from Sel.

Clicking on the message, a picture appears on my screen and I have to stifle a moan at what I see. Selene is in the hot pink number I picked and she's staring seductively at the camera. My dick once again hardens as I type out my reply.

MILLER

> You better get that and I want you to wear it out of here. I'm going to fuck you in the parking lot before I drop you home.

No sooner do I hit send and her reply comes in.

SEL

> You're going to have to wait, I'm so turned on, I need to relieve the pressure

Another message comes in and it's a picture of her sitting in the chair I was in, her pink panties have been pushed to the side and her finger is deep inside her pussy. Pocketing my phone, I race back to the lingerie department but I'm stopped by the department manager with a stern,

"Please leave or I will call security and have you escorted off the premises and banned."

Reluctantly, I exit the store and make my way to my car. I shoot off a text to Selene, letting her know what happened.

MILLER

I just got kicked out, my dick and I will be waiting for you in the back seat of my car

SEL

Sucks to be you, I just had the most amazing orgasm

I'll be there after I find my prom dress

"What the fuck?" I hiss.

MILLER

You better be joking

SEL

I never joke about shopping ... toodles.

MILLER

Get your fucking ass out here now, Sel, or I'm leaving

SEL

Fine, leave. See you at school tomorrow.

"What the fuck?" I sneer. Slapping the steering wheel, I know Sel, she means it. That girl can shop up a storm like the best of them, she makes the *Clueless* chick look like an amateur. Deciding to give her ten minutes, I mindlessly scroll on my phone because I've fallen for *that* trick before and that's not a mistake, or tongue lashing I wish to endure again.

Luckily I did hang around because a few minutes later, she exits the store but she's not alone, Van der Cunt is with her. The old fuck's hand rests low on her back, inappropriately low, and it raises my hackles. He really is a creepy old fart. What Sel sees in him, I will never know. Like always when she's around him, she's smiling. Laughing. She looks so carefree and happy, she used to be like that with me but of late, unless we're fucking, we're fighting.

Sitting here, I watch them walk to his car. She climbs into his Mercedes after he opens the passenger side door for her. He taps her on the ass and she giggles, she fucking giggles. With anger building, I shake my head and growl, "Fuck this."

I put my car into gear, press my foot down on the accelerator, and peel out of the parking lot, pissed that she chose to get a lift with him and not me.

Over the next few weeks, our relationship changes. Each day, I can feel Selene pulling farther and farther away from me. Hell, she didn't even come to the end of year basketball gala. She made some weak-ass excuse about a headache, but she was fine for the after-party. No headache in sight but the morning of prom, my world crashes into a million pieces.

> SEL
>
> We're over, Mils.
>
> We're on different paths and hockey will always come first.
>
> I can't do this anymore.
>
> Don't call me.
>
> Just forget you know me.

Immediately I call her but she's already blocked me. "What the fuck?" Grabbing my car keys, I yell bye to Mom and drive over to her place. When I get to the gates, they're closed and the security guard steps out. "You're not welcome here anymore, Mr. Wentworth."

"Since when?"

"Since Ms. Salvatore advised me so."

"Please," I beg, "I need to see her."

"I'm sorry, I have my orders."

"Fuck you and fuck her," I growl.

Shaking my head, I slam my car into reverse and high-tail it out of there. Thankfully there's no school today since it's prom day. Heading back home, I raid Dad's liquor cabinet. With a bottle of vodka in my hand, I head up to my room and drown my sorrows.

A few hours and half a bottle later, Mom comes into my room. I'm sitting on the floor, my legs bent and I rest my arm on my knee. "Miller Dominic Wentworth, what on earth are you doing?"

"She dumped me," I snap at my mom.

"I get you're upset but do not take that tone with me." She drops down next to me. "Wanna talk about it?"

"What's there to talk about, she broke up with me."

"Did she say why?"

"Some shit about wanting different things and that I'll always put hockey first."

"Well, hockey is your first love."

"No, she is ... was."

"Ohh, baby." She pulls me into a sideways embrace and, like a little bitch, I cry into her shoulder. "This is your first heartbreak and it certainly won't be your last, but drinking yourself into a stupor won't fix it. Now, go get in the shower. I'll make you a greasy lunch to soak up all the alcohol, and then you're going to get dressed and go to prom with your head held high like the gentleman I know you are."

"But it hurts, Mom." She looks at me as if to say, you don't know the meaning of true heartbreak, because she does. When Dad died, Mom lost a piece of her soul too, but she got back up and now she lives for him too. It's not quite the same, but I need to live for me.

"I know, but don't let her ruin prom, you only get one."

Mom's right, I can't let her ruin things. I worked hard to graduate and I deserve to celebrate all that I've achieved. Pushing myself upright, I mumble a "Fuck her," to myself and begin the process of sobering up so I can attend prom with my friends and celebrate all that we've achieved. But after prom, I can get drunk.

Arriving at prom is a somber affair, but thankfully people don't ask me where *she* is. Entering the ballroom, I walk up to JJ and Lexi. I'm a little wobbly on my feet because I necked the bottle of champagne that was in the limo I got for Sel and me. I also managed to sneak the rest of the bottle of vodka I took earlier, and I may have topped up the punch when I got here. I sling my arm around JJ's neck and ruffle his hair, something I know pisses him off. "It's prom, fuckers, complete with spiked punch." He pushes me away from him and my gaze lands on Lexi. "Damn, Knight, who knew you were so fine?"

"Back off, Wentworth," he growls at me, such a protective fucker.

"Down, boy," Lexi placates him, looking all lovey-dovey at him, and my heart aches because I no longer have that. "You don't look too bad yourself, Miller, but if you want to see graduation, I suggest you focus on Selene, you know, your girlfriend and not me."

"If she was still my girlfriend, I would," I morosely whine like a little bitch.

Both of their eyes widen at my words. "What happened?"

"She dumped me, some bullshit about us being on different paths and hockey will always come first."

"That's rough, man, I'm sorry," JJ tells me, pity in his eyes and that's a look I hate. It was the same look we got when Dad died, and now it's the look I get for being dumped at prom.

Lexi reaches out and takes my hand, squeezing in that reassuring way. "Her loss, Miller. You'll find Mrs. Wentworth when you least expect it."

"It is what it is." But I don't believe what I'm saying. "I need a drink," I mumble to myself and I stagger toward the spiked punch bowl. Chugging back three glasses in quick succession, I raise my arms in the air, let out a "Woo Hoo," and make a beeline for the dance floor.

Selene never appears at prom, in fact, she disappears completely. No one knows where she goes, not even her parents.

5
EVIE

...a few months later

I'M in the thick of my mid-semester exams and my phone won't stop ringing. "Leave me alone," I growl at the device before shoving it under my textbook and focusing back on the paragraph I'm trying to memorize. I still have a few years left on my degree but I really do not want to fail anything. The thought of another semester makes me shiver. I want to be out there, practicing, not studying. This course is hard, so fucking hard, and as much as I want to rip my hair out right now, I fucking love it. But so help me God, I will throw my phone out the window if it rings again.

No sooner do I finish that thought and it starts to vibrate and ring from under my book. Sliding the device out, I decline the call. Then I pick it up, and turn it on to silent. Something I should have done at the beginning.

Rubbing my forehead in frustration, I drop my pen, stand up, and stretch. My back cracks like I'm an eighty-year-old woman, but that stretch felt ohh so good. Picking up my empty mug, I head into the kitchen to make myself another coffee. I think this will be cup number five today and, right now, I'm pretty sure there's caffeine running through my veins and not blood. My diet at the moment consists of coffee, carrots and ranch dip, coffee, Double Stuf Oreos, and coffee. Normal eating and exercising will resume after my exams and Thanksgiving.

Speaking of Thanksgiving, this will be the first time heading back to Chicago since Sel disappeared, and I don't know how I feel about that. One day she was there, having her final dress fitting for prom, and the next, she was gone. There's been no trace of her. My gut is telling me she's still alive, but where the hell is she? I just wish she'd let us know she's okay. It's the not knowing that's the hardest. I thought we were closer than that but in saying that, I know we weren't super tight sisters, but it hurts nonetheless. I miss her but, at the same time, I hate her for leaving without saying anything.

And how Mom and Dad handled things, don't get me started on that. I'm thankful I live on the other side of the country in California and away from "that" life. Growing up in one of the mafia families had its ups and downs. Yes, I never wanted for anything, but I always wondered if my friends were my friends because of me or because of who my father was in the city. You'd think with the contacts my father has that he would have found Sel, but they haven't been able to find her. It's almost like he just gave up. I know if my child was missing, I would move heaven and hell to find them. No stone would be left unturned. And if something happened to them, anyone who hurt them, their blood would be spilled ... guess there is a little mafia in me after all.

Shaking off those thoughts, I pour myself another coffee. With my cup of happiness in hand, I head back to my dining room table to finish studying for tomorrow's exam when my phone starts to vibrate across the table. I've had enough and my frustrations boil over. Picking it up, I answer with an angry, "What?" I spill coffee on myself in my haste to answer.

Placing my mug on the table, I wipe my hand on my leggings and shake my head. Walking over to the sofa, I drop down and flop back into the cushion with my phone to my ear, but I'm met with silence. Normally, I'd hang up but something is telling me I need to stay on the line. My Spidey senses are telling me that whoever is on the other end of this call needs me. I can't explain it, I just know this is important. "Is anyone there?" I ask again, breaking the silence.

"Eves, it's me," my sister timidly whispers down the line.

"Sel," I screech, sitting up straight. "Where the fuck have you been? You just disappeared. I've been so fucking worried." My tone is harsh and knowing my sister, I know she'll get on the defensive so I lower my tone and meekly add, "I've been worried. I've missed you. Please come home." My words and sentences all flow into one jumbled mess, and I have no clue if she even understood what I just word vomited.

"I miss you too," she replies, her tone sad.

"Where are you? Why did you leave? Are you in trouble? Come home." I rapid fire the questions at her, one after the other.

"I ... I had to get away but, Sel, I ... I'm in trouble and, and I ... I need my big sister."

"I'll do what I can, what do you need?"

"I need money," she sniffles.

"Please come home," I plead with her. "Money will not fix whatever mess you're in," I tell her. That was one difference between my sister and me, she always thought money and wealth is what makes a person. That it will fix things, but money isn't everything. Where she flaunted our wealth, I snuck in under the radar and did what I could to help others. She would always look down on me for it but then, in the same breath, she'd help when she would think no one was watching. Underneath her bitchy princess-like exterior, was a person with a heart of gold.

"I can't, Eves. If h..." She drifts off, not finishing her sentence.

"He who?" My mind drifts to Miller and I wonder if he's who she's running from, but he was just as distraught when she disappeared as we all were. Plus, he's a puppy dog, he might be a hockey player but underneath all the padding and muscles, he's a sweet, sweet boy. He took Sel's disappearance harder than anyone because he was the last person she contacted before she ditched her phone and left. He blames himself that he didn't realize she was in trouble.

"It doesn't matter who, I just, please, Eves, please help me."

"You know I will, but I'm in the middle of studying right now, can you—"

"Of fucking course you blow me off. You'll help some random person but when me, your sister, needs you, you tell me you're in the middle of studying." I can feel her anger through the phone and no matter how many times I try to interrupt her, she just goes on and on about me being selfish and not caring. "Fuck you, Eves!" she shouts into the phone. "Forget you have a fucking sister," she sneers and that statement hurts. "Just forget I fucking called."

Before I can say anything, she hangs up.

"Fuck," I hiss. Rubbing my forehead, I close my eyes and take a deep breath. Typical Sel, always making it about her. I was going to ask her to give me an hour, but no, Selene wants everything dropped right there and then for her. Clicking on the number that she called me from, it rings and rings and rings. Deep in my soul I know she's not going to answer, but I have to try.

I click redial three times and nothing. Hanging up, I call Dad. "Evie, what can I do for you?" he says in greeting.

"Dad, Sel just called me."

"Where is she? Why did she leave? Is she in trouble? Is she coming home?" He rapid fires similar questions to what I fired at her, and I'm kinda shocked he cares. "Soph," Dad calls out. He's huffing, no doubt running to find Mom. "She called," he tells her. "Sel called Eves."

"Where's my baby?" I can hear Mom in the background. When I hear the desperation in her voice it guts me because I fucked up, I had her and ... and, now I don't.

"Where is she, Eves?" Dad asks.

"I don't know, she hung up on me when I was trying to say give me a sec. She ... she thinks I don't care," I cry into the phone. "Dad, she sounded so broken, but I was right. She *IS* running from someone."

"Who?" he asks me.

"I don't know. She clammed up when I asked and before I could ask anything else, in typical Sel style, she hung up when I wouldn't drop everything to immediately help her." A tear falls onto the top of my hand, I didn't even realize I'd started to cry. I sniff back in a very unladylike manner and bat at my tearstained cheeks. "Dad, she hung up," I morosely add.

"At least now we know she's alive."

This is true, trust Dad to bring a sense of happiness to

the scenario, and I find myself smiling through my tears. "I told you she was." I sniffle again but at the same time, I'm pissed at myself for not getting more information from her because, once again, Selene disappears into the void and we have no clue where she is, or who she's running from.

6
MILLER

PRACTICE TODAY WAS GRUELING, but I wouldn't give this up for anything. I was born to be a hockey player. With my bag over my shoulder, I say my goodbyes to the team and head out to my truck. Dumping my things in the bed, I climb into the driver's seat, I'm about to put the key into the ignition when a voice from the back startles the ever-loving shit out of me when they murmur, "Hey, Mils."

Lifting my gaze to the rearview mirror, my eyes bug out of my head when I see Selene sitting in the back of my truck. A hoodie covers her head, but I'd recognize those eyes anywhere. "Am I hallucinating right now?"

She shakes her head and chuckles. "No, I'm really here."

"Why?" I ask, my tone harsher than I intended. But the woman who dumped me via text the day of prom, and disappeared three months ago, is currently sitting in the back of my truck. Staring at me, without a care in the fucking world. She destroyed me three months ago when she dumped me and left, and now, she's in the back of my truck without a care in the fucking world.

"I ... this was a mistake," she says when the silence becomes suffocating. She moves and reaches for the door handle to climb out, but I quickly flick the lock, trapping her and preventing her from leaving. "Please, Mils," she begs, "let me go ... I ... I shouldn't have come."

Turning to face her, I look at her. I really look at her. She's just as fucking sexy as I remember, even with the black rings under her eyes and pale dirty skin. Hell, she could be in a potato sack and she'd still be one of the most beautiful women I have ever seen. Looks aside, right now, she looks scared and frail and meek, not the confident ball-busting girl I remember. I know something, or someone, caused her to dump and run and even though I'm mad, I can't let her go. "No, you came here for a reason and I want answers." She blankly stares at me. "Plus." I lower my voice and smile at her, hoping I can charm her just like I used to. "You look like you need a hug." Her eyes well with tears and her head begins to bob up and down.

"I'd love a hug," she squeaks out.

"Come here," I offer.

Quicker than the Flash, she climbs into the front and straddles my lap, just like we used to. She burrows her head into my neck and begins to cry. Her body shakes as she breaks down. "Shhhh, Sel," I coo, "I've got you."

I haven't held Sel in months, but having her in my arms again feels like coming home. To be honest, since I arrived at college, I've turned into a bit of a manwhore. Taking face-less woman to bed night after night, only for me to kick them out come morning because I'm nursing a broken heart. Selene broke me doing what she did. Even though I'm hurting, seeing her and holding her as she falls apart makes all the hurt go away. She's clearly going through something.

Me being an angry asshat isn't going to help her and it won't make the hurt I felt go away. She needs me and like my mom and dad taught me, I'll be here for her.

"Sel, babe, please talk to me."

"I can't tell you because ... because you'll hate me."

"I could never hate you," I tell her, but we both know I'm lying.

"The text messages you sent after I broke up with you say otherwise."

"I was angry and confused."

"I'm sorry," she mumbles. "For everything. If I had any other choice I would have stayed, but I didn't."

"Are you safe now?" I ask but I already know the answer.

"Considering I can never go home again, no."

"What can I do?"

"Just hold me."

"That I can do." Placing a gentle kiss on her head, I tighten my embrace around her. Silently, we sit in my car, hugging.

"This is nice," she quietly voices, breaking the silence before she burrows farther into me. My body is beginning to cramp and I'm about to ask her what she needs when she says, "Is ... is there somewhere we can go and we can talk? I'll tell you what I can."

"I can get us a hotel. I live in the dorms and my room-mate is an obnoxious jerk."

"I ... I don't have any money."

"I've got it but I need you to tell me one thing first."

She lifts her head and looks at me, nodding. "I can't tell you everything, but I'll ... I'll tell you what I can."

"That will do to start." She shuffles off my lap and moves into the passenger seat, "Did you, umm, want to call your parents?"

"No, I ... I don't want to speak to them."

"What about Evie?"

"My sister is in the middle of exams and doesn't have time."

"She would—"

"I called her, she said as much, so I hung up on her and I decided to come here and see you. Hoping with each mile that passed that you wouldn't turn me away too."

Reaching over, I cup her cheek. "You can always count on me, Sel."

She leans into my palm, turns her head, and kisses it. "Thank you."

Pulling on her seat belt, she buckles up and I pull out of the parking lot and head across town toward Luxe; a five-star hotel because I remember Sel won't do anything below five stars.

After checking in, we make our way up to the fifteenth floor and enter our suite. Sel looks around, assessing things, just like she used to but then she shocks me when she says, "This is too much." She's shaking her head and looks like she's ready to bolt.

"You've changed your tune when it comes to hotels."

"Well," she hisses, anger washing over her. "When you have no money and take what you can get, things like star ratings don't mean shit."

Raising my hands in surrender, I go to apologize but she's shaking her head again before she drops down onto the edge of the sofa and covers her face. She starts to cry again, and I hate seeing her so frail and broken. "I'm sorry, Mils. I ... I just ... I, shit."

"It's fine," I tell her. "Why don't you have a shower and I'll order us something to eat and drink?"

"Are you sure?" I nod and smile at her. This is not the girl I remember, and I hate seeing her like this.

"Thanks," she softly replies. Walking over to me, she kisses me on the cheek and cups my face, like I did to her earlier in my car. "You really are a good guy."

Before I can say anything to refute that notion, she walks into the bathroom and closes the door behind her.

Ordering room service, I kick off my sneakers and jump onto the bed and begin to mindlessly scroll through the channels while I wait for our food and for Sel to finish in the shower. No surprise, our food arrives first. Grabbing a fry, I pop it into my mouth just as the door to the bathroom opens. Craning my neck, I look in her direction and watch as steam billows out of the doorway. Standing there, wrapped in a fluffy hotel towel is a fucking angel. She's skinnier than when I last saw her but still fucking gorgeous.

"Food's here," I say but really all I want to do is rip that towel off of her, pull her into my arms, and kiss her from head to toe. I want to worship her like the goddess she is.

Hesitantly she walks over to the table, picks up a fry, and pops it into her mouth. She moans and the sound heads straight to my dick. I have to arrange the boys in my sweats because taking advantage of her right now is not something I'm going to do. She's emotional and fragile, she doesn't need me to act like a Neanderthal.

Ignoring me and my dick adjustment, she reaches toward one of the silver domes and lifts the lid. A smile appears on her face when she sees chicken tenders and ranch. "You remembered."

"It's easy to remember when tenders and ranch is also your favorite." For our first date, we went to this little diner and we both ordered tenders and ranch. Each of us chuckled when we realized we had the same favorite food.

"I miss Martha's tenders," she says with a sad smile.

"Yeah, me too," I agree. Then I try my luck and add, "You can have them again too, you know."

She shakes her head. "I can never go home, Mils. Never."

"Why?" I ask again, but I already know she won't answer.

"It's safer if you don't know."

"But how can I help you if you don't let me in?"

"I don't need your help, Mils."

"Then why are you here, Sel?" Her mouth drops open and I can see her thoughts whirring away in her brain. "You need me, Sel, so let me help you."

"I ... I." Her eyes well with tears again. "I just..." But she can't talk as she begins to sob.

Pulling her into my arms, she wraps hers around me tightly and like in my truck earlier, she breaks down. Once she has no more tears to cry, she lifts her head from my chest. She runs her fingers over the soaked material of my shirt. "Sorry," she whispers. Lifting her gaze to mine, she smiles. "I must look a mess."

Reaching up, I wipe under her eyes, "You look just as beautiful as I remember."

Silently we stare at one another and then before I can stop myself, I lean toward her and press my lips to hers. She freezes at the contact and before I know it, she pushes me away and slaps me across the face. The sound of her palm colliding with my cheek echoes around the room. "I ... I'm sorry, Mils but I can't do that. I ... shit, I'm sorry."

"No, no, it's fine. I shouldn't have done that."

She stares at me again and then meekly murmurs, "I wish we could go back."

"Me too," I tell her. "Me too. For now, let's just eat, get a good night's sleep, and then we can tackle whatever you need in the morning."

"Thank you."

Silently we eat and once our bellies are full, we snuggle

on the sofa and start watching a rerun of *The Big Bang Theory*. One minute we're lying together on the sofa and the next, she pushes me to my back and she's kissing me. We're making out and dry-humping each other, just like we used to. "Please," she begs.

Without saying a word, I scoop her up into my arms and carry her over to the bed. Sitting down on the end, she straddles me, pressing herself against my growing erection. Within seconds, we're both naked and she's riding my dick. I thought after she slapped me for kissing her this was off the table, but then again, when it comes to Selene and me, we have, err had, a very volatile relationship.

After two orgasms, we happily drift off to sleep. Selene is naked and in my arms and for the first time in a long time, I feel content. However, when I wake the next morning, the bed next to me is empty and there's a note with two words waiting on the pillow beside me.

I'm sorry!

Once again, my heart has been broken by Selene fucking Salvatore.

7

EVIE

THE SOUND of incessant knocking at my front door startles me awake. Glancing at the clock on my bedside table, I see it's just before five in the morning. I groan and grumble a pissed-off, "Someone better be dead," as I climb out of bed. This time of the morning should be illegal. Slipping my feet into my slippers, I shuffle down the hallway toward the door. The person on the other side is still frantically banging on the wood. The insistence of their knocking has me starting to panic that something is really, really wrong.

Without checking the peephole—sorry, Dad—I swing it open and my eyes widen at who I see standing there. All thoughts of sleep, at it being stupid a.m., and of being pissed off at being abruptly awoken evaporate when my early morning visitor says, "Hey, sis."

Standing before me, looking like a homeless hobo, is my

sister. She's here, in my doorway at stupid a.m. with a child in her arms. "Selene, yo—"

"You need to protect him," she screeches, thrusting the child in her arms at me. "Protect him with your life."

"What's going on?" I ask. Taking the small child from her, I cradle him to my chest but I somehow manage to grip her wrist before she pulls away. "Selene, talk to me … please." I look at my panicked sister and I just know; she's going to run again. I add another, "Please. Stay."

After what feels like an eternity, she sadly smiles at me and I know, well, I think, she's going to stay. I've never seen my ball-busting sister look so broken and scared. It causes my inner momma bear to bubble to the surface. When she nods, relief at seeing her agree courses through me. "Come inside. Come inside."

Again, she nods and smiles but that lip lift, it doesn't reach her eyes. Selene always had a bright and infectious smile, seeing her meek, like this, cuts me deep. Stepping aside, I usher her into my apartment, quickly closing the door behind her. She turns and stares at the closed door. She steps toward me and I think she's going to leave, but instead, she reaches past me, flips the lock, and turns the deadbolt.

"Coffee?" I ask, not sure what else to say or do. I'm standing here, holding a child I have no clue who he is, but one thing I do know; I would lay down my life for him. I have no idea where this protective feeling comes from but it's strong. It's like how I know, no matter what, I'm going to help my sister. Her disappearing isn't just her throwing a Selene tantrum, someone has her on edge. If she's ruffled and here, she's really, really screwed, especially with how the call with her two years ago went.

"Please, and maybe a sandwich. It's been a few days since we ate."

"What?" I screech. "How come?"

"Things have been tough," she mumbles.

"Whatever you need, I'll do it," I tell her. "Both of you will be safe here."

"Thanks, sis." She walks over to me and brushes a tendril of hair off the little boy's face. "This ... this is Tyler, my son."

"I'm an aunty?" I ask. She nods and smiles at the little boy in my arms. This smile reaches her eyes, and I can tell she loves my nephew with everything she has. And when Sel loves something, she loves it with her whole being.

"Mmmhmpf, I'm sorry I kept him a secret, but I had, well, have no choice."

"Tell me everything."

She shakes her head, "I can't tell you anything, it's safer if you don't know, but I need you to look after him for me for a while. I need you to protect him with everything you have."

"I will," I tell her. "But what do *you* need?" I emphasize you because as much as I will look after Tyler, I want to be there for her too.

"Just promise me," she cries, ignoring my question.

"I promise," I assure her, nodding emphatically. Reaching out, I take her hand in mine and squeeze. "But how can I protect you?"

"It's too late for me, just"—she bats at a tear on her cheek—"just look after Tyler. Please."

"I promise." Squeezing her hand again to reiterate my promise, she squeezes back. "I'll pop him in my bed and get you that coffee and sandwich."

"Thank you," she replies, relief and exhaustion evident in her tone.

With my promise made, I walk into my bedroom and place Tyler down in my bed. Pulling the covers up to his chin, I stare down at my nephew. He looks so peaceful and, like earlier, I know I will do anything for him. Pulling the door closed but leaving it open a crack, I head back to the living area. I'm surprised to find Selene still standing in the same spot, a part of me expected her to disappear while I put Tyler down. Walking over to her, I pull her into my arms and hug her. She's frozen for a moment but, eventually, she hugs me back. Then I feel her body shaking, she's crying. "Shhhh," I whisper, "I've got you."

"I ... I don't know what to do, Eves. I can't keep running, it's not good for him, and I'm so tired. So, so tired."

"What can I do?"

"Give me a time machine so I can make a few different choices."

"If I could, I would," I tell her, and I mean that. I've missed my sister. Yes, she and I have a volatile relationship but she's my sister and, at the end of the day, I would do anything for her. "How about for now, I get you that coffee and we go from there?"

"Sounds good," she agrees, "and once I'm caffeinated, maybe a shower?"

"I can go one better and offer you a bath." Her eyes widen in delight. Selene was a bath junkie when she was a teenager. Our joint bathroom was always filled with bath salts and candles.

"I've missed you," she murmurs.

"I've missed you too." Pulling her into my arms, I give her another hug. Then, I take her hand and I pull her into the kitchen. Pointing to the stools, I silently tell her to take a seat while I make coffee. I turn toward my coffee machine and grab the water canister. Stepping over to the sink, I see Sel has jumped up onto the counter instead of taking a seat. "I see you're still a rebel," I tease.

"Once a rebel, always a rebel," she tells me, and I can't help but laugh.

"And I wouldn't have you any other way."

"Oh my God," Sel declares, walking back into the living area after taking another bath, "that was heaven." She's had a bath every day since she and Tyler arrived.

"Sis, you say the same thing after every bath."

"What can I say, I'm easy to please."

We both chuckle. "You look, happy," I tell her.

"I am happy," she pauses. "And I have you to thank for that."

"You don't need to thank me. We're family, and family helps family."

"I don't deserve your help. Not after all the shit I've pulled."

"We all make mistakes," I tell her, just as Tyler cackles from the floor in front of the television. "Hope you don't mind, I gave him some chocolate."

"You're his aunty, it's your prerogative to give him chocolate and things I wouldn't."

Aunty, I'm an aunty ... and so far, I love it.

Tyler is still mesmerized by those dogs on the television. He's obsessed with this hit show from Australia, *Bluey*. While he's off watching Bluey and Bingo and their adventures, I make Selene and me another coffee and we sit at my dining room table. I still have no idea where she's been these last few years, and the need to know is killing me. I've been able to deduce she's running from someone. I'm guessing

Tyler's father has no idea he exists, call it gut instinct, so I broach the topic head-on. "Can I ask about Tyler's father?"

"You can, but I ... I can't tell you anything. It's safer for everyone if you don't know."

"Doesn't he have a right to know?"

"I guess, but ..."

"He's married?" She shakes her head. "An asshole?" Again, she shakes her head. "Then why? Surely he'd help?"

"He'd be an amazing dad," she agrees, smiling sadly. "But no one can know I had a baby. It's safer this way."

"I still think Dad can help."

"No," she shouts at me in a tone I haven't heard in a very long time. When my sister is passionate about some-thing, she goes in guns blazing, and keeping Tyler's baby daddy identity a secret seems to fall into that category. "They definitely cannot know, if he..."

Reaching over, I cover her hand with mine. "I won't say anything, but I really think they can help." She shakes her head and I sigh in frustration. Apart from putting a roof over their heads and feeding them, I don't know how else I can help her. "If you won't speak to them, what about Klaus Van der Kündt, you and he were always close. You—"

"No," she interrupts me with a venomous hiss. "Not him. Ever." Her reaction to me mentioning him surprises me. Her relationship with him was always intriguing. At one point, I thought they were sleeping together, but I quickly shook that idea off. Not only is he old, but he's Dad's best friend and that's just eww ... except in books. Age gap in books is hot. "You have to promise, no one is to know I'm here or that I have a child."

"I promise," I reaffirm. "But for what it's worth, I think Mom and Dad could help."

"No. End of story."

Selene hops up, knocking the chair over in her haste to

get away from the conversation. She joins Tyler on the sofa, effectively ending the topic. After placing our empty mugs in the sink, I join my sister and nephew on the sofa. We snuggle in and spend the next few hours lazing about watching cartoons.

The sound of my phone ringing causes Selene to freeze. Fear mars her face, and I hate the simple sound of a phone ringing causes her such panic. Pulling it out of my pocket, I smile when I see it's Mom. "Hey, Mom," I say in greeting.

"Hey, baby," she replies. "How are you?"

"I'm good," I tell her.

Selene waving her arms like a lunatic garners my attention, and when I look at her, she mouths, "Do not tell her." Nodding, I focus back on Mom. "Sounds like a busy week—" but before I can ask my next question, Tyler comes barreling back into the room and jumps into my arms.

"Loclate. Loclate," he singsongs in that cute lil' voice of his.

"Is that a child?' Mom questions.

"Yes, a friend from school is here." Selene grabs him and pops him on her lap, quietly telling him to shush.

"Ohh, I didn't realize you had company, I'll let you go."

"I'll call you back once they've gone."

"No rush, I was just checking in." She pauses, then morosely adds, "Today is Selene's birthday." My eyes flick to my sister and I smile when Mom adds, "I miss her."

"I miss her too, Mom, but I'm sure she's safe."

"I wish I had your confidence," she cries. "Klaus is still looking for her."

"He is?" I ask. "I didn't realize Klaus was so invested." Sel's eyes cut to mine. They're wide like saucers and I notice, just like the other day when I asked about him, she curls into herself. She's holding on to Tyler like his life depends on it and suddenly, it all starts to make sense. "Look, Mom, I've got to go but I'll call you later."

"Okay, sweetheart, I love you."

"Love you too, Mom."

Hanging up, I turn to my sister and before she can say anything, I ask her outright, "Is Klaus his father?"

8
SELENE

"IS KLAUS HIS FATHER?" Her question causes me to pause, I was wondering if, well, when she'd ask me this. Evie isn't stupid and how I reacted when she mentioned reaching out to him, that wasn't my finest moment.

"No, he's not," I honestly tell her. Thank the fucking Lord that psychopathic dickwad, egotistical asshat is not Tyler's father. There was a scare once but thank fuck it was a false positive on the home test, but convincing him that it was a false positive was difficult. Thankfully, I got my period and I could prove to him I wasn't lying, but after that he refused to use protection with me. Little did he know, I was still on the pill. I swapped from taking a tablet daily to the injection so he was none the wiser ... Shame on me though, because when I left, I didn't have access to my injection anymore, and what do you know, Tyler was conceived.

"Then is he who you're running from?"

"No, he's not," I tell her, but I can tell from the look on her face she doesn't believe me. Hell, I don't even believe me. "Look, Eves, the less you know the better. Just know, I'm doing this for Tyler's and my safety. The less you know, the better. And I promise, one of these days I'll tell you but for now, I can't tell you anything."

"You know, if you tell me who and why I can help you better."

"No," I growl at her, "I won't bring you into my shit."

"Considering you're hiding here, I'm already in it."

"I know, and I hate that I've brought you into my shit but, Eves, I ... I'm just so tired." Being on the run when it was just me was hard but now, with Tyler, it's even harder. Shelters are good for a few nights but they won't house you forever. I can't get a job because I have no one to watch Tyler. I can't get benefits because I can't use my identity, and I can't get a fake one because I have no money. Money is the root of all evil. It's funny, I used to take our wealth for granted, but now I'd give anything to have enough just to survive. The old me was a spoiled, selfish bitch. The new me is a poor bitch, but at least I have my integrity.

"And that's why you need to give me something. Being on the run isn't good for him, or you." I hate that she's right, and I know if I give her something, she can help, but I can't risk *him* finding us. "Look, I hate to do this but I have to get to a study session at the library with Wren."

"Who's Wren?" I waggle my eyebrows at my sister, hoping she's getting a little action from this Wren person.

However, that thought is squashed when she says, "She's," Evie emphasizes that word, "a friend of mine from school. How about on my way home, I grab things to make Alfredo with chicken and shrimp for dinner?"

"I'd love that," I excitedly singsong, "but I'll grab the ingredients while you're out and I'll cook. It's the least I can do."

"I'd love that," she singsongs mockingly back at me, and I can't help but chuckle.

"I might even take this lil' guy to the park."

"He does love the swings," my sister says with a big smile. "Think of me slaving away over my books while you two have a blast." She bends down and kisses Tyler on the head, then she pulls me in for a hug. Wrapping my arms around my big sister, I hug her tight. In her arms it feels like all will be okay.

She grabs her things and heads out for her study session, leaving me alone for the first time since I arrived here. The quiet is deafening and while Tyler watches *Bluey*, I start thinking about what could have been and what would have happened if *Klaus* was Tyler's father.

Memories of the day he shattered my heart with what his plans for me were filter into my mind in all their Technicolor heartbreak...

...Collapsing onto the bed next to him, I lie here, puffing. Sex with an older man is amazing. "That, was, wow," I pant.

"Mmmhmpf," he nonchalantly replies. Turning to face me, he stares at me and when he looks at me like that, I feel like everything is right in the world.

Smiling back at him, I mumble, "I love you." Reaching up, I run my finger along his cheek. "I wish we didn't have to hide."

"Me too, baby, but your dad would kill me for sleeping with you. Hopefully, when you give me a male heir, that will all change."

"What?" I ask, confused and taken aback. I've only just turned eighteen, I'm not ready to be a mom, and he's still married. How will that work? "You want me to have a baby?"

"Of course I want you to have a baby."

"But I'm only eighteen."

"Well, I need a male heir and my wife keeps punching out girls. I need a male heir and you, my dear, are going to give me a son. Then your father will have no choice but to merge with my family and, finally, I'll have it all."

"You ... you only want me for a baby and access to my dad's wealth and turf?"

"Why else would I be fucking an eighteen-year-old?"

"I don't know," I hiss, "maybe because you love me?"

"I love fucking you, does that count?"

His words are like an arrow to the heart, but I know he loves me. "I ... I thought..." Tears well in my eyes at the look on his face. He means it, he loves fucking me, he doesn't love me. That pisses me off because I'm not someone he can just use. "I ... I won't be used like that."

"You're a woman, Selene. All you're good for is producing an heir and sex."

"But—"

"No buts." He looks at the clock on the wall and hisses, "Shit, I'm going to be late. I'll text you when I'm free next."

He places a quick kiss on my lips, climbs out of bed, and leaves me here, heartbroken and crying. I thought we had something special, but it turns out he just wants me for my uterus and what my dad can offer. I'm such a fool.

Shaking off the memory of the day it all started to fall apart for me, I focus on the lil' man before me, giggling away at the adventures of Bluey and her sister. Getting pregnant at eighteen wasn't on my bingo card, but then again, neither was becoming a dirty secret to a psychopathic dickwad, egotistical asshat. This is so not how I pictured my life going but I wouldn't change a thing. Tyler is the best thing to have happened to me, and it was the wake-up call I needed. Seeing the positive sign on the seven, yes seven, tests I took was the beginning of the end for me. I was already on the run and then, because of a mistake I made revisiting the past, I became pregnant while on the run. At the same time, it was a blessing because it was what I needed to keep me going.

Do I feel guilty keeping him a secret from his father? Yes, I do, but I need to protect him. My job as a mother is to look after him, and that's exactly what I'm doing. Maybe Eves is right and I need to go home and see Mom and Dad. I might talk some more with her, but for now I need to get to the store so I can make us Alfredo with chicken and shrimp for dinner.

Strapping him into his car seat, I make my way to the store. I shoot off a text asking if Evie needs anything else. I'm on my way to the registers when my phone pings with a text. "Perfect timing, Eves," I mumble as I pull my phone out.

UNKNOWN

How's my baby momma and son doing?

My eyes widen at the text on the screen.

ME

Wrong number

A reply comes in immediately.

UNKNOWN

Nice try, baby

grainy picture of me pushing a stroller

"Shit. Shit. Shit," I hiss. Quickly I save his number and

no sooner do I hit save and another message comes in. Three in a row to be exact.

VAN DER CUNT

Did you think you could hide him from me forever?

I want my son

I will find you and when I do, I will make you pay for keeping my son and heir from me.

Dumping the shopping cart in the middle of the aisle, I grab Tyler and race out of the store. Looking around to make sure no one is following me, I walk the long way to my car, just to be safe. Once Tyler is safely in his seat, I climb into the driver's seat.

With tears in my eyes and a racing heart, I bring up the picture and study it. I'm relieved to see it's from a few months ago when I was in the Midwest. "We're safe, Buddy," I tell my son in the back but why does he think Tyler is his? Surely he can math and figure out it's impossible for him to be but then again, he is a conceited old fuck. I don't know how I ever found him attractive. He's no silver fox, that's for sure. He's definitely a grey geezer or as my friend Ali calls not-so-good-looking old guys, a charred potato.

Looking in the rearview mirror, I watch Tyler and I make a decision. "I think we need help from Poppy, Buddy. But before I go get help, I need to make sure you're safe. I need to make sure that you'll be looked after if anything should happen to me."

He babbles, "Momma," and I know that's his way of agreeing.

Bringing up Google, I search for a lawyer nearby and

when I find one, I punch in the address to my navigation and I make my way over to J Burrows Attorney at Law. With it being a small firm, I was able to see Mr. Burrows straightaway. Without batting an eyelid at my story, he helps me get all my affairs in order. In the event of my death, custody of Tyler will go to Evie and, for now, I'm handing parental control over to her. I write her a letter, outlining all my misdeeds and I beg her to look after Tyler.

By the time I leave the lawyer's office, the sun has set and I have several missed calls and texts from Evie wondering where I am. I know I should tell her something but, right now, I need this time with my son.

He and I are at the park, I'm sitting on the swing and he's in my lap. Tears stream down my face as I talk to my lil' man. "Tyler, baby," I sniffle. "Mommy loves you so very much, but I need to go away for a while. Aunty Evie is going to look after you until I get back. I know you're going to be a good boy for her 'cause you're the bestest little boy in the world." I wipe at my nose with the back of my hand. "You are my greatest achievement and everything I've done has been for you. This isn't goodbye, it's see you later. I'll be back as soon as I can, Buddy."

Kissing him on the head, I hold him tightly to me. A cool breeze picks up and I know it's time to go. Heading back to the car, we climb in and I head back to Evie's.

Just as we pull up, another text comes in.

VAN DER CUNT

I will find you, save us all the effort and let me know where you are.

I'm taking my son back and if you put up a fight, I won't hesitate to end you or anyone in my way

"Like fucking hell you will. Tyler is mine," I hiss at my phone, flipping it off.

Climbing out, I grab Tyler from his seat and I head up to Evie's apartment. Standing outside her door, I take a deep breath but before my hand reaches the handle, the door swings open. As soon as I see my sister, my eyes well with tears and I all but throw Tyler into her arms. "You need to protect him, Eves. You need to protect him with your life." I thought I was okay with my decision but now that I'm faced with it, I'm shit scared.

Never have I felt fear like I do right now. His last message freaked me the fuck out. I won't let Evie get hurt because of me. Deep down, I think I always knew this would come back to bite me in the ass. He's the head of the Van der Kündt family and he always gets what he wants. He wants a male heir and it seems he's convinced my son is his. Thank fuck he isn't Tyler's bio dad, but convincing him that he isn't is going to be difficult. That's why I have to go home, I need my dad's help.

"What's going on, Selene?"

"I wish I could tell you but, for now, the less you know the better it will be." My sister has been amazing this past week but, looking back, I never should have dragged her into my drama. I really am a shit sister. "Just, keep him safe. Promise me," I plead with her.

"I promise." She nods emphatically. My sister is the best person I know and Tyler will be safe with her. She will guard him with her life and that's all I care about right now. "But how can I protect you?"

"It's too late for me, just—" The tears I've been holding at bay start to fall. If I don't get out of here, I won't ever leave, and I cannot do that to her, or to Tyler. "Just look after him."

Leaning over, I kiss him on the head and pull my sister

in for a quick hug. "Thank you," I whisper. "I'll tell you everything soon, I promise." With that, I walk away from the little boy who holds my heart and from my sister, who I know will give her life for her nephew.

Racing down the stairs, I climb back into my beat-up car and pull away. This is the hardest thing I've ever done, but I'm doing this for Tyler. He will be safe with Evie and it will allow me to fight my demons so we can have a better life together.

9

EVIE

"HONEY, I'M HOME," I call out after my study session with Wren. She and I might be studying two very different things, but that girl has a way of making you want to succeed. She's going to be great when she graduates. "Hmmmpf," I mumble, "They must still be out." Grabbing my phone, I shoot off a text.

Throwing my phone onto the counter, I head into my room to grab a shower. Stepping under the spray, I wash away the day. Stepping out, I dry off, and pull on my yoga pants and a slouchy tee. Slipping my feet into my slippers, I shuffle back to the main area and furrow my brows when I see that Selene and Tyler still aren't back.

Picking up my phone, I see my messages are unread. Deciding to call, I press on her name but it rings out and I get her voicemail, "Only crazy people call, text me like a normal person."

Shaking my head, I chuckle at her greeting, if you can call it that, and send another text.

> EVIE
>
> Just me texting like a normal person, let me know where you are … please

Then I quickly send another,

> EVIE
>
> Do you need me to start on dinner?

Dropping down onto the sofa, I turn the television on and *Bluey* is still playing from earlier. I get sucked in watching the show, I was only introduced to it a few days ago, but I can see the appeal. It's a fun lighthearted program but I was shocked to discover Bluey is a girl, totally thought she was a he.

A noise outside garners my attention, and I wonder if Selene is struggling with the groceries and Tyler. I jump up to help, but when I open the door and see my sister, I know something is wrong. It's confirmed when she thrusts my nephew at me and shouts, "You need to protect him, Eves. You need to protect him with your life."

Tyler snuggles into me and, for a few brief seconds, I feel content. Then I look back at my sister and the hair on my neck stands on end. Something is off. "What's going on, Selene?"

"I wish I could tell you but, for now, the less you know the better it will be. Just, keep him safe." She's pleading with me, fear laces her words.

My head nods on its own. "I promise." She smiles at my words. "But how can I protect you?"

"It's too late for me, just—" She begins to cry, I reach for her but she shakes her head and takes a step away from us. It's as if my touch will cause her to fall apart. "Just look after him."

"I will, I promise." Taking a deep breath, I reach for her hand but she pulls away from me. "Maybe it's time to go home. Mayb—"

"No." She shakes her head. "I can never go back to Chicago.

Selene leans in and kisses Tyler on the head, her lips linger longer than usual. She pulls away and looks to me, offers me a silent thank you, and then she turns and walks away.

Standing here with my nephew in my arms, I step further outside and watch my sister walk away from me, not knowing it would be the last time I ever see her alive.

10
MILLER

JJ CHIPS the puck across the ice and with precision only JJ can manage, it slides directly toward me. Like a moth to a flame, the puck comes straight to my stick and I make a break for it, but out of nowhere one of the defensemen from the other team crashes into me. One minute I'm skating down the ice and the next I'm flying through the air, until I'm not. My body is slammed against the boards on one side and on the other side, a six-foot-three, fully padded body crushes me into the boards.

Being Kronwalled sucks.

Do not recommend.

Zero stars.

Being Kronwalled is part and parcel of playing hockey, but it definitely is better when you're the Kronwaller and not the Kronwallee.

Being Kronwalled hurts but when your knee goes one way and your body goes the other on the way down, it makes it a super shitty Kronwalling. A painful sensation rips through my knee and leg. I go down like a sack of shit. All I can focus on is the sharp pain on the inside of my knee, and I know I've done some serious damage.

My vision begins to dot but I blink it away. I refuse to pass out in front of a stadium full of people. Closing my eyes, I take a deep breath and when I blink my eyes open again, I see a figure hovering above me. Rapidly blinking, the figure above me comes into focus and I see JJ staring down at me. "You good?" he asks.

"Yeah, just thought I'd take a nap."

"Always knew you were a lazy shit," he teases.

"Eat a dick, asshole," I throw back at him. Then I add, "I think I'm gonna need a hand up. My knee's fucked."

Lifting my head, I look down at my knee. Without me having to say anything, he just nods, looks to one of the other guys, and they help me up. Somehow, I manage on one skate because putting any pressure on my left leg hurts like a bitch. The guys get me off the ice and into the treatment room. Lying on my back, I stare at the ceiling and just know I'm gonna be out for a few weeks.

Yep, a few hours later, after being transported to the hospital, it's confirmed—I have a grade two MCL sprain, and I'll be out for three weeks to a month. My future is going to consist of a leg brace, physical therapy, and taking it easy while I slowly recover. Yeah, not on my watch will I be taking it easy. Well, I will be for the next few days but I will be back in two, maybe three weeks. I'm not going to let a slight injury keep me down.

"Don't push yourself," JJ warns me when we get back to the hockey house from the hospital.

"I won't," I reply without looking at him.

"Yeah, and I'm a virgin," Byron says from behind JJ.

"Bullshit you are," I throw back at him as he and JJ help me down onto the sofa. Byron Schneider is the resident manwhore of the house and campus, with the unofficial nickname of "Casanova." His bedroom is a revolving door of puck bunnies and older women. He doesn't just limit his extracurricular activities to the bedroom. When it comes to Byron, any surface will do in order to get laid. Come to think of it, I'm pretty sure he fucked on this couch at the last party we had.

Carefully I lift my braced leg up onto the coffee table and lean back, trying to get comfortable, but when you're a person who always sits with their left leg tucked under them, this is pure torture.

"You need anything?" JJ asks.

"A time machine so I can go back to that game and not get Kronwalled into the boards ... and maybe sterilize this couch."

"Don't worry," Byron says, coming back into the room with a bottle of water for me and a bottle of pain pills, "I've cleaned it." He hands me the water and pills. I throw the pills to the side; I don't need them for now. "I learned my lesson after the foursome on Thanksgiving last year."

A shudder runs through me as memories of that incident slam into me. It's like being Kronwalled all over again. Byron, a few guys, and I stayed here for Thanksgiving. I went out for lunch with my family and the ones who stayed home all chipped in and made dinner together. Word got out that some of the guys were "all alone" so some bunnies came over and, well, let's just say, no one got dessert—except for Byron, the couch in the basement, and the three bunnies.

When I got home, I went downstairs to grab some beer and what I walked in on will be seared in my brain forever. I vowed to never ever sit on the couch in the basement again ... or eat pumpkin pie.

The next three, yes, three weeks fly by but at the same

time, the minutes tick by ever so slowly. I follow the team doctor's orders. I do the therapy that's required, plus extra at home and, tonight, I'm back on the ice for the first time since my injury. I cannot wait to get back out there because life is good when I'm on the ice.

11
EVIE

FINALLY, after eleventy billion years, well, it feels like I was studying for eleventy billion years, I'm a fully qualified orthopedic surgeon with a sports focus—just like I always dreamed. Thankfully, I was only one semester behind after taking time off to help get Tyler settled but, if I'm honest, I would have deferred indefinitely if it meant Tyler was safe.

My studies may be over, but now I'm onto the next part of my journey, my fellowship. Next week, I'll be starting my two-year fellowship at Limitless Therapeutic Rehabilitation and Wellness Center in Brookvale, Nevada. It's a rehabilitation facility that specializes in sports injuries, and I cannot wait to get my hands on some smashed-up bodies.

Rumor has it Marshall Kerr, the famous race car driver and Hottie McHotterson, is there recovering. He had a horrific racing accident and shattered his hip a while back—what I wouldn't have given to be part of the team that worked on him. To be in the operating room when they pieced him back together again would have been amazing. Like a lot of people who have accidents, he got into his head—douche. What should have been a quick recovery—had he stuck to the management plan originally laid out for him—he would be back on the track by now.

Tyler will be starting at a new daycare but when we walked in, I felt at ease. I still hesitate leaving him alone, what with the little Selene told me, but here in Brookvale no one knows us. We should be safe.

Tyler continues to surprise me with how clever he is and it amazes me how much like Selene he is. His mannerisms remind me so much of my sister. Not a day goes by that I don't think of her. It's been a year since she left Tyler with me and while the time has gone fast, it's also dragged.

When I was offered the job at LTRWC, I hemmed and hawed about taking it. I was worried if we left LA and Selene came back for Tyler, she wouldn't know where we were. Considering the paperwork she surprised me with soon after she left, I don't think that'll ever happen. To be on the safe side, I left contact details with Mr. Burrows at the law office, who turned my world upside down just after she left.

It feels like it was only yesterday the courier knocked on my door and dropped off the paperwork that changed my life...

... I've just gotten Tyler down for a nap. He's been really out of sorts the last few days but, then again, his mom has disappeared and he's only known me for a few days. But in saying that, I know I would lay my life down for him. He and I are going to find a new normal, and I will make sure he's safe and happy and fed. I have to say, looking after a kid at twenty-six wasn't on my bingo card, but here I am.

Leaning against the doorframe, I watch him sleep. I've

always thought people who said they did that were weird, but I find myself doing it quite often.

At his age, they're so little and not jaded. They still have their whole lives before them. I wonder what Tyler will be when he grows up? Will he follow in my footsteps and go into medicine? Or will he want to be a mechanic or a fireman or a chef? The world's his oyster and I cannot wait to see him grow and thrive.

A knock at the door startles me. Pulling his door closed, I head to the entrance and swing the door open. "Can I help you?"

"Evie Salvatore?" he asks.

"That's me," I tell him. He pulls out a yellow envelope and I wait for him to say, "You've been served" like they do in the movies but instead he pulls out a clipboard and growls, "Sign here, please."

He points to a line with my name on it and hands me a pen.

Taking the pen from him, I sign next to my name and after returning his pen to him, he hands me a yellow envelope. Without another word, he turns and walks away.

Closing the door, I head over to the couch and sit down. Looking at the envelope, I see it's from a lawyer I've never heard of. Opening the envelope, there's a letter on letterhead from the lawyer and a stack of papers behind it. Skimming the letter my eyes widen, "What the fuck?" I mumble to myself then I go back to the top and read it again. Word for word this time.

Dear Ms. Salvatore,
We are acting on behalf of your sister,
Selene Salvatore. She has instructed us to
begin the process of signing parental
rights over to you, Evie Salvatore, for her

son, Tyler M Salvatore. Ms. Salvatore is
aware that by doing so, she will relinquish
all rights, including the loss of decision-
making authority over the child's upbring-
ing, education, welfare, and potentially
the cessation of financial support obliga-
tions. Furthermore, Ms. Salvatore is aware
that she cannot talk to or see the afore-
mentioned child until the child turns eighteen (18) years of age. The child also
cannot inherit any property from their
parent under state estate planning laws,
unless that parent explicitly denotes such
inheritance in a will, which Ms. Salvatore
has done.
A copy of the will and testament for Selene
Salvatore has been attached for your
reference.
In the coming weeks, you will be required
to appear before a judge to finalize the
adoption of the child in question. My
office will be in touch when we are given a
court date.
If you have any questions in the meantime,
please do not hesitate to contact my
office.

Regards,
Dominic Burrows

After the initial shock wore off and speaking at length
with Mr. Burrows, we came up with a game plan. A few
weeks later, the judge signed off on everything and I offi-

cially became Tyler's new mom, with the records sealed so as to protect Selene and Tyler.

Taking that semester off to get Tyler settled was the best decision I made. Dad did what he always does in order to get his way and made a donation to the school that pretty much gave me free rein to do what I wanted, but I don't like to use his connections to get ahead. However, this was one time I was happy he is who he is.

After moving into a new place with a backyard for Tyler, he and I settled into a routine. It was an adjustment, that's for sure, but the more time I spent with him, the more I fell in love with my nephew, I mean son. I hate that I'm keeping his paternity a secret, and at times it's hard because he looks so much like Sel. Luckily for me, I live two thousand miles away from our hometown and anyone who might put two and two together.

It's funny, I keep expecting someone to jump out and tell me I've been punked, or that I'll receive another yellow envelope from Mr. Burrows telling me it was all a mistake and I need to hand Tyler back to my sister, but I don't know if I could do that. He's mine in every way, and I would lay my life down for him.

Every day I hope my sister will reach out but I know her and after signing everything over to me, I know that's not going to happen. On several occasions I've sworn I've seen her hovering in the distance, but it's all a figment of my imagination because she never materializes.

Wherever she is, I hope she's safe and happy.

12
SELENE

...two'ish years later

EVIE AND TYLER have been in Brookvale for almost two years now, I'm still amazed the three of us ended up in the same town. I mean, Brookvale, Nevada is literally in Bumfuck, Nowhere. I nearly tripped over my feet when I was walking into town and saw them at the park together.

Tyler is so big now, the pictures I see online of him don't do him justice. Even though I took off and signed over my parental rights, I still keep an eye on them. Hiding in the shadows, I watch over him like a guardian angel.

He's growing up so quickly and my sister is doing an amazing job. Word on the street is she's kept who he really is a secret, and I love her all the more for that. Goes to show she really is a better person than me. Yes, legally I'm not supposed to see him, but there's no harm in a little spying every now and then. Besides, Tyler is, and always will be, my number one priority. I may have signed away my rights, but he's my son and I love him unconditionally. I know I did the right thing leaving my son with my sister, even if it was the hardest thing I've ever done.

But like all secrets, they never stay hidden.

After leaving them at the park, I made a monumental mistake and was discovered by one of Klaus's men when I let my guard down. Klaus hasn't stopped looking for me, he's even had someone watching Evie from time to time. Luckily, I managed to make my escape but that guy is good, hence, why I'm currently in my car and on my way home. If Klaus is still looking, that means he thinks he knows something, and now that I've been seen in the same town as Eves and Tyler, it's time to face the music. I can't do this alone anymore, I need my dad's help.

Driving all night is probably a stupid thing to do, but I can add it to the already long list of stupid things I've done in my lifetime. My eyes are getting heavy. I'm so, so tired and it's not just from the driving. Being on the run for so long is mentally and physically draining. I'm finally adult enough to know I need my dad's help. I haven't seen my parents in years. I know they'll be happy to see me, well, I hope they will be. However, when I tell them everything, they're going to be so disappointed in me. I just hope I haven't caused too much damage with the choices I've made. Klaus and the affair. Having Tyler. Leaving Tyler with Eves. Surely they will understand and Daddy will help me, right?

I'd do anything for Tyler, which gives me hope that Daddy will be there for me too. At the end of the day, I'm his daughter, a disappointment of a daughter, but still his daughter. Hopefully, the surprise of being biological grandparents and not grandparents by adoption will soften the blow of all that I've done.

I've seen how they are with him and they're just as I expected them to be. Doting and soft, just like they were with Eves and me when we were younger, before I fucked it all up.

Pulling into a dingy motel, I grab a room for the night. Paying cash, I take the key from the young clerk and head to my room. I think I'm asleep before my head hits the pillow. I sleep for twelve hours straight, kicking myself when I wake up for sleeping so long.

Getting back into my car, I hit up a drive-through and get the biggest coffee they have on the menu. Chugging back the sludge, and that's the best way to describe what they served me, with a crappy caffeine hit, I get back on the road.

With each mile that passes, it sinks in that I'm going home. Deep down, I know I'm doing the right thing and if this all goes well, I can have a relationship with my son again. Dad will pull strings, like he always does, and legally he'll be mine. Then Tyler and I can be a family again.

Three days later and I'm still on the road. All I've done is drive, eat, sleep, and repeat. I'm beyond exhausted but I've nearly reached my destination. I've played several different scenarios around in my head on what will happen when I get home, and I have no clue which one of them will be the correct one.

Needing gas, I pull off the freeway and stop at the first truck stop I see. After filling up, I park my car and head into the diner attached for a quick bite to eat and another coffee. The waitress sees the photo of Tyler I'm holding and we chat about my son and how gorgeous he is. I tell her he's the smartest little boy and I cannot wait to be reunited with him.

With a full tummy and a to-go coffee the size of my head in my hand, I get back on the road. A smile appears on my face when I realize I'll be home in just a few hours.

I'm singing along to "Don't You (Forget About Me)" by Simple Minds and after I belt out the last line, a sense of unease washes over me. Looking around, I realize I'm the only car on the highway and that unease intensifies when a car suddenly appears behind me. They follow me for a few miles, slowing when I slow and speeding up when I speed up.

Rounding a bend, they flick their lights on to high beam, blinding me. "Asshole." Glancing in the mirror again, I sigh in relief when I notice they've turned them down, but when I focus back on the road in front of me, I nearly crash into a car stalled in the middle of the road.

Yanking the wheel, I swerve and somehow miss the car in front of me. "Dickhead," I growl, but that uneasy feeling slams back into me. My heart begins to race so I push my foot down on the accelerator and when I look in the rearview mirror again, the car following me is now right on my tail.

Pushing my foot down, my speed creeps up and up. I'm going much faster than the designated speed limit and with the pitch blackness of the sky, what I'm doing is highly dangerous. Spotting a sign telling me there's an exit up ahead, I speed up. Reaching a curve in the road, I follow the exit off the road but the car behind me rams my bumper, causing me to swerve. I turn the steering wheel, trying to straighten up, but I overcorrect and my car begins to spin and spin and spin.

My head bounces off the side of the car and my vision becomes blurry and unfocused. After what feels like an eternity, the car finally comes to a stop when the passenger side slams into one of the big trees along the side of the highway.

My movements are sluggish but my gut is telling me one thing, Klaus has found me.

Lifting my hand to my head, it comes away bloody and it hurts like a bitch. I think I have a concussion. With all my effort, I manage to get the driver's door open and climb, well, fall out of the car. It's started to rain, again, and the ground beneath me is muddy and boggy. Pushing myself upright, I stumble away from my car but I slip and fall down. My body hurts from a combination of the crash and fatigue from driving across the country nonstop. I manage to roll over onto my back. Closing my eyes, I take a deep breath as the adrenaline rush of the accident begins to wear off, leaving me lethargic and exhausted. A shadow appears above me and when I open my eyes, I stare into the eyes of the man I've been running from, Klaus Van der Kündt. His smarmy smiling face is the last thing I see before he raises his foot and everything goes black.

13
EVIE

"COME ON, BUDDY," I call out to Tyler, "time to get going."

My lil' man and I are off to the park, something we do every Saturday. Hearing his little giggles on the swing is always a highlight of my week.

"Coming, Mommy," he calls out from his bedroom. It's still surreal hearing him call me Mommy, but he doesn't know any better. To be honest, I wouldn't have it any other way ... plus, him calling me Mommy plays into the ruse that I *am* his mother. I vowed to my sister to watch over him, love him, and keep him safe, and that's exactly what I'm doing. I love Tyler as if he was my own and, to everyone, he is mine.

I'm helping Tyler with his shoes when my phone rings. I smile when I see Dad's face on the screen. "It's Poppy," I tell Tyler and his lil' face lights up with excitement.

"Hey, Dad," I greet when I answer.

"Evie, sweetheart, it's Dad," he says, just like I knew he would.

"I know, the screen flashed your name," I tell him and normally that would get a chuckle out of him but not this time. Immediately, I know something's wrong. "What's happened?"

"It's … it's your sister," I hold my breath waiting and then he says two words that shock me. "She … she's dead."

"Wwwwwhat?" My eyes flick over to Tyler, and when I see his smiling little face dads news hits me and I stumble. Tears well in my eyes.

"She died in a car accident, sweetheart."

"No," I cry, shaking my head as I process what he just told me. "She … she …no." I feel numb, closing my eyes I hope that when I open them I'm in bed and this was just a nightmare, but when I do, I'm not in bed. I'm standing in my living room, my phone pressed to my ear and Dad is once again telling me that my sister is no longer with us.

"She's gone, sweetheart. She crashed her car along the I-80, well, that's what the authorities are saying. However, from what Mike tells me about the scene, I know a hit when I see a hit."

"It … it has to be a mistake. Maybe it was someone who just looks like Sel. We all have a doppelgänger out there, this was hers. It … it has to be."

"It's not, Eves. She's gone. My baby is gone."

"No, no, she can't be … T…" I can't finish the sentence because no one knows Tyler is hers. "You're wrong," I tell him, shaking my head as tears begin to cascade down my cheeks. Dropping down onto the sofa, I lift my hand to my chest and I feel my heart beating. "I'd feel it in my heart if she was gone, Dad." *Tyler would feel it,* I tell myself but he's only four, he wouldn't know, would he? "It has to be someone else," I plead. "They're wrong, it's not her."

"I saw her with my own eyes, sweetheart."

"She was in Chicago?" That news shocks me because she was adamant she'd never go back there. So if she was back, something bad must have happened.

"It looks like she was coming home, but it seems an enemy of mine intervened and took her out before my baby returned."

"Dad, I ... I saw her a few years ago, she ... she mentioned she was running from someone. Do-do you think they finally found her?"

"Maybe but, Eves, this wasn't just a car accident, she was found next to her car. They're saying she managed to stumble out and then collapsed, but if that was the case, she wouldn't have been flat on her back, staring up at the sky. Someone did this to my baby and I'm not going to stop until I find who did this to my baby girl. No one touches my family and gets away with it. I've taken men out for far less but taking my daughter from mc, that is un-fucking-forgivable."

"Don't do anything stupid, Dad."

"When it comes to my family, nothing is off-limits."

A silence falls between us, but it's broken when Dad informs me about the arrangements he's made for Tyler and me to head home for her funeral. We say our goodbyes and when I hang up, I look down at my sister's son. How-how do I tell Tyler his mother is dead?

"Mommy, why are you crying?"

Hearing him call me Mommy makes the tears fall harder. He climbs into my lap and wraps his little arms around my neck, hugging me just how Sel used to when we were little. That action has me breaking down completely. Hugging my son, I cry over the death of my sister ... and his mom.

Pulling myself together, I look into his little face.

"Buddy, we're going to go on a plane trip and see Nanna and Poppy."

"Planes go in the sky," he tells me. He jumps off my lap, lifts his arms, and zooms around the room. His innocence is just what I need right now, and it feels like my sister is still here with me.

Picking up my phone, I call my boss at the center and tell her my sister died, and I need a few days off to attend her funeral. She passes on her condolences and tells me to take all the time I need. Did I mention my boss here is pretty fucking amazing?

I spend the rest of the day focusing on Tyler. I hug him harder when I tuck him in, and I watch him for longer than I usually do. He doesn't even know that he lost his mom. As much as I'm his mom, Sel was his mom too ... and now, she's gone. My eyes well with tears once again. I don't have any energy to do anything else, so I climb into my bed and cry myself to sleep.

The next morning, I pack bags for Tyler and me. Dad has arranged for a car to pick us up, just after eleven, to take us to the private airport a few miles out of town. I've just zipped up my suitcase when there's a knock at the door. Tyler is watching television but when he hears the knocks, he jumps up to answer it. "Hey, Master T," Tony from the center says in greeting to my lil' man.

"Tooooony," he singsongs, throwing himself into his arms.

"How you doing, lil' man?"

"Mommy and I are going on a plane," he excitedly tells the chef from work, who has become a good friend of mine.

"I heard," he says. When he lifts his gaze to mine and I see sympathy reflecting back at me, I start to cry again. He shuffles into my apartment, closing the door behind him, and engulfs me in a Tony hug. "Let it all out," he whispers. Wrapping my arms around him, I cry just as hard as I did last night. "I'm sorry for your loss."

"Thanks, Tony," I mumble when I pull back from him. He swipes under my eyes, drying my tears.

"I take it you and your sister were close?"

"We told each other everything and kept so many secrets," I tell him, secrets I will take to the grave now.

"She sounds wonderful. Do you need me to do anything while you're gone?"

"Maybe water my plants." He looks over to the peace lily sitting on my bench and scrunches his face.

"Looks like there's going to be two funerals," he jokes.

"Too soon, Tony, too soon. But yeah, I'm not a very good plant mom."

"Luckily for T-man, you're a great human mom, and one of the best orthopedic surgeons I know."

"How many orthopedic surgeons do you know?"

"Just one, but she's the best, therefore, I don't need to know any others." For the first time since I got Dad's call yesterday, I find myself smiling. "There's that smile I love."

"It feels wrong to be smiling."

"Look, I didn't know your sister and I've never lost anyone super close, but I think she'd want you to keep smiling. She wouldn't want you being sad. Yes, you can be sad for a while but when you get back, no more sadness. You will live extra hard for her and you'll tell T-man all the stories about his amazing aunty—" I sharply inhale at him referring to Sel as T's aunty. It's like another punch to the gut and he looks at me quizzically.

"She loved T so much," I sniffle as I say that. "She would have done anything for him," I morosely add, "just like I will."

"If she's anything like her big sister then she's an amazing woman. Now, who wants caramel slice?"

"You sure know the way to a girl's heart." Tony's caramel slice is like crack and, right now, it's just the pick-me-up I need because when I get home from my sister's funeral, it becomes harder than I ever thought.

14

MILLER

ALONGSIDE MY BUDDY, JJ, he and I are both back in Colorado for the retirement celebration of Coach Johnson, our college coach and mentor. To be honest, I always thought Coach would die while coaching. To this day, he still remains one of the best, if not *the* best coach I have ever had, and I couldn't not be here for it.

Lacing up our skates for one final practice with Coach Johnson, I'm assaulted with a ton of memories and I find myself smiling as I reminisce back to my times here in Colorado. Like the first time, and the million others since, that feeling of exhilaration washes over me. I wonder if it will ever fade away?

Playing in the NHL has been my dream since I watched my first game, and I can say with utmost certainty, my ultimate dream of playing in the league has come true. It sucks JJ and I aren't on the same NHL team right out of college but hopefully one day, we will be teammates again.

I still remember my first game with the Legends against JJ and the Crushers. It was so odd to be playing against him after being on the same team for so long, but at the same time, it was great to crush—pun totally pucking intended—him and the Crushers.

"Holy shit," JJ gasps from beside me.

"Holy shit, what?" I ask my best friend.

"It's Selene," he says the one name I was hoping to never hear again. I clench my teeth and breathe in deeply, I was hoping to never hear her name uttered ever again in my presence. She broke my heart, twice. Why he wants to bring her up now, all these years later, is beyond me. "Mom just messaged me, she died a few days ago."

"I'm sorry, what?" Surely I didn't hear him correctly. "Did you say she died?"

"Yeah," he nods, "and it looks like it was foul play."

"What do you mean?"

"Her family think she was murdered but, then again, what do you expect from a mafia family? You dabble in that shit and stuff like this is bound to happen."

"Dude," I snap at him, "she died."

"Dude," he throws back at me, "She broke your heart ... twice. She doesn't deserve any or my sympathy, let alone yours."

"That's a tad harsh," I sneer at him. My reaction to him dissing her now she's dead is confusing because, just a few seconds ago, I was feeling the same way he is now. Yes, she broke my heart, but she was murdered by the sound of things. No matter how shit of a person she is, was, that's a sucky way to die. "A girl is dead and her parents lost a child. Yeah, she might have been a bitch but she wasn't always like that. I still maintain she was in trouble and if she was murdered, I was right."

"You and your bleeding heart. No wonder the bunnies love you so much."

"What can I say?" I shrug. "I'm a sensitive soul, and I

know how to handle my stick. On and off the ice." I waggle my eyebrows at him.

"You, my friend, are a tool."

"Yet you and the bunnies still love me."

"Yeah, but I've taken one too many pucks to the head, and the bunnies, well, they can't be held accountable for their lack of taste when it comes to the opposite sex."

"If you two ladies are finished flirting," Coach hisses from the doorway to the tunnel, "we have a practice to get to."

"Yes, Coach," we both call out at the same time. Then we look at one another in a "we're fucked" kind of way, just like we used to. We finish lacing our skates and head out to the ice where Coach Johnson hands us our asses one last time.

Two grueling hours later, we shuffle back into the locker room. "Holy shit," JJ breathlessly pants, "Coach really ran us hard today."

All I can manage is to nod my head but even that takes a ton of effort. "I forgot how sadistic Coach Johnson was."

"Yep." JJ agrees. "But, holy shit, did I miss training with him."

Removing my skates and pads, I shuffle to the showers and as soon as the hot water beats down on my back, I sigh in pleasure. Closing my eyes, I'm assaulted with images and memories of Selene—the good and the bad. I can't believe she's gone. She was so young and had her whole life ahead of her. She may have broken my heart, twice, but no one deserves to die young, even a bitch like her.

Finishing up my shower, I hop out, dry off, grab my things, and call out to JJ that I'll see him back at the hotel, and I head out. Climbing into my rental car, I call Mom. "Hey, honey, how was your last practice with Coach Johnson?"

"Tough," I tell her. "Like always, he put us through our paces but my mind was elsewhere."

"I take it you heard about Selene?"

"Yeah, I did. Is it true she was murdered?"

"Officially it was a car accident, but her father is claiming otherwise."

"So it's possible she wasn't murdered?"

"I ... I don't know, honey."

"It could explain why she disappeared." That's all I've been able to think about since JJ told me the shocking news earlier. I think back to the last time I saw her, when she popped up in the back of my truck, and she was scared. Which is not Selene-like at all, she was always feisty and on top of things. Surely she hasn't been running for all these years?

"It could, but we may never know." Mom pauses. "Are you coming home for the funeral?"

"I think I want to, but I don't know."

"She was your first love," Mom reminds me. "It might give you closure if you do."

"I'm fine, Mom," I hiss.

"I never said you weren't but you were, and still are, hurt by her actions. Maybe saying goodbye is what you need to close that door so you can move on and be happy. Find a nice girl so you can settle down and make me a meemaw."

"Mooom, I'm only twenty-two, not fifty-two. There's plenty of time for all that lovey-dovey, till death do us part crap."

She laughs but she also has me thinking of what the future will be like for me. Is the whole white picket fence and two point five kids in the cards for me? "Just think about coming home, if not for the funeral just to visit. I miss you."

"I miss you too, Mom, and I promise I'll think about it."

Then I change the subject and ask about Roman, my little brother, who is currently thirteen going on thirty-three. We chat for a few more minutes and when we say our goodbyes, I throw my phone into the cup holder and I pull out of my spot. Before heading back to the hotel, I take a tour of my old haunts here in Colorado, including the amazing Lair, home of the Colorado Dragons. Their stadium is one of the best ever designed. You walk down to the rink as if you're entering the dragon's lair, but instead of heat, you're hit with the chill from the ice.

My mind is all over the place, I'm so deep in thought I nearly run up someone's ass at a red light. Then I cuss out Selene Salvatore once again, even from beyond the grave she's screwing with my life.

15
EVIE

STANDING out on the patio with a cup of coffee in my hand, on the morning of my sister's funeral, is not something I expected to do at twenty-nine, but here I am. I still can't believe she's gone. This gone is different than before because this gone is gone-gone. As in, she's never coming back.

My eyes well with tears, again, but before I breakdown, again, Tyler comes running up to me. "Mommy, Mommy, look what Marfa gaved me!" In his hand is a chocolate croissant.

"That was your mo—aunt's favorite breakfast treat," I tell him. Walking over to the lounger, I plop down onto the end of the chaise and pull him into my arms. "Can I have a bite?"

With a nod, he shoves the buttery flaky treat into my mouth and I take a bite. "Mmmmm," I emphasize how yummy it is.

He takes a bite and follows suit with a cute exaggerated "mmmm," of his own.

"Motherhood suits you," Mom says, joining us outside. She stands next to me and looks down at Tyler and me. I wish with everything I have I could tell her the truth. It might make the hurt she's feeling right now a little less, but I promised Selene I would keep his parentage a secret and I will, until my last dying breath.

"He's hard not to love," I tell her, ruffling his hair. He wiggles free and wanders over to the edge of the pool. He bends down to run his little fingers across the surface. "Careful," I call out to him just as Martha appears with a tray. On the tray is a carafe of coffee—bless her—and a plate of croissants, chocolate croissants. She places everything down and as I eye the chocolate pastry, my eyes well with tears. "The chocolate ones were her favorite," I tearfully mumble.

"She would have eaten them for breakfast, lunch, and dinner if we allowed her to," Mom says. Her eyes glaze over and a tear falls. Standing up, I walk over to her and wrap my arms around her. She falls apart in my arms and I find myself crying too. A few moments later, little arms wrap around our legs. Looking down, I smile through my tears at seeing my son hugging Mom and me.

Mom squats down and pulls him into her arms. "May you never feel hurt like this." She kisses him on the forehead and stands up. She wipes at her cheeks and smiles. "The car will be here to take us to the church at ten." She takes the coffee Martha prepared for her and walks back inside.

"Is she going to be okay?" I ask Martha as she hands me my coffee.

"She will be. She's a Salvatore."

With that, she heads back inside to finish preparing for the wake later on today. Sitting back down, I sip on my coffee and watch Tyler chase a butterfly. It makes me think of Selene and her secret butterfly tattoo. It feels like a sign that she will help me watch over Tyler.

Today has been one of the toughest days I have ever had to endure.

Seeing my parents so heartbroken is, well, heartbreaking, and I hate there's nothing I can do to ease their pain. *There is, you can tell them Tyler is their biological grandson, that would help.* Shaking off that thought because I won't betray Selene, I smile when I see Tyler coming around the corner but behind him, chasing him, is the last person I expected to see, Miller Wentworth. I haven't seen him since, well, I can't remember when the last time I saw him was but one thing is the same, he's still fucking hot. He's now sporting a scruffy beard and I'm not usually one for facial hair but, fuck me, he's rocking it.

A waiter walks past and I snag a glass of red wine off his tray. I don't normally drink red wine but when you bury your sister, the rules don't apply. Sipping on my wine—which isn't half bad, by the way—I stand here and watch Miller and Tyler together. I find myself smiling, something I haven't done since returning home. They're animatedly talking about something and seeing Tyler so happy and carefree makes me happy too. At the same time, it guts me that Selene will never see her son grow up. It also makes me curse her out for not giving me more. Who is his dad? Who was she running from?

The longer I stand here and watch them together, it does something to my heart. Actually, I'm pretty sure it's seeing Miller for the first time in years that has my heart thumping and my panties wet—just like they used to be when he was around. Just like back then, I shove those feelings back down because he's here grieving the death of his high school girlfriend. And I'm grieving my sister. He and I will never be.

"Whose kid is that?" Klaus joins me.

"Pardon?" I ask, he's standing way too close for comfort and I don't like it. His head nods toward Tyler and Miller. "He's mine," I tell him.

"When did you pop out a kid?" he questions in a vulgar manner, eyeing me suspiciously as he sips on what is presumably vodka.

"I didn't, I adopted him."

"You adopted?"

"Yep," I nonchalantly reply. I've never been a fan of Mr. Van der Kündt and, right now, with how close he's standing and how he's interrogating me about my son, it's giving me the creeps.

"Really?"

"It wasn't anything I thought would happen but yes, I did."

"Why?"

"My friend died and she left her son to me."

"Why?" he repeats the same question again, and the way he's interrogating me has the hairs on the back of my neck standing up. The feeling that *he* is who Selene was running from slams into me like a freight train. Surely she didn't get involved with a married man? She was always reckless but she'd never do that, right? "I asked you why," he sneers when I don't answer him.

"She, umm, she had no family," I tell him. "She and I became close and when she got sick, she asked me to take care of him."

"You a lesbian now?"

"No," I scoff, disgusted that he would accuse me of that and, even if I was a lesbian, it's none of his fucking business. Besides, love is love and as long as it's between consenting adults, who gives a shit? "It is possible for two women to be friends."

"And who did you say this friend was?"

"I didn't say." Thankfully, at that moment, Dad walks over to us. He hands me another glass of wine and I eagerly take it from him. Chugging back half the glass, he eyes me but doesn't say anything.

"Sorry for your loss," Klaus says to Dad. They each shake hands.

"Thanks for being here to lay my baby girl to rest." Dad pulls me into his side and presses a kiss to my temple. I have to admit, I like his protection from Klaus. "May you never have to bury one of your daughters."

"Such a sad thing to lose a child in an accident like that." Klaus's words lack sincerity and that feeling of unease and suspicion rears up again.

"Accident, my ass," Dad growls. "My baby was murdered and when I find who did it, they'll be sorry they messed with me. No one harms a Salvatore and walks away."

"Anything you need, and I'm here."

"Thank you, friend."

The two of them start to discuss how to find the culprit. I want no part of this conversation and feel it's inappropriate to be having it here and now. Slipping out from Dad's arm, I excuse myself and walk over to Tyler and Miller. Snagging myself another glass of wine along the way, I drop down into a squat next to them. "What are you two discussing?"

"Hockey," Tyler excitedly squeals.

"Of course you'd be talking hockey." I shake my head.

"What can I say," Miller nonchalantly replies with a shrug, "it's what I know."

"I wanna play," Tyler says, gripping my cheeks in his little hands. Popping my glass down beside me, I cover his hands on my cheeks. This lil' monkey has been my lifeline today, whenever I was close to breaking down, he'd always appear and make the darkness disappear. It's almost as if Sel is here, guiding him, and me.

"I don't think there's a rink in Brookvale, Buddy, but we'll see what I can do."

"I wanna hockey." He stamps his little foot. He's so much like Selene when he gets mad, it's moments like this that make me miss her even more. And now, there's no chance to ever see her throw a tantrum when she doesn't get her way.

"Don't speak to your mom like that," Miller scolds, my first instinct is to yell at him for parenting my son, but there's also a part of me that likes him defending me. Obviously realizing he may have overstepped the mark; he looks to Tyler. "I'm sure your mom will do what she can and, if not, I'm sure there's another sport you can get into."

"I wanna hockey," Tyler shouts, louder this time.

People around us all look to the little boy starting to get angry, but I know he's just tired. Hell, even I'm tired. Being emotional really takes it out of you. I'm about to scoop him up and take him upstairs for a nap when Martha swoops in.

"Let's get you down for a nap," she says, lifting him up into her arms and blowing a raspberry on his cheek.

"I can do it," I say, standing up.

"I've got him." Without another word, she heads toward the house with a now giggling little boy.

"Super Martha to the rescue," Miller says, when Martha and Tyler are out of earshot.

"She really is a saint," I tell him. "I'm going to miss her when I go home."

"And where is home these days?" he asks, handing me the glass of wine I popped down. Our fingers brush and a spark jolts between us. It must be the wine because surely I did not just feel that. Chugging back what's left, I look around for a waiter and, as luck would have it, one is walking past. He takes my empty glass and when I look at his tray, all I see are tumblers of scotch. A shudder runs through me at the thought of scotch but before I can think on it, Miller takes my hand and tugs. "Come with me."

With his hand in mine, we weave our way amongst the guests and head inside. With my hand clasped in his, we sneak down the hallway and head toward the library. Stepping into the room, I close my eyes and breathe in deeply. This room was always a safe haven in the house, and one that Selene would spend countless hours in.

Miller closes the door behind us and drops my hand when the door clicks shut. I mourn the loss immediately but I quickly shake that thought off because this is nothing but him being nice. He makes his way over to the drink cart in the corner. He pours himself a whiskey and me another glass of red. I really shouldn't have another one, I'm borderline tipsy right now but, to be honest, I just want to numb the pain of burying my sister.

Walking across the room, I drop down onto the love seat in the corner and tuck my legs up underneath me. I think about Selene and what she went through these last few years. There was always a part of me hoping Selene was just being dramatic with everything going on in her life, but I have a feeling she held many things back. Now I'll never know why she left Tyler with me, or who she was running from.

Miller walks over with our drinks and hands me my glass. "To Selene," he raises his glass in a toast.

"To Selene," I repeat.

Bringing the glass to my lips, I take a sip and savor the rich flavors of the merlot. Lifting my gaze to Miller's, I nod to the seat beside me. Without acknowledging my request, he drops down next to me. Our legs brush and like earlier, a spark ignites between us.

Silently we sit here, drinking. It's not awkward, it's kind of perfect—to be honest—and it's exactly what I need after today.

From the corner of my eye, I notice Miller staring intently at me. Taking another sip, I turn my head toward him. The air around us crackles and becomes heated. Our bodies begin to move toward one another but before anything can happen, the door to the library opens and my dad walks in with Mr. Van der Kündt.

"WHAT ARE you two doing in here?" Mr. Salvatore asks Evie and me when he notices us sitting here in the dark of the library. We look suspicious because we nearly kissed ... well, I think that's what was about to happen before they interrupted us.

"Just taking a breather," Evie tells her dad. "Today has been ..." She drifts off and sighs. On instinct, I reach over and take her hand, giving it a squeeze. I don't know what compels me to do so but now that I have her hand in mine, I'm glad I did.

"I get that," he tells her. "Miller." He turns his attention to me, dropping his gaze to my hand holding Evie's and then it flicks back to my face. "It was good of you to come. I know how close you and Selene once were." He still has that fatherly tone. Once again, I feel like I'm eighteen years old, about to get a talking to from him regarding the virtues of his daughter ... and reminding me he knows how to make people disappear.

Standing up, I step toward him and offer him my hand. "I'm sorry for your loss, sir." This is the first time I have seen him today to offer my condolences.

He nods his head and shakes my hand. No longer do I see that scary guy; I see a broken man grieving the loss of his daughter. It's so surreal being back here and being caught in the library with one of the Salvatore daughters. However, unlike years ago, Evie and I were not making out ... even if the air felt electric seconds before they arrived.

"Miller," Sophie singsongs my name as she walks in, joining us and, like always, bringing an air of grace with her. "You came." She pulls me in for a hug, and I can't help but wrap my arms around her. It feels like it was only yesterday she saw me and hugged me in this manner.

"Mrs. S, how are ... shit, that's a stupid thing to ask. I'm so sorry for your loss."

She smiles at me but it's filled with sadness. She takes my hand and squeezes. "I'm fine, well, as fine as you can be when your baby girl is ... is..." She begins to sniffle and I hate I'm the cause of her anguish but, to be honest, I think this is how she's been reacting to everyone since she received the news about Selene. "Sorry, I just can't help it."

"No need to apologize at all, losing a child must be tough."

"May you never experience it," she whispers, wiping at her eyes. "Umm, Daniel, people are starting to leave."

"I'll be there in a minute." He smiles lovingly at his wife.

Their love for one another hasn't changed since I saw them last. Selene used to always say she wanted a love like they had. I wonder if she ever had that before she died? She was the last woman I ever loved. Ever since she stomped on my heart, it's just been a revolving door of nameless and faceless woman. My eyes drift to Evie, she's staring off into the distance again, and in this light she looks beautiful, broken but beautiful.

The sound of the door closing garners my attention and when I look around, I see everyone else has gone, and it's just Evie and me alone here in the library.

Walking over to the drink cart, I pour myself another drink and I grab the bottle of wine. Walking over to Evie, who is now by the window, looking out in the backyard, I take her glass and refill it for her. "Thanks," she murmurs and then looks back out the window. "This was always Selene's favorite room."

"I know," I agree.

"I remember one time, she was in here reading and left to go meet you. I came in here to do some schoolwork and I closed her book. When she got home, later that day, she lost it at me because I didn't use a bookmark."

"At least you didn't dog-ear a page. I did that once and I was lucky to walk away with my balls attached."

"You're a monster," she teases. "You never, ever, ever dog-ear a book, you always, always, always use a bookmark. And anything will suffice, a scrap of paper. A receipt. A birthday card."

"A Kindle," I offer. She laughs and looks at me quizzically.

"I saw a meme posted online once and it was a picture of a pile of books and someone was using a Kindle as a bookmark."

"Well, I guess that's better than dog-earing a book." She takes another sip. "You know, you lose hotness points for that comment." She laughs, it's only a small one but it's nice to see and hear her happy, even if only for a moment.

"So you think I'm hot, huh?" Her cheeks darken at my teasing.

"You know you are, Mr. Big Time Hockey Dude."

"I think you mean Mr. HOT," I emphasize the word hot, "Big Time Hockey Dude."

"Aaaand there goes any hotness you had ... plus, you can't trust a word I say right now, I'm a lil'"—she holds her thumb and index finger close together—"tipsy schmipsy right now."

"So you're telling me you have beer goggles on?"

"No." She shakes her head. "Wine goggles." She giggles at her own joke and I find myself laughing with her.

"You know, you're not as uptight as your sister always said you were."

"Thank you ... I think."

She walks back over to the love seat and drops down onto it, sloshing her wine over her hand as she does. Placing her glass on the table next to her, she brings her hand to her mouth, sticks out her tongue, and licks thc dark liquid off her hand. Standing here, I watch as her tongue slides over her skin and suddenly I'm imagining her tongue licking up my shaft, circling the head and ... Nope, I need to stop those thoughts, we're at my ex-girlfriend's wake, who also happens to be Evie's sister.

A groan gets stuck in my throat and when Evie looks at me, I turn around so she can't see the boner I'm currently sporting. Subtly—I hope—I readjust my dick and walk over to the drink cart because more alcohol is clearly what I need right now.

Topping up my glass, I chug it back before refilling it again. Grabbing the decanter, I make my way over to where Evie is sitting and drop down beside her.

"Why did you groan just now?"

"No reason," I say, hoping it comes off casually but my tone is all off.

"No one groans like that for no reason. It was almost

as if you were ..." She stops herself from finishing her sentence when she realizes what she was about to say. Her eyes drift south and they lock on to my dick. My still hard dick because I cannot get the image of Evie running her tongue over my dick out of my head. "Ohh, wow, umm."

"Yeah, sorry about that, but I"—I shake my head—"never mind, you don't need to know."

"Tell me," she whispers.

"I—"

"Please," she interrupts me and places her hand on my thigh. I can feel her hand searing into my skin. Looking over at her, she's silently begging me with her eyes. Deciding "what the hell," I tell her.

"When you were licking the wine off your hand, I was imagining you were licking my dick."

"And that made you hard?" I nod. "Why?"

"Because you're hot and it was fucking hot watching you lick your hand."

A silence falls between us and then, out of nowhere, she says, "I'll do it. If you, umm, want me to."

"Do what?" I question because, surely, she isn't offering to lick my dick.

"Lick your dick," she confirms. My eyes widen because she *is* offering to lick my dick for me. If this was any other time and she hadn't freely admitted she was tipsy, I would take her up on her offer because Evie Salvatore is fucking hot. I always thought she was when I was with Selene, with her chocolate brown eyes that draw you in, her button nose, and kissable lips. And don't get me started on her tits. Where Selene was flat-chested, Evie's breasts are plump and full. All of that aside, I'm not an asshole and as much as it pains me, I reject her offer. "Thanks for offering, but I'll be fine."

"Ohh," she dejectedly replies, and I hate the sadness laced in that one word.

"Besides, we haven't even kissed. I mean you should at least kiss a girl before you let her lick your dick."

"Yeah, okay," she mumbles from next to me and then, suddenly, she's straddling my thighs, gripping my cheeks, and she's kissing me.

Evie

Salvatore

Is

Kissing

Me.

Her lips press to mine and her tongue seeks access to my mouth. If I wasn't also a little tipsy, I'd be pushing her away but when a sexy older woman is straddling you and kissing you, you kiss her back. Threading my fingers up into her chestnut brown locks, I hold her to me and kiss her back. I push my tongue into her mouth and suck on her tongue as she rocks her hips against me. It's too much but, at the same time, it's not enough.

Sliding one hand down her back to her waist, I lift her up and flip her onto her back. Laying her down on the love seat, I cocoon her underneath me and continue to kiss her. Pressing my knee between her thighs, she gyrates her hips, rubbing herself on my leg.

My cock hardens between us the longer we kiss. She moans into my mouth and then she mumbles, "I'm coming." Her body stiffens beneath me and she once again lets out a guttural groan. When her body relaxes, I separate our lips and I lift myself up. We both open our eyes and stare at one another. Our breaths are hurried just as our breathing returns to normal. I see the moment it registers in her brain and she realizes what just happened. She pushes on my shoulder and pleads, "Let me up."

Lifting myself off of her, she shimmies to the side, rolls off the love seat, and races out of the library. Standing here, I watch her retreating form as guilt slams into me. I just made out with and dry-humped my ex-girlfriend's sister to a climax at her wake ... I really am an asshole.

17

EVIE

WAKING THE NEXT MORNING, I have the hangover from hell. Wine hangovers are the worst, and combine it with the guilt of what I did, I feel like the shittiest human being to ever have walked the earth. Who makes out and dry-humps their sister's ex at her wake?

Shaking off the memory of last night, I pad into the bathroom and have a shower. Hopefully, the hot water will wash away the guilt and memories of what I did last night. FYI … it doesn't.

Once I'm showered and dressed, I head downstairs in search of coffee and my lil' man. Seeing his gorgeous lil' face will make me smile. Giggles can be heard coming from the kitchen and when I walk in, I stop mid-step because sitting at the island counter is Mom, Tyler … and Miller.

"What are you still doing here?" I snap, my eyes widening at how rude I sound but right now, I'm panicking that Mom will know what I did yesterday with Miller, and I don't want to upset her more than she already is.

"Miller passed out in the library last night," Mom

informs me when Miller just sits there silently. "He's having some breakfast and then he'll head home."

"Ohhh," is all I can manage because I can't look at him. If I do, I'm sure there will be a flashing billboard above my head exclaiming to the world what I did last night. Nodding at Mom, I walk over to Tyler and place a kiss on his head, "Morning, my lil' monkey."

"Morning, Mommy," his little voice singsongs and it instantly calms me.

"Morning," Miller drawls from next to him.

"Morning," I utter, not looking at him. I will never be able to look Miller Wentworth in the eye again without remembering what his tongue feels like in my mouth, or what the scratch of his beard feels like on my face ... I wouldn't mind knowing what that scratch feels like between my thighs, no, Evie. *Bad, Evie. Stop thinking about Miller kissing down there or about kissing him ever again.*

The coffeepot is calling me, so I kiss Tyler one more time and make my way over to the coffee nook and make myself one. Behind me, I can hear Mom and Miller talking about hockey and his life. Apparently, his agent has a deal in the works that will be great for his career. Thankfully, he's on the other side of the country because, in a few months' time, Tyler and I will be moving to New York. Doc Michels has invited me to come and work with him at the NY Crushers and be a part of his amazing program, which helps athletes recover quicker. When he made the offer, the more than generous offer, I jumped at the chance without even thinking about it. Don't get me wrong, I've loved my time at LTRWC, but I want to be more hands-on with the patients from when the accident first occurs. I don't just want to focus on the recovery aspect, I want to be part of the rebuild, as such. And this offer from Doc Michels allows that.

After what feels like an eternity, Miller finally says goodbye and leaves. Being around him this morning was awkward, to say the least. I'd like to say it was the wine and grief that made me turn into a hussy last night, but deep down it was those unrequited feelings for him. Over the years that man has somehow managed to become hotter. And his kisses? Soooooo much better than I ever imagined, but I have to put him in the past, where he belongs.

Fingers clicking in my face and the sound of Mom's voice saying, "Earth to Evie," snaps me back too attention.

"I'm sorry, what?"

"You were off in la-la land, everything okay?"

"Yeah, I'm just tired. So much has happened and with the big move coming up, I just feel overwhelmed. Then I feel selfish for feeling overwhelmed because Selene is gone and she's never going to feel overwhelmed again. And she'll never get her dream job and I—" I sniffle. "I just miss her and I hate that she's gone."

"Ohhh, honey," Mom coos, pulling me into her arms. "It's okay to be overwhelmed and happy. Your sister would want you to be happy and as for being overwhelmed, that's okay too. You're allowed to feel that way, especially with everything that is going on. I think if you didn't, that would be something to worry about."

"I know, it just sucks. Why couldn't some pedo or murderer be the one to die? Why did a sweet, sweet girl like Sel have to be taken from us?"

"The world works in mysterious ways, Eves. One day there will be a silver lining to her death but, in the meantime, all we can do is remember her fondly and keep on living."

"How are you so calm and okay with this?"

"Sweetheart, I may look like I have it all together but I assure you, on the inside, I'm broken and crying and angry and so many other emotions there's too many to list. No parent should ever have to bury their child. I know Tyler isn't biologically yours, but may you never experience losing him." Looking over at him, I smile. When I look back to Mom, I see she's smiling too. "It's funny," Mom interjects, "sometimes when I look at him, I see Selene, but then I blink and it's gone. My mind is playing tricks on me because I wish she was here."

"You know, I do too," I say in agreement, but if only she knew how right she was. It's on the tip of my tongue to confess all, but then Dad walks in and he's talking to someone on the phone. He's angry, again. It feels like all I've seen from him is anger since I got here but, then again, his youngest daughter was murdered and the police are ruling it an accident. If I know my dad, he will not rest until he has all the answers. When he discovers the truth, there will be hell to pay for whoever took his little girl from us.

18

MILLER

IN THE FEW months since Selene's funeral, I've found myself in a funk of sorts. Her death caused me to open my eyes and reevaluate my life. Her passing made me realize I want what she will never get to experience, a chance to find love and have a family.

Memories of experiencing how much of a fucking deviant her fucking smoke show of a sister is have plagued me nightly. I always knew she was a deviant after what happened at Sel's eighteenth back in the day, but doing what we did in the library takes that to the next level. Yes it was highly erotic but at the same time so, so wrong. *Who hooks up with their dead ex-girlfriend's sister at her wake? Then again, who focuses on their girlfriend's sister while she's blowing him?*

Like always, when I'm alone and memories of her riding my leg play in my mind, my dick hardens and I have no choice but to jerk off like a horny fifteen-year-old. My dick has seen more hand action than vagina action, and that's saying something, considering my reputation with the bunnies.

Slipping my hand into my sweats, I grip my dick and give it a few pumps. Freeing my cock, I get comfy and get to it. Just as my strokes pick up speed and I start to feel that tingly feeling low in my balls, my phone rings but I ignore it.

My dick is my sole focus right now.

Closing my eyes, I imagine Evie's hand wrapped around my shaft. It's her wrist flicking back and forth, squeezing the tip before sliding back down again. Focusing on the image of her kissing me and riding my leg, I rub myself in sync with her imaginary rubs on my leg.

Sooner than is acceptable for an almost twenty-four-year-old, I come all over my hand. As soon as I finish, I grab a discarded shirt and wipe myself clean.

Climbing off my bed, I pad across the carpet and into the bathroom to wash my hand. Glancing at my reflection, I notice my cheeks are flushed and I look tired. I don't feel tired, I feel alive and ready to conquer the world.

My phone beeps, indicating that whoever called before has left a message. Heading back into my room, I grab my phone and click on the voicemail icon. "Miller, it's Jaxson, give me a call when you get a chance."

Deleting the message, I click on his name and call him back straightaway, hoping he has news regarding the deal he's been trying to secure for me. "Nice of you to call me back," Jaxson says in lieu of a hello.

"Hello to you too, Jaxson, sorry I missed your call. I was, ummm, busy."

"I'm sure you were," he teases. "Just make sure to wrap it before you tap it."

"It wasn—"

"I don't want to know what it was or wasn't, but considering you're calling me within five minutes, either you suck in the sack—"

"I'll have you know; I can wield my stick on and off the ice just fine, thank you very much."

"Methinks the player doth protest too much."

"Shut up," I hiss. "What was it you wanted to chat about?"

"I have news," he tells me.

"And?" I probe, running my hand over the scruff on my chin, it's a little longer than usual but I think I'm digging the scruffy lumberjack look. For the last few months, Jaxson has been in negotiations with several teams since my contract with LA is coming to an end after this season. As much as I love the Legends, I never really felt at home here in California. To be honest, I really want to go to New York to play for the Crushers, with JJ. Jaxson has another client who plays for the Crushers and he wants out. So he's been tirelessly working to do a swap between the two of us and now that he has news, I'm hoping the deal is finally done.

"All parties have agreed, Miller, you're officially a Crusher."

"Are you shitting me?"

"I wouldn't do a thing like that," he says with a chuckle, and we both know he's full of shit. Jaxson Scott is one of the most laid-back guys I know but at the same time, he knows his shit. It's why he's the most sought after agent at Life's Too Sport. He always has his clients' best interests at heart and, luckily for me, he's always secured the deals I've been chasing.

"You and I both know that's a lie but that aside, I'm over the moon right now. Thank you for always looking out for me."

"It's my job. I'm sending over the contract, look it over,

but it's all the standard stuff. You can't talk about this with anyone until it's made official, but come next season—"

"I'll be living in New York."

"We'll have to catch up for drinks when you get here. Now, I'll let you get back to whatever you were doing when I called."

Shaking my head, we say our goodbyes and then I hang up. Tossing my phone down onto my bed, I fist pump the air. You can't wipe the smile off my face right now. Finally, the deal is done and, come next season, once again JJ and I will be on the same team.

My agent seriously is the best.

Now if only I could find a lucky lady to settle down with. This player's off the ice lifestyle is becoming redundant. This move is exactly what my dating life needs, a fresh start. A new city for a new chance at love. Only time will tell.

19

EVIE

IT'S BEEN a week since returning to Brookvale after the funeral and life has become even more hectic. Tyler and I have settled back into our routine, but I do wish we had more downtime. He's once again thriving, and I really hope our move doesn't disrupt him too much.

Today has been call after call with my new boss, Doc Michels. Seems he's keen to get started before I'm officially part of his team. He's working with the NY Crushers and he's heading up this amazing program to help athletes recover quicker. He wanted to pick my brain on things I noticed and what we've been doing with Marshall Kerr now he's putting in the effort. As much as it was thrilling, it was also tiring.

When Tony asked if he could take Tyler for the afternoon, I was so flipping happy. Tony dotes on my son like a loving uncle, and he treats me like his niece. It's nice to have a family of sorts here, and I'm going to miss him like crazy when I move.

Grabbing myself a glass of wine, I head into the bathroom for a relaxing soak in the tub. Pushing aside all of Tyler's bath toys, I put the plug in and turn the tap on. Since I don't get a chance to relax often, I don't have any adult bubble bath, so I squeeze in some Hot Wheels bubble gum scented wash and climb in.

Leaning back, I close my eyes and sip on my wine as the tub fills. Like always, since we returned from Sel's funeral, whenever I close my eyes, memories of making out with Miller filter into my brain. I remember the feel of his body pressing into mine. The feel of his tongue pushing into my mouth. The scratches of his beard against my skin. My clit throbs at the memory and my heart starts to erratically beat.

Sliding my hand under the water, I slip it between my legs and press down on my nub, trying to abate the growing arousal. A moan passes through my lips, and the sound turns into a guttural growl when I push two fingers inside.

Placing my glass down, I squeeze my breast as I begin to finger myself. Swiveling my hips, water sloshes about as I bring myself closer and closer to release. Miller's name squeaks out as I tumble over the edge.

Collapsing back against the side of the tub, I lie here, breathlessly panting. Like clockwork, the guilt at getting off to thoughts of my sister's ex slams into me, and I go from feeling euphoric to feeling like a piece of shit. I never should have acted on my feelings for Miller because now, I feel like the worst sister in the world. Thankfully, I'll never see Miller Wentworth again, so there's nothing to worry about.

It's officially moving week. Normally, I feel organized and on top of things when it comes to moving, but this time I feel like a chicken with its head cut off whose feet are stuck in cement. Don't get me wrong, I'm super excited for the move. Dream job. Dream city. Dream apartment, but at the same time I'm overwhelmed with the dream job, dream city, and dream apartment.

Speaking of apartments, the one I've rented in Hell's Kitchen is perfect for Tyler and me. It's not as close to the stadium as I would have liked, but it's secure and the views are pretty spectacular. The building has an amazing kids' play area, a pool, and there's even a courtyard.

I've always loved New York, The City that Never Sleeps. Mom too is excited because New York is closer to Chicago, making it easier for her to visit.

"Come on, Buddy," I sing out after taping up another box. "Let's go into town and get some dinner." Cooking is the last thing I feel like doing and a burger and beer sound great right about now.

Tyler comes racing out of his room, he's still wearing the Scofield Racing hat Marshall gave him a few weeks back. The team owner came to town and, for the first time ever, Marshall left the facility ... on two feet. Seeing him up and about was a feat to see, and I have no doubt he'll be back in his car very soon.

Tyler and I enter the diner and I smile when I see Marshall and E in a booth, looking very chummy together. He looks up and when he sees me, he does that head nod thing guys do, and I find myself mimicking it back. Knowing if Tyler sees him, he will interrupt their date, I steer him in the opposite direction and make sure he's sitting facing away from Marshall and E.

He's become obsessed with car racing in the last few weeks. It's a nice reprieve from his hockey obsession but I'm sure once I arrive in New York, hockey will be his number one again. For now, he pretends to drive everywhere, *broom brooming* and screeching all over the place.

We place our orders and I help him color while we wait for our food. I'm going to miss small-town life but, at the same time, I'm looking forward to having everything I need at my fingertips once again.

Tyler and I are just finishing up dinner when Dad calls. "Hey, Dad," I say when I answer.

"Evie, it's Dad." He says this every time he calls and like always, I reply with, "I know, Dad, your name came up."

"I'm in Brookvale, where are you?"

"You're in Brookvale?"

"That's what I said. Where are you?"

"Tyler and I were just getting dinner. We'll be home in five."

"I'm staying at the Brookvale Inn. Can you meet us there?"

"Sure, I'll be there just after I settle the check."

"See you then." He hangs up before I can say anything else.

As I help Tyler pack up the crayons, I wonder why Dad is in town. And why didn't he let me know he was coming? Maybe he's here to help me pack up but that's unlikely, Dad isn't one for packing boxes. He'd pay someone to do it, or he'd have one of his men do it for him.

After settling the check, Tyler and I head outside. "We just have to make a stop on our way home, Buddy." Tyler just nods, takes my hand, and like clockwork he starts with his *broom brooms* as we walk toward The Brookvale Inn. It's just around the corner from where we had dinner so we make it there in no time at all.

As we walk up the driveway, I realize I don't know what room Dad is in. It doesn't matter because he's in the parking lot, pacing back and forth with his phone to his ear. He looks up and when he sees me, he smiles, but I can tell he's angry from the fiery look in his eyes. "Room seven," he mouths and points to the door behind the black Escalade.

Walking to the room he pointed out, I open the door and when I step inside, I see the last person I expect to see. "Klaus, what are you doing here?"

"I'm here with your father. He got a lead on Selene, and color me surprised when she was last seen here. In Brookvale. Where you live." He sneers the word you and I don't like his tone ... or him. "Something you want to share?"

"Selene was in Brookvale?" I question, shocked and confused that she was here. Tyler lets go of my hand and starts to zoom around the room, oblivious to the confrontation happening between the two of us.

"What are the chances that she and you end up in the same bumfuck nowhere town?"

"Selene was in Brookvale," I repeat. "But why?"

"You tell me," he hurls at me. "You're hiding something and I want to know what you know. Why was she running? What aren't you telling me? Where was she all this time?"

"I ... I don't know anything," I stammer, wishing Dad was here because there is no way Dad would let him speak, well, interrogate me like this. "I didn't even know she was here. Are you sure she was in Brookvale, Nevada?"

"Positive," he snaps.

She was here, I smile to myself and look over at Tyler. She has been watching him, us, but why didn't she reach out? I know she was scared but she came to me once before, why not again? I know legally she couldn't but I would never keep her from Tyler. She's his mom.

"Don't play dumb," he hisses. Those words and the tone he used has me snapping my head back toward him. He's eyeing me suspiciously and I don't like the look in his eye. "Why did she come and see you?"

"She didn't," I defend. "I didn't even know she was here."

"Don't lie or hide anything from me, girlie. I will find out why she left and if I find out you know, I will make you suffer and there will be hell to pay—"

"And it won't be my daughter paying anything," Dad shouts, walking back into the room, slamming the door behind him. "You need to back up and watch your tone, Klaus."

"She knows something," Klaus shouts at Dad, spittle flying out of his mouth. "She fucking knows."

"That may be so, but you will not speak to my daughter like that. She's not one of your men—"

"I don't give a fuck who she is. If she knows something, I want to know what she fucking knows." He turns his attention to me. "I will get it out of you, one way or another."

Before Dad or I can say anything, he marches to the front door, wrenches it open, steps outside, and angrily slams the door behind him. The force causes the walls to rattle and for Tyler to stop in his zoomy zoom tracks. His little eyes open wide and his face is etched with fear.

"It's okay, Buddy," I tell him. Walking over, I squat down in front of him and he throws himself into my arms. "Hey, it's all right."

"That man's mean," he whimpers into my neck.

"I know and I'm sorry he scared you, but he's helping Poppy with something and just got a little angry."

"A lot angry," he says, pulling away from me.

"Yes, a lot, but sometimes adults get angry."

"Maybe he needs a nap. I get mad when I'm tired."

"Maybe he does," I agree. "Why don't you watch some cartoons while I chat with Poppy?"

"Okay, Mommy." He races over to the sofa and pops the television on.

"You're good with him," Dad says, smiling at me.

"I learned from the best," I tell him. "Now, can I have a hug?"

"You're not too old to hug your dad?"

"Never," I tell him as I wrap my arms around his waist. He hugs me back and I find myself smiling into his chest. "Now, what's going on? Selene was here? In Brookvale?"

"It seems so," he tells me.

"Are you sure? I mean, Brookvale isn't that big, surely I would have seen her."

"Your sister is, was, the best at hide-and-seek, she was probably hiding in plain sight."

"What was she into, Dad? She..." I can't say that, he and everyone else think the only time I've been in touch was when she called me just after she left. "She could have come to me; I would have helped her. No questions asked."

"I know you would have, and I wish I had answers but..."

"I don't think we ever will," I finish the sentence for him. "Why is Klaus here?"

"He hasn't stopped looking for her, or for her killer."

"But why?" I think back to Selene's letter and I wish I could tell Dad what I know, but she would hate me for telling him what I know. I also have a feeling, sharing what I know would just make things worse. Especially considering how he acted just now, thinking I know something. If he ever finds out I know more than I'm letting on, it's not going to end well. It's best if I just keep my mouth shut.

"He's a good friend, Eves."

"It just seems weird," I honestly tell Dad.

"It can be as weird as it needs to be. I just want answers, and I will not rest until I find out what happened to my daughter."

With the heaviness regarding the why of Dad's visit

over, he accompanies Tyler and me back home and, shocking the shit out of me, he helps me pack up the last of my kitchen.

"Are you sick?" I ask him when the last of the glassware has been packed into a box.

"No, why?" He looks quizzically at me.

"You're helping pack. Isn't packing beneath you? Shouldn't one of your minions be here packing while you sit back and drink scotch and smoke a cigar?"

"I think you're confusing me with Klaus. I'm very hands-on when it comes to—"

"Taking out the bad guys but when it comes to domestic things, you are like a newborn calf, wobbly and—"

"Excuse me, young lady, I will have you know that I can hold my own. I'm not some helpless calf, as you so eloquently put it."

"Mmmhmpf," I sass, "but for what it's worth, thank you. I muchly appreciate it. I've really struggled with packing up and working and looking after Tyler."

"Why didn't you ask for help? I would have sent some minions, as you call them, to assist you."

"That's not my life, Dad," I tell him. He knows I'm not a fan of the other part of our life. However, I know without that part, I wouldn't have had a lot of the things I had growing up. Now that I'm an adult and a mom, I want to do things my way. The legal way.

"I know you hate that part of my life, but it's all I know. I would never push it onto you, and I'm so proud of you for achieving your dream, on your own per se." He's referring to the donation he made to the school and them allowing me to take a leave of absence when I took the semester off for Tyler. If Dad knew it was for his biological grandson, he would have done even more to help. But I promised Sel I would keep it a secret, and I always keep my promises, even in death.

Shaking off the thoughts of secrets and Sel, I hand Dad a glass of wine, well, a coffee cup of wine since we just packed the glassware. Together, we catch up and, before I know it, Dad leaves and I'm climbing into bed.

Thankfully, I don't see Klaus again before they head back to Chicago. The morning before they leave, Dad, Tyler, and I have breakfast together, and then Tyler and I head home to meet the movers because it's officially moving day.

When the movers are done, Tyler and I hop into the car and begin our road trip across the country to New York ... if only I knew what was coming in the next few months in The City that Never Sleeps.

20

MILLER

NEW YORK really is The City that Never Sleeps and I love it. I've been here in The Big Apple for just under a week, and I already feel at home.

I'm all settled into my new forty-third floor apartment in Hell's Kitchen. I would have liked to be closer to the stadium, but I fell in love with the views and the in-house gym when the agent showed me around. My apartment is also for sale but I want to see if I like the building and area before I make a big purchase like that, but after the short period of time I've been here, I could definitely see myself calling this place home.

Tomorrow is my first official day with the Crushers, but this afternoon I'm meeting JJ and a few of the other guys from the team at Squires Tavern for a catchup. Apparently, this place is the best sports bar in the city. This will be our last chance to let loose before training commences for the upcoming season.

I'm nervously excited about it, both the season and this meetup. Colton Bolton and I, yep, that's his name, are the new guys. It's always nerve-wracking being the new guy, but I'm hoping since I know JJ, it won't be so overwhelming.

Heading downstairs, I step out onto the street and I'm immediately hit with the hustle, bustle, and noise that is New York City. Thankfully the soundproofing in the apartments is top-notch because when I'm in my apartment, I hear nothing. Hailing a cab, I jump in, and after giving him the name of the bar, he pulls out into traffic and whisks me across town.

When I arrive, JJ and Kallen, the team's goalie, are arriving too.

"You made it," JJ says, pulling me in for a one-armed bro hug.

"Said I would," I tell him. "Kallen," I offer in greeting and outstretch my hand.

"Wentworth," he says with a nod, shaking my hand in return.

The three of us head inside and the guys make a beeline to a table where a few of the other team members are, as well as their girlfriends. When we reach them, JJ throws his arm around my shoulder. "It's so good to have you here."

"It's good to be here."

Looking around the table, I see Jett Jensen and his "fake" girlfriend Margot, Anton Seaton, who recently retired, and Colton Bolton—LOL—wonder if I will ever be able to say his name without chuckling, plus a few others who I unfortunately don't know.

"Drinks?" I offer.

"I'll get the first round, you get the next one." Before I can say I can get my own drink, JJ is off toward the bar.

Taking a seat across from Jett, I watch him and Margot. They're awfully chummy for "fake" dating, and I'm about to ask about it when a girl slides up next to me. "Well, well, well, look who made it to The Big Apple." Turning my head, I smile when I see Lexi Knight grinning brightly at me and looking as gorgeous as ever.

"Lexi," I singsong, "long time no see."

Standing up, I pull her in for a hug and, like clockwork, JJ growls, "Hands off."

"I see some things haven't changed."

Lexi giggles and lets me go. She slides over to JJ and slips her arm around his waist. He kisses her on the head, and I find myself smiling at my school friends. It's nice to see them happy and in love again, especially after JJ broke her heart, back in the day. I still maintain he was a dickhead but JJ is a stubborn one, and he was sure he was making the right decision. Guess fate had a plan for them after all since they're together again.

"Get a room, you two," Lexi calls out. When I glance to where she's looking Kallen and Chelsea are making out. Kallen is hooking up with the coach's daughter. That's ballsy if you ask me, but I will admit, the two of them look happy and in love.

Next time I date, I want it to be someone with less drama … and not the daughter of someone who holds my career in the palm of their hand.

The afternoon flies by and as I sit here with my new team, sipping on my beer, I feel at home. This move was just what I need and, now, I really can't wait for tomorrow.

"Fuck me," I pant, dropping down onto the bench in front of my cubby after throwing my training shirt to the floor next to me. "That was hardcore."

"Coach was definitely in a mood today," JJ states from beside me.

Stretching out my leg, I rub my knee. Ever since my injury a few years back, it aches on occasion, and today is that occasion. Thank God my building has a heated spa and pool. Looks like a bit of aqua therapy will be in order this afternoon.

Closing my eyes, I rub my knee, but then I hear a voice I would recognize anywhere saying, "...and his recovery is on track. Surgery went well and if he sticks to the plan, he should be back on the field before the start of next season." When I open my eyes again, they widen completely and my mouth drops open because walking out of the treatment room with Doc is none other than Evie Salvatore. She's here in the Crushers locker room before me in leggings and a polo, looking just as sexy as I remember. "Evie," I blurt out her name and stand up.

She turns her head in my direction and when she sees me, her eyes widen just like mine. "Miller," she utters my name in a shocked tone. "What are you doing here?"

"I was traded," I tell her. "What are you doing here? I thought you were living in Bumfuck, Nowhere?"

"I ... I moved here a few months ago when Doc offered me a position on his medical research team."

"Ohh," is all I manage to utter because I'm shocked to see her. My eyes roam over her and, fuck me, she's just as gorgeous as I remember ... Then I remember the last time we were together and what we got up to. Before I can say anything else, what sounds like a kid pretending to be a race car zooms into the locker room and when I look toward the noise, I see Evie's son. He has a race car in his hand and he's zooming it all over the place. And right now, he's zooming it up Kallen's leg and across his lap.

"Tyler," Evie scolds him, "wheels on the ground, not on people." She looks to Kallen with a "sorry" look on her face.

"It's fine, Eves." Hearing him call her Eves pisses me off, but I have no right to be pissed and the feeling confuses me. "Oddly enough, it feels good on my muscles." He chuckles. "Maybe you guys need to look into *broom-broom* therapy."

"You're a dick," JJ says from next to me, but most of the guys are chuckling at his *broom-broom* therapy suggestion.

"You saids a bad word," Tyler interrupts them and holds out his hand to JJ. JJ sighs but reaches into his locker and hands over a quarter. Dropping the coin into his outstretched palm Tyler smiles sweetly, turns, and walks over to a jar in the corner. Removing the lid, he drops the coin into it and then skips away without a care in the world. *Ohh, to be young and carefree again.*

"What was that all about?"

"We're not allowed to swear around the kid," JJ tells me. "If we do, we have to put a quarter into his swear jar."

"He's gonna be a rich five-year-old if he hangs around with us," I say, earning a few chuckles from the rest of the team.

"You'll lean to swear without swearing," Kallen informs me. "Chels uses puck in place of f..." he pauses, "uck. There are actually many creative ways to swear without swearing."

"Guess I better google them then." Then I look down over at Tyler. "Hey, T-man, can I just make a donation to the cause and call it even?"

"Nope," Evie says, joining us. "Fair's fair. You swear, you pay up."

"Is Doc paying you so little that you need your son to extort hockey players?" I tease.

She just shrugs and taps the side of her nose in a "guess we'll never know" kind of way, and I can't help but chuckle. "It's good to see you, Miller," Evie says.

"You too, Eves, you too." She gives me another one of her megawatt smiles, and then walks over to Tyler. She takes his hand. "Come on, lil' man, let's go home and, if you're lucky, we might go for a swim since it's still early."

He hisses a lil' "Yesss," adding a few extra s's, and does a fist pump.

"Bye, everyone," Evie calls out with a wave.

Tyler does a lil' wave too and calls out, "Later, duuu-udes." Adding a few extra u's to the word.

A chorus of "later" and "bye" echoes in the locker room and then they're gone. What are the chances that the one woman I've not been able to stop thinking about is here in New York? Is this kismet? Or is the universe just fucking with me?

21

EVIE

OF ALL THE teams he could have been traded to, Miller Wentworth is traded to my team, well, not my team but the team I'm working with. When I heard my name and *that* voice, I was shocked, but instantly the vibration of his voice caused goosebumps to rise. Then, when I turned around and looked up, there he was. Standing there in all of his six-foot-two sexiness, my knees went weak, but somehow I managed to stay upright.

We talked and discussed things but, for the life of me, I have no clue what we actually spoke about because Miller Wentworth is in New York, and it's messing with my head ... and vagina ... like it always does.

Tyler managed to earn a quarter from JJ and then Miller teased me about needing the money, which was secretly funny because we both know my family isn't short of cash. Regardless of my financial status, curbing the potty mouths of these players is something that needs to be done. I love how all the guys on the team happily pay up and play along when Tyler hears them swear. I'm positive the kid has super-power hearing when it comes to swear words.

After drooling over Miller and him paying up, I tell him with a smile, "It's good to see you."

"You too, Eves, you too." When he calls me Eves, holy shit, I swear I could come in my pants. I know that's not very ladylike, but his voice is low and smoky and just perfect. So perfect I could listen to him read the phone book.

Before I make a fool of myself in front of Miller and the team, I make my escape with the help of Tyler and the promise of a swim. When he readily agrees, he takes my hand, we say our goodbyes, and together we head to the parking lot. Tyler climbs into his seat and once he's strapped in, I pull out of the parking garage and we make our way home.

Driving in New York is an experience I don't think I will ever get used too. Dad offered to pay for a driver for us, but I want to make it on my own. Plus, I like the independence of having my own car. Parking in my allocated spot, Tyler and I climb out and head to the elevator. While we wait for it to arrive, my mind drifts back to Miller. Of all the teams, he's here. Is this kismet? Or is destiny once again fucking with me? Regardless of his looks, I cannot go there with him. He's my sister's ex and that's a big no-no. I already crossed that line by making out with him, but that's as far as it will ever go. He and I will never be.

The ding of the elevator snaps my attention away from dreamland and after ushering Tyler in, he pushes the buttons for our floor and the metal car whisks us up to our floor. Tyler races out as soon as the door opens and after I unlock ours, he darts off to his room. Dumping our things on the counter, I put away our lunch boxes. Then I open the refrigerator, trying to decide on what to have for dinner.

Closing the fridge, I come face-to-face with my son. His little hands are on his hips and he has a stern look on his face. "Can I help you?"

He looks at me matter-of-factly, "You said we can swim."

"I did," I confirm, trying to hold back a laugh because the serious expression on his face right now is very, very cute. "And what must you do if we go for a swim?"

With a sigh and an eye roll that rivals his mother's when she was a teenager, he says, "I have to promise to eat alllllll of my wegetables and go straight to bed."

"That's right, now, go get changed and then we can head down."

"Yesssssss," he hisses. Fist pumping the air like he does whenever he gets what he wants. He once again races down the hallway and into his room to get changed.

At a much more leisurely pace, I make my way into my room to change. I slip into a black-and-silver halter bikini before I throw a cover-up dress over the top.

Once we've both changed into our suits and Tyler has his floaties, we grab our towels and head down to the pool. It's still warm out, but I love that the pool is heated because it takes the chill away when I have to get in with Tyler.

We enter the pool area and I nearly trip over my feet when my gaze lands on none other than Miller-fucking-Wentworth. A shirtless Miller Wentworth. Is the universe trying to punish me? First he transfers to my team, and now he's here. In my pool. In my building.

"Miller," Tyler calls out when he spots him.

Miller turns toward us and his eyes widen when they spot Tyler and me. Standing up, he walks toward us and I notice his gaze roams over my body. My skin sizzles at the intensity from his stare. The stare he isn't even trying to hide. "What are you guys doing here?"

"Mommy said we can swim so we're swimming, but I have to promise to eat my wegetables tonight."

"I love veggies," Miller says, crouching down to talk on his level. "I think broccoli is my favorite."

"Eeeeew," Tyler makes a gagging sound and scrunches his face up. "I like carrots."

"Carrots are another good one—"

Tyler interrupts and I just know what he's going to say next. "I loves corn too 'cause it makes your poo colorful."

"It does," Miller agrees with a chuckle, then he adds, "You know, you should love all veggies 'cause eating your veggies will help you to grow up big and strong."

"Like you," Tyler states.

"Yeah, like me."

"Come on, Tyler," I call out. "Leave Miller alone."

"It's fine," he waves me off, "it's nice to have some company."

"You want to hang out with a four—"

"Almost five," Tyler interjects, smiling brightly.

"Sorry, almost five-year-old and his mom?"

He shrugs. "I haven't met my neighbors yet, and I kinda don't really know anyone here except the guys on the team."

"Same," I agree. "If it makes you feel better, Tyler and I have been here for a few months now and I still haven't met my neighbors either. I'm not even sure someone lives in the apartment across from me."

"Same for me," he agrees, before looking around to see if we're alone. When the coast is clear, he leans in and whispers, "New Yorkers aren't the friendliest of people. No one smiles and they avoid eye contact like the plague."

A laugh breaks free. "This is true, but I promise to look you in the eye and say hello should we pass one another in the lobby or here in the pool area."

"Deal," he agrees.

Placing our things down on the lounger next to Miller, I take a seat and pull out our towels, just as Tyler whines, "Can we swim now, Mom?"

"I didn't hear the magic word in there."

He sighs dramatically and then he grips my cheeks in his little hands. "Please, Mommy, can we swim now?"

"Yes, but only because you asked so nicely."

"Yesssssss," he hisses with a fist pump. He grabs my hand and pulls. Once upright, I lift my cover-up over my head, dropping it to the lounger. Then I pull my hair up into a messy bun before I offer Tyler my hand. He pops his in mine, and together we walk over to the pool's edge. Tyler stands next to me, staring at the water. He's brave but he's also only four, almost-five brave.

"Do you want me to hop in first?" He nods. Sitting down on the edge, I slide into the water and gasp as my body sinks down. "Shit, it's cold."

"You saids a bad word," Tyler points out.

"I did and I'm sorry, I'll pop a quarter in the jar when we get upstairs."

Miller laughs and my eyes dart over to him. He's lying back in the lounger, aviator sunglasses covering his eyes. He's wearing board shorts that sit low on his hips, showcasing his abs and "V" muscles that send women—hello, I'm women—crazy. No wonder they signed him for that underwear commercial.

He sits up and lowers his sunglasses and it hits me. I was just caught checking him out. "Shit," I hiss.

"You saids a bad word again."

Turning my attention back to Tyler, I smile at the little tycoon. "I know, sorry. Now, you ready to dive in?" He excitedly nods and, before I know it, he's launched himself into the air and he's diving into the water. Breaking the surface, I pull him into my arms and tickle him. He giggles and before he even asks, I grab under his arms and call out, "Ready." Then I lift him up and I throw him up into the air. He squeals in delight before he once again, crashes into the water.

"Again, again," he asks when he paddles over to me.

We repeat the motion a few times and, thankfully, he wants to stop because my arms are sore. Wading over to the side, I lift myself up and sit on the edge, watching as Tyler paddles around the pool. Leaning back on my hands, my head drops back and I close my eyes. The afternoon's sunrays warm my skin, and I take a moment to suck up the vitamin D and just enjoy the afternoon.

I love my job allows me time with Tyler like this. I'm sure things will change once the season officially starts and we'll be tending to injuries and monitoring the recoveries. I know it's bad to be excited about injuries but without players getting hurt, I wouldn't have a job.

Before I know it, Tyler's bottom lip is quivering and there's a chill in the air. When Tyler and I exit the pool, I deflate when I notice Miller left, and he left without saying goodbye. Packing up our things, we head upstairs where Tyler eats all of his veggies and due to all the swimming this afternoon, he's asleep before his head hits the pillow.

Pouring myself a glass of wine, I sit in the living room and stare out the floor-to-ceiling windows, gazing down at The City that Never Sleeps ... and thinking about Miller. I've always loved him and now that we're together again, the love I felt all those years ago is back. But we can never be because he's my sister's ex, right?

22
MILLER

SEEING Evie at the pool area was a shock, that's twice today she's shocked me. I thought I was hallucinating at first but when Tyler called out my name, I knew I wasn't because I do not daydream about him. His mom, on the other hand? Well, I haven't stopped thinking about her since I saw her in the locker room earlier today

Grabbing a mineral water, I'm limiting my beer consumption now that training has started, I pad over to the floor-to-ceiling window. Twisting the cap off my water—the sound isn't the same as popping the top off a beer—I take a sip and place the bottle down on the side table. Resting my arm on the glass, I stare out the window and gaze down at the street below. The sun has set, leaving the sky inky black. The street below is lit up from the streetlights and head-lights of the cars. People watching from this height isn't as much fun because they look like teeny tiny Lego men and women. It's not the same because you can't see their facial expressions.

Closing my eyes, I breathe in deeply and suddenly I

have a vision of Evie in my mind. She's in nothing but that sexy as fuck swimsuit she was wearing earlier. She has one leg bent and she's leaning against the glass provocatively, giving me come hither eyes. Walking over to her, I gently glide my palm down her side and back up again. Her nipples pebble and she whimpers at my touch. Leaning forward, I suck on the taut peak through the thin material of her suit. Her whimper turns into a moan when I gently bite down on the tip. "Yes," she mewls as I cup her pussy with my hand. Pushing the material aside, I run the pad of my finger up and down her slit. Another throaty hum quickly turns into a guttural rumble.

My eyes fly open when I realize it was me making the noises and then it hits me, I just came all over the window to my fantasy of Evie.

Pulling my shirt over my head, I clean up the glass as best I can then I walk into my bedroom to wash off the chlorine from my earlier swim ... and the shame of what I just did.

Of course, the first person I see when I walk into the locker room this morning is Evie. It's as if fate is messing with me. First, I sleep through my alarm and then my truck wouldn't start, so I'm running late and in a mood.

"Morning," she calls out when she looks up and sees me.

"Morning," I repeat back.

"Wentworth. Gym. Now," Coach McQueen bellows from the doorway to the gym. McQueen has a bark just as good as our head coach, David Maxwell. Between the two of them, I'm not sure who is scarier. One thing I do know, they're a dynamite coaching duo and I cannot wait to work with them this season.

"Uhhh ohh," Evie singsongs, "someone's in trouble."

My lips lift into a grin and I shake my head. One sentence and all my anger from the morning dissipates.

Dumping my bag in front of my locker without unpacking, I head into the gym and thank the heavens I'm already in my workout gear. McQueen barks out orders and we all scatter and get to it.

He pushes us hard, harder than usual.

"Someone needs to get laid," Colt murmurs under his breath, but Coach McQueen has superhero hearing or something because he marches over to Colt. Standing toe to toe, he gets up in Colt's face and shouts at him about showing respect to his elders and demands that he drop and give him fifty.

Not arguing, Colt drops and gives him fifty, but the newbie doesn't know how to keep his mouth shut. When he stands up after doing fifty push-ups, he stares at Coach, grinning and cheekily utters, "That all you got?"

"Ohhh shit," Kallen whispers, while the rest of us stare on in shock. Everyone knows you never talk smack to your coach. And you never throw down a challenge like that. Standing here, we all brace ourselves for what's to come next but, shocking the shit out of everyone, Coach McQueen just turns around and walks out of the gym.

"I showed him," Colt boasts, breaking the silence that fell over the rest of the team.

Kallen shakes his head. "You're fucked," he chortles.

"What do you mean?" And for the first time, Colt sounds and looks scared.

"I think it's best if you just find out for yourself," Kal says, slapping him on the back before exiting the gym.

"JJ?" Colt asks.

"What Kal said," JJ replies before mimicking someone getting their neck sliced.

"It can't be that bad, right?"

Wrong! It was worse … for all of us. That afternoon on the ice, Coach McQueen pushed us hard, harder than I've ever been pushed in a training session. Each and every one of us silently cursed Colton-fucking-Bolton for this punishment.

A few of the guys puke from being pushed so hard, Colt included. And when Colt vomits, McQueen walks over to him, squats down before him, and staring into his eyes, he says, "That enough for you?"

Colt stares back at Coach, and we all stand here and wait with bated breath to see what he will say and, thankfully, he learned his lesson. He just nods and mumbles a, "Yes, Coach."

"Let that be a lesson to never talk back to your coach." McQueen taps him on the cheek, stands up, commands us to do ten more laps, and without another word, he walks off the ice.

Finishing out my laps, I make my way back to the locker room and drop down in front of my cubby. My body hurts in a way it's never hurt before. All I can think about is the spa when I get home, but I need to shower first because I stink.

Shuffling to the showers like I'm an eighty-year-old man, I step under the spray. The water beats down on my body and washes away the stench. Tilting my head back, the water hits my face and I let out a moan.

"You beating off in there, Wentworth?" JJ asks from next to me.

"I couldn't get it up even if,"—*Evie*—"Buffy herself was naked and in here with me."

"I hear ya," he agrees, but I'm focused on the fact I immediately thought of Evie and not my all-time celebrity crush on Buffy, aka Sarah Michelle Gellar. "If I had the energy, I'd beat the fuck out of Colt."

A chorus of "Hear! Hear!" echoes around the showers.

"I'd beat myself up," Colt pipes in. "Sorry, guys, but lesson learned."

"Beers are on you next time we all end up at Squires," someone sings out, again, earning a chorus of "Hear! Hear!"

"Deal," he agrees without argument, and I really hope he's learned his lesson because there is no way in hell I will survive another practice like that.

23

EVIE

THIS WORKING full time and raising an almost five-year-old on your own is harder than I thought it would be. Tyler and I have just gotten home and all I want to do is curl up with a glass of wine and my Kindle, especially after the argument I just had with Tyler. He wants to go for a swim, but I'm too tired to take him and it's nearly dark outside. Thankfully, I sweet-talk him with cooking mac 'n' cheese from scratch using my mom's family recipe for dinner. That manages to settle him and he finally calms down. I get him set up with *Bluey* and I head into the kitchen to start on dinner.

Turning on the pan, I drop in a dollop of butter and, when it's melted, I whisk in some flour and my secret ingredient—nutmeg. Once it's bubbling, I begin to whisk in the milk and heavy cream. It's bubbling away nicely, so I reduce the temperature and let it slowly simmer.

While I wait for the sauce to thicken, I pour myself a glass of wine. Leaning against the counter, I take a sip but as soon as the liquid hits my tongue, I spit it back into the glass and groan. It's horrible, worse than mushrooms horrible. I took a chance on a new one when I was at the store earlier this week. The purple label was cute but that's all that's good about this wine.

Placing the glass down on the counter, I use a little more force than necessary—but it really is shit wine—and the stem breaks, causing me to slice my hand open—this is why I like stemless glasses.

"Shit," I hiss as blood begins to drip down my hand onto the counter.

Grabbing the tea towel, I race into my bedroom and into the en suite. Crouching down, I pull out the first aid kit from under the sink and make a mental note to move this out to the kitchen. Removing the cloth, blood drips all over the place and, within seconds, the sink looks like a scene from *CSI*. "I don't have time for this," I whine.

No matter what I do, the blood will not stop pouring out of me.

Finally, after all the gauze in the first aid kit has been used and thrown in the sink, the bleeding stops. Popping a Band-Aid on, I start cleaning up when there's a knock on the door. Exiting my bathroom, I head to the door and when I open it, my eyes widen when I see a shirtless Miller standing there. "Miller," his name comes out in a rush, but then I see he's holding Tyler's hand. "Tyler," I utter his name in shock, and it's a few octaves higher than usual. "What ... what are you doing outside?"

"I found him in the hallway when the elevator doors opened."

"You live on this floor?" He nods and points to the door across the hall from mine. "But how did you find Tyler? He was inside. Watching *Bluey* while I cooked dinner." Just as I say the word dinner, the smoke alarm in my apartment starts to blare. "Shit," I hiss.

Turning my back on Tyler and Miller, I race into the kitchen and my eyes land on the pan on the stove top. The kitchen is full of smoke, which is pouring out of the pan. Seems when I cut my hand, I didn't turn off the element and now dinner is burnt and ruined, and my kitchen is full of smoke. Plus, I'm going to get fined from the building for setting off the smoke alarms.

It's the straw that breaks the camel's back. After tossing the burnt pan into the sink and turning the faucet on, I slide down the fridge, bring my knees up, lower my head, and I begin to cry.

Sitting on the floor in my kitchen, I sob and sob.

Lifting my head, I tilt it back and stare at the ceiling. Closing my eyes, I inhale deeply and recenter myself. My eyes fly back open when I hear running water coming from the bathroom down the hall. Pushing myself up, I race down the hallway but I slow my steps when I hear Tyler, "That's too much Hot Wheels bubbles, Mommy will get mad."

"It'll be our secret," Miller suggests, and I find myself smiling at their little secret.

"Did I make Mommy cry?" Tyler asks, and my heart breaks at hearing him sound so sad.

"Nah," Miller placates him. "Sometimes adults just need to cry, but you do know that leaving the apartment by yourself was a silly thing to do, right?"

"But I wanted to go swimming," Tyler tells him.

"And I get that, but you need an adult with you when you go swimming, and there's also stranger danger and tricky people to worry about."

"What's that?" Mister Twelve Million Questions a Day asks.

"Well, ummm, it's like, shit." Peeking into the bathroom, I smile when I see Tyler standing there in his swim shorts with his hand out. I still can't believe the lil' shit tried to go swimming by himself.

Miller pulls out his wallet and drops a quarter into his outstretched palm. "Getting back to sticky strangers. Shit, I mean, stranger danger and tricky people, it's umm, well, it's staying safe from people you don't know by following some rules."

"What rules?"

"You never go anywhere on your own or without telling a grown-up. Never leave with a stranger without telling someone you know. Never get in their car. Never accept gifts or treats from people you don't know, and never give them your personal information. But most of all, they should never ask you to keep a secret or do something that makes you feel unsafe."

"But why?"

"Not everyone is a nice person, and I'd hate to see something bad happen to you."

"You're nice too."

"Thanks, Buddy, now, how about you jump into the tub?" Tyler nods and he hooks his fingers into the top of his swim trunks and removes them, when Miller screeches and swats at his hand. "No, no, leave your trunks on."

"For my bath?" Tyler asks. Both of us furrow our brows in confusion. Standing here, I wait and wonder where this is going to go.

"Well, yeah, I ummm, I don't think I should see you naked."

"Why?" Tyler asks. "We both have pee pees. Is'd yours a flat one like Cate's?" I chuckle to myself as I think back on the day when we found the two of them in the bathroom together. I never expected to have to have an anatomy conversation with two four-year-olds. When I told Coach McQueen about it, he warned me in no uncertain terms to, "Keep my son away from his daughter." He wasn't impressed when I informed him that it was his daughter who started the innie/outie pee-pee experiment.

"What?" Miller exclaims, "No ... I ... shit." Tyler pops his hand out for another quarter. "I'll give you five bucks later."

"It's only a quarter, silly."

"Call it interest."

"What's that?"

Stepping into the bathroom, I rescue Miller. "Look at all those bubbles," I say, garnering the attention of the two of them.

"Miller did it," Tyler says without batting an eyelid.

"Way to throw me under the bus, Buddy."

"There's no bus in here," Tyler states, and I can't help but chuckle at Miller's blank expression.

"Just get in the tub," I tell Tyler.

"Yes, Mom." Without another word, he climbs into the tub and starts splashing about. This must be the cleanest bathroom in all of New York because it gets a clean each time Tyler has a bath.

"Ten minutes," I tell Tyler. "Can I, umm, talk to you, Miller?"

He nods and without another word, he follows me back into the main living area.

"Thank you for ... just thank you. I don't know what I would have done had it been anyone else who found him."

"He's a smart kid, he would have found his way back to you."

"I know but"—I shake my head—"I need to be more careful. I'm just glad it was you."

"I have to admit, I was shocked when I stepped out of the elevator and found him waiting in the hallway."

"Well, I was shocked when I opened the door and found you with him."

"This next question comes with no judgment, but what happened?"

"I was making dinner and I broke a glass, and while I was fixing up the cut, he decided to go for a swim." He nods his head. "You must think I'm a shitty mom."

"That'll be a quarter," he teases, with a chuckle. "And no, I don't think that at all."

"That makes one of us," I tell him.

"Shit happens"—he raises his hand—"and yes, I'm aware I owe eleventy billion dollars to the kid's jar."

"How about we call it even for saving my son?"

"Deal, but, Eves, stuff happens. You just need to learn and move on." He pauses and then asks, "Are you sure you're okay? You kinda broke apart just now."

"I, umm ..." How do I tell Miller I was simply overwhelmed and burning dinner was the catalyst that sent me over the edge? Basically, I needed a good cry. I don't know what it is, but sometimes you just need to give the tear ducts a clean out by letting the tears flow freely. You just need to let out all the pent-up emotions trapped inside and, after falling apart, you're magically okay again. Thankfully, I'm saved from having to tell him that because from down the hallway a little voice calls out, "Moooooooooooooommm, I'm ready to get out."

"I guess I better go so you can get him out of the bath."

"Thanks again, Miller, I really appreciate it."

"Anytime and now that you know I'm just across the hall, holler if you need anything. I'll leave my number on the counter for you."

"Thanks."

Turning my back to him, I walk down the hallway feeling a little lighter after my meltdown. Who knew that all I needed to reset my mind was for my son to go wandering and have my long-time secret crush rescue him, and me, while I break down in my kitchen?

MILLER

GRABBING A PEN OFF THE COUNTER, I jot my number down, then the pan in the sink catches my eye. A memory of Evie on the floor falling apart hits me, and I can't in good conscience leave this mess for her to clean up. Dropping the pen on the counter, I step into the kitchen and get to cleaning up the pan. Once it's all sparkly again, I pop it back on the stove as it doesn't feel right to go through her cabinets.

From down the hallway, I hear Tyler, "Are we still having mac 'n' cheese for dinner?"

"I, ummm, I don't think I have any more ingredients to make it since I burned it."

A dejected, "Ohhh," follows and that one word guts me. Poor kid, couldn't go swimming and now he can't have mac 'n' cheese for dinner. "Does that mean I have to have broccoli now?" I chuckle to myself when I think about our conversation down at the pool the other day.

"I don't know what we'll have now, Buddy, but let's finish up here and then I'll organize something for dinner."

"Okay," he replies. Then he starts talking about frogs and makes ribbit sounds.

Not wanting to intrude any further, I exit their apartment and cross over to mine. Opening the door, I walk into my kitchen and grab a bottle of water. Twisting the cap off, I take a sip just as my stomach growls. Grabbing my phone, I quickly place an order for delivery from the Italian place around the corner.

While I wait, I quickly grab a shower and slip into gray sweats and a Crushers tee. No sooner do I walk out of my bedroom and there's a knock at my door.

Walking over, I open the door and as soon as I open it, I'm hit with the most delicious smells. "Fuck, I love that smell," I tell the delivery guy.

"You're ... you're Miller Wentworth."

"I am," I tell the starstruck fan. He just stands there, holding my food, staring at me open-mouthed. It's still so surreal that people get like this around me 'cause, well, I'm just me. But then I think about the first time I met Rick. His team was playing in Chicago, and JJ and I won meet-and-greet tickets from the local radio station. It was finally our turn and when I walked up to the table, I just stood there and mutely stared at him. Rick being Rick, he made me not feel like a dick, and I always told myself that if I made it big, I would never make people feel stupid for being starstruck. "Do you think I can get my food?"

"Ohhh, yeah, shit," he stammers. His hand is shaking as he passes the bags to me. Placing them on the hall table, I grab my wallet, pull out a bill, and hand him his tip. When he looks down at the money in his hand, his eyes widen farther. "A fifty?" Nonchalantly I shrug. "Thanks, man." His mouth opens and closes a few times and before he speaks, I know what he's going to ask. "Do you, umm, think I can grab a pic?"

"Sure," I reply and his smile widens even farther.

Quickly he whips out his phone and we snap a few pics. After thanking me profusely and wishing me luck for the upcoming season, he walks off grinning. Closing the door behind me, I too smile because I'm about to eat the best lobster linguine I've ever eaten. With the delivery bag in hand, I walk across the hall and, for the second time tonight, I knock on Evie's door.

"Coming," a sweet voice calls out. "Miller," she breathlessly says my name when's she opens the door. "What are you doing back here?"

Holding up the take-out bag, I inform her, "I brought dinner."

"W-w-w-what?" she stammers in confusion.

"Dinner," I reconfirm. "I got dinner for you guys."

"You really didn't need to do that."

"Well, I did because you burned yours and we can't have Tyler eating broccoli."

"You heard that, did you?"

"While I was cleaning the pan."

"Which you really did not need to do."

"It was nothing. Now, are you going to let me in?"

"Depends," she playfully replies.

"On what?"

"Only if there's garlic bread in there as well."

"Of course, you cannot eat pasta without garlic bread."

"Then, please, come in."

Stepping into her place, I walk over to the island counter and start unpacking the dishes.

"Did you order everything on the menu?"

"Not everything but we have lobster linguini, puttanesca, ravioli Milanese, chicken carbonara, and for the lil' man, mac 'n' cheese. There's also an arugula salad, broccolini sautéed in garlic butter and last, but not least, three cheese-stuffed mushrooms. Ohh, and for dessert, tiramisu." She makes a face. "You don't like tiramisu?" She scrunches her face up again and shakes her head. "But you're a coffee fiend."

"I love coffee but tiramisu is gross."

"That's just weird."

"No, it's not," she defensively refutes. "It's like people who like peanuts but not peanut butter, or people who hate avocado but love guacamole."

"Nope, those people are weirdos too. Okay, well, if tiramisu is gross, what's your go-to dessert?"

"Easy, chocolate mousse."

"Noted for next time," I tell her. She smiles at the possibility of next time and I have to say, I'm excited for a next time too. However, before I can think on that too much longer, Tyler pokes his head over the back of the sofa. When he sees me, his little eyes brighten and I find myself smiling back at him. "You hungry, Buddy?"

"Staaaaaarving," he adds a ton of extra a's and I have to admit, it's kind of cute.

"Well, go wash your hands while Mom and I dish up."

He nods, jumps off the couch, and runs down the hallway. A few seconds later I can hear him singing, "Washy-washy little hands, rub them like a marching band..."

"Like a marching band, what the hell?"

Evie shrugs her shoulder. "Beats me, but if it gets him to wash his hands, he can sing whatever he wants."

Evie spoons some mac 'n' cheese onto a plate for Tyler, then she adds some salad and a slice of garlic bread. "You're a good mom, Evie Salvatore."

She lifts her head and stares over at me. "I ... thank you. Some days I feel like I'm failing him. Why Sel-she—" She stops herself. "It's just hard."

"You're doing this alone, therefore I can only imagine

how hard it must be." I pause and then ask the question that has plagued me since I discovered she had a kid. "Can I ask about his dad?"

"Not around," she says but doesn't offer anything else.

I'm guessing it's a touchy subject and not wanting to put a damper on the evening, I push the million and one questions I have aside. "Well then, that makes you even more amazing in my eyes."

"I don't know about that. He ran away tonight."

"He didn't run away," I emphatically state.

"Potato. Vodka."

"Isn't the saying potato. Potatho?"

"I think you can say whatever you want but at the end of the day, my son ran away."

"He just wanted to go for a swim," I remind her, but I can tell from the look on her face, she's still torn up over what happened earlier. I'm not a parent so I can't tell her how to feel or even gauge how I would feel, but things happen and at the end of the day, Tyler is safe and happy. "How about we focus on the fact Tyler is fine ... and now you both get to have dinner with me."

"How did this become about you?"

"It's always about me, baby, now, try this." Forking a piece of broccolini, I lift it to her mouth. "Open," I command and surprising me, she opens. She wraps her lips around the fork and I pull it away. She moans and with the almost erotic vision of her lips wrapped around the fork and the sexy sound that slipped past her lips, I have to subtly rearrange my dick. *Down boy*, I internally berate myself. Thankfully, Tyler comes racing down the hallway and climbs up onto the stool next to me. "Do I have to eat that?" He points to the broccolini and scrunches his face up.

"No," Evie tells him, "but you have to have some salad."

"But no broccoli?"

"No, no broccolini."

He smiles sweetly at his mom and digs into the plate Evie slides across to him. Evie hands me a fork and I dig in too. Evie moans with each new dish she tries, and it's one of the most uncomfortable meals I've ever encountered. Hiding a raging hard-on from her and Tyler is hard—pun intended—when you're only wearing sweats but hardness aside, it was the most fun I've had in a long time.

After dinner, Evie helps Tyler brush his teeth and I clean up the kitchen for the second time this evening. I've just popped the last of the plates into the dishwasher when I hear a pleading, "But I want Miller to tuck me in."

"Not tonight, Buddy. It's already past your bedtime, you don't wan—"

"I want Miller to tuck me in!" he shouts even louder.

Tossing the tea towel onto the counter, I walk down the hallway toward the commotion. "What's going on in here?" I ask, resting my shoulder against the doorjamb.

"I want you to tuck me in but Mom said no," Tyler whines.

"Well, what your mom says goes, buuuut, if it's okay with her, I'm happy to do it. Only if tomorrow you eat all of your veggies and clean your room."

Tyler nods his head and looks to Evie. "Fine," she relents. Leaning over, she kisses him on the forehead and we swap places.

"Cool sheets," I tell him as I sit on the edge of his dinosaur-themed bed. Tyler has dinosaur sheets, a dinosaur duvet, and a stuffed T-Rex. I've never tucked a kid in before so I have no clue what I'm supposed to do.

"That's Declan," he tells me.

"Declan the T-Rex, cool. I always liked the long-necked ones."

"They're boring, I personally—"

"Tyler," Evie warns from the doorway.

He lets out an exaggerated sigh and it reminds me so much of Selene. *Seems the Salvatore genes are strong in him.* "We can discuss dinosaurs another time. You need to get a good night's sleep so you can grow up to be big and strong."

"Like you," he declares.

"Yeah, like me and your mom." Ruffling his hair, I smile down a the lil' dude. "You know, Tyler, your mom's pretty awesome." Looking over my shoulder at Eves, I add, "You're lucky to have her." Turning my attention back to Tyler, we bump knuckles and I pull his duvet up to his chin. He snuggles in and closes his eyes.

Sitting here, I watch him for a few moments and then stand up and walk out of his room.

"That was pretty easy," I tell Eves, just as from behind me, Tyler asks, "Can I have a glass of water?"

"Easy, huh?" she teases. She peeks around into the room. "It's on your bedside table. One sip and then sleep."

"Yes, Mom," he deadpans and I can't help but chuckle.

He has his drink and then Evie and I walk back into the main living area. "You didn't need to clean up," she says when she realizes the kitchen is tidy.

"It was nothing," I tell her. "Can I say something and I really hope it doesn't upset you."

"Ummm, yeah, but I can't guarantee I won't get upset."

"Just now, Tyler reminded me so much of Selene. His mannerisms were like I was looking at a mini male version of her." When I look up, her eyes are wide open and she's standing there, mute. I feel like I've upset her. "Shit, I'm sorry, I shouldn't have said that. Speaking of your dead sister like this is pretty shitty."

She shakes her head. "No, it's fine, it's just, I miss her so much. She's missing out on so much of Tyler's life, and I hate she's not here to see him grow up."

"Yeah, it does suck, but I bet she's up there watching over him and you." She smiles at that thought. "That's better."

"What's better?"

"You smiling." Her smile widens and then she yawns. "Sorry," she says through another yawn.

"I'll get out of your hair," I tell her. "Thanks for a great night."

"I should be the one thanking you. You saved Tyler and then you cleaned up my kitchen, twice. And to top it off, you brought dinner. Even if your dessert taste is questionable."

Picking up the container of tiramisu, I smile. "I'm going to enjoy this in peace when I get home … just don't tell Coach."

"Your secret is safe with me." With that, I bid her a good night and head across the hall and into my apartment.

Tonight was not what I expected but I have to say, hanging out with Evie and Tyler was fun. After eating my dessert—and yes, I ate all of it—I jump into the shower and I jerk off to visions of bending Evie over in the locker room and fucking her from behind. That's an image that'll play on repeat in my head for the rest of my life, much like the fantasy from the other night of us fucking up against the windows in my apartment.

I'm so fucked when it comes to this woman and now I know she lives across the hall from me, I think I might be screwed.

25
EVIE

THE NEXT FEW weeks pass by uneventfully, thankfully, but ever since Tyler took off, I've been paranoid over his safety. Why Sel thought I was the right person to look after him, I will never know. I mean when we were growing up, I couldn't even keep a cactus alive, how did she think I'd keep a human being alive?

Thankfully, my new friend Kennedy, Coach McQueen's nanny—and more, if my Spidey senses are correct—hooked me up with Cassandra. She comes in a few days a week to help me with Tyler and, oh my fucking God, this woman is a literal angel. She's so good with him, and I recently discovered she makes the most amazing guacamole. One afternoon Kennedy, Cassandra, and I will need to indulge in her famous guac and a few margaritas together.

Another godsend, Miller. That's not something I ever thought I'd say. It's almost like he has this sixth sense radar to know when I'm about to fall apart because just as I reach the breaking point, he swoops in and saves me. I've lost count of the number of times he's appeared at my door with dinner or breakfast.

Watching him with Tyler has my ovaries going into overdrive. What is it about a sexy as puck—damn you, Chelsea—man lying on the floor playing dinosaurs with a four-year-old? For never having been around kids before, he's brilliant with Tyler.

In another life, I'd push for more, but it feels wrong to go after my sister's ex. Plus, I'm like seven years older than him and a single mom. A hockey player in his prime doesn't want to be tied down with that, but luckily for me, dreams are free.

Arriving home, I toss the mail on the counter and a yellow envelope catches my attention. Picking it up, my eyes bug out of my head when I see the return address details. Quickly, I get Tyler into the bath and while he's splashing about, I pick up the envelope I haven't been able to stop thinking about. The last time I received an envelope like this my life changed in a way I never imagined, and my gut is telling me the same is about to happen again.

Tearing into the package, I pull out the papers and immediately begin to read.

```
Dear Ms. Salvatore,
Please accept my sincerest condolences on
the passing of your sister. I only met her
the one time but she was a breath of fresh
air. When she told me her story, my heart
broke for her, and I did all I could to
keep her son safe.
Recently there was some water damage at the
office and when I was going through every-
thing, I found an envelope tucked in the
back of my cabinets. This letter should
```

have been sent to you when we finalized the adoption all those years ago. I do apologize for this and hope it can shed some light and give you the closure you need as to why your sister did what she did.
Again, my apologies for this mix up.

Regards,
Dominic Burrows

Looking back into the envelope, I see another envelope and pull it out. Looking down at it, I gasp in shock when I see my name written in my sister's handwriting. With the pad of my finger, I rub over the ink. Tearing open the second envelope, my eyes fill with tears when I see Selene's handwriting before me. She always had such beautiful penmanship and with tears in my eyes, I begin to read.

My dearest Eves,
This is the hardest thing I have ever done, but I can't do this to Tyler anymore. He needs stability and you are the only person in the entire world who I would trust with my son. I know this may seem rash and crazy, even for me, but know me handing him to you is for the best. You were right in that I was running from Klaus. He and I had been having an affair. I was hopelessly in love with him but it turns out, all be wanted from me was a male heir. Thankfully, I left before that could happen but right before I did leave, there was a scare. Thank fuck, I wasn't pregnant that time. I knew I needed

to stop seeing him but I also knew he wouldn't just let me go, so I made the hard decision to leave.
I promise you with all that I have, he is NOT Tyler's father. Tyler's bio dad is ...

"Holy fuckballs," I hiss, my eyes and mouth drop wide open in shock. Covering my mouth, I pull out a chair at the island, drop down onto it, and continue to read.

He and I hooked up one weekend a few months after I left and that's when I got pregnant. He was doing so well with his career and I couldn't ruin that for him, so I did it on my own ... until I couldn't.
That last week with you was the best week I'd had in a long time, but Klaus somehow found me. That's when I knew I had to run again, but this time I couldn't take Tyler with me. Leaving him and signing him over to you is the hardest thing I have ever done, but as a parent you will do whatever it takes to keep your child safe. As much as it hurts, leaving Tyler with you is the best for him. You are the best person I know and, as I said earlier, there is no other person in the entire universe I would trust with my most precious treasure. I may have fucked up my life, but I will not fuck up his.
I know you will love him unconditionally and maybe one day, when Van der Cunt is dead, we can be together again. Until that day, please, please look after him as if he was your own son.

I love you and him to the moon and back. You will
forever be in my thoughts and heart.
Love always,
S
PS. Please, please, please, keep this secret

"I will," I mumble to the empty room, "I will."

Like when Sel asked for me to keep Tyler's identity a secret, this is another secret I'll take to my grave.

WIPING my face with my towel as I exit the gym, I bend my neck to the left before moving it in a tight circle, stretching it out. Dropping down in front of my locker, I wince in pain. My knee has been a little twingey the last few weeks. It seems to happen when the weather turns cold. The cooler temps tend to aggravate the tendons in my knee. Knowing I need to get it looked at, or risk further injury, I toss my towel onto the bench and switch from my sweaty gym shirt and into a Crushers tee.

Standing up, I walk into the medical room looking for Lexi, but I stop mid-step when I see a perky ass pointing up in the air. Standing in the doorway like a creeper, I watch for a few moments and when they reach to the side, a smile appears when I realize who the perky ass belongs to.

"Hey, Eves," I call out, stepping into the room

She looks over her shoulder and when she sees it's me, her eyes widen. "Miller," she says my name in a tone I haven't heard before. "What are you doing here?"

"I was looking for Lex, but you might be able to help."

She turns to face me. "Lexi should be back soon." Like before, her tone is off and rather than talking to me, she squats back down and focuses intently on the box before her.

"What's up?" I question, she's acting really strange right now.

"Nothing, why?"

"You seem ... different."

"I'm fine." I eye her because everyone knows when someone says they're fine, especially a woman, they're anything but fine.

"You sure about that?"

"Yes, I'm sure. Just busy."

"Need a hand?" I offer.

"I'm fine." There's that word again. Staring at her, I try to decipher what's up, but I can't get a read on her. I know it's nothing to do with Tyler because if it was, I'm pretty sure she'd come to me. When it comes to the lil' guy, she and I are on the same page. I don't know what it is about the kid, but I feel protective over him. I would do anything for him, and for her, so her being weird is eating at me. "What's up with you?" I ask again.

"Nothing, I'm—"

"Fine," I interrupt her.

"Seriously," she snaps. "I'm busy and I have a million and one things to do, and right now you're being annoying. So please, just fuck off."

Outstretching my hand, I look her directly in the eye. "That'll be a quarter." She purses her lips, trying to hide a smile. "But since the swear Nazi isn't here, I'll let it slide."

"How noble of you," she deadpans.

Offering her an exaggerated bow, she laughs, and when I stand upright again, I notice her smile is wider now. "That's better." But before we can continue our conversation, the woman I was looking for enters. "Miller, what can I do for you?" She runs her eyes over me, squints, and points to my leg, "Knee?"

"How the fuck did you guess that?"

"That'll be a quarter," Evie says, outstretching her hand.

"Hey," I protest, "I just gave you a freebie."

"Not all of us are famous hockey players making mega bucks, now, cough it up."

"Harsh, Eves. Harsh." I cover my heart pretending to be wounded.

She shrugs. "I'll come back and unpack this and leave you guys to it." Without another word, she exits the treatment room and closes the door behind her.

"Okay, up on the table and let me have a look," Lexi says.

"She okay?" I ask as I climb up on to the table.

"I thought she was off today too but she did say Tyler had a rough night last night, so she might just be tired."

Nodding, I make a note to check in on them when I get home this afternoon. I don't like the idea of her struggling, but I get the feeling it's more than just being tired. Shaking off thoughts of Evie and what could be up with her, I focus on Lexi. She asks me questions about my previous injury and, as I tell her, she pokes and prods at my knee. Thankfully, she doesn't want to order any scans because, like I thought, it's just the change in the weather messing with it. She sets out some stretches for me to do daily and before I leave she asks, "What are your intentions with my friend?"

"I ... I don't know to be honest. I like her but at the same time, I feel guilty because I used to date her sister."

"Miller, Selene broke your heart ... twice and, need I mention, she died. Whatever you and Selene had, it's in the past, but just know Evie and Tyler are a package deal."

"I know that and the fact she has a kid doesn't bother me in the slightest."

She stares at me, processing what I just told her. "You are good with him," she agrees. "But just don't hurt her."

"She'd need to let me in for that to happen but she's always holding me at arm's length."

"So swoop her off her feet. Make her feel like she's special."

"So I need to become a sap and be like JJ is with you?"

"Basically." She nods and a goofy loved-up look washes over her.

"That look looks good on you, Lex. I'm glad you and JJ got your second chance."

"Me too," she agrees, "me too. And maybe it's time for you to get yours too."

Waving bye to her, I grab my things and head home. All I can think about is what she said about Evie and me, but is it weird to hook up with your dead ex-girlfriend's older sister?

27

EVIE

TODAY IS Tyler's fifth birthday, and to say he's excited is the understatement of the millennium. This afternoon we're hosting a pool party for his birthday and people will be here very soon. The morning started with waffles for breakfast and presents. His main present is coming soon because I struggled to put it together but, like always, Miller swooped in and saved the day.

Like he always does.

He really is a super dad in every sense, but he will never know because I can never tell him. I swore to keep Tyler's parentage a secret and at the time it was just regarding who his mother was, but now I'm hiding the truth about both his parents. Am I doing the right thing keeping this from him?

Probably not.

But if I tell him that's going against my sister's wishes, and this is one of the last things she ever asked of me. I feel like I need to honor that, even if Miller is an amazing father.

I'm nervous to see him because, while we were putting Tyler's bike together the other night, we almost kissed. But

Cassandra interrupted us, preventing me from acting on my crush. Besides, there are so many reasons why he and I can never be. One, he's my dead sister's ex. Two, he's the father of my child. Three, I'm too old for him and, four, he's Tyler's dad and I can never tell him he is.

My head is a mess, overthinking about everything, and now I'm doubting that we even did almost kiss ...

...Cassandra has taken Tyler to the park so I can put together his bike—who knew bikes came like Ikea furniture and needed to be put it together with Allen wrench thingies and plier scissor thingies. I'm not very handy—as per my thingie knowledge—but I'm a capable thirty-two-year-old woman, I can put a bike together, right?

WRONG!

As it turns out, no, I cannot put a bike together. The instructions may as well be in Finnish because nothing makes sense. "Grrrrrrrr," I growl, tossing the wrench thingy down.

A knock I've come to know and love echoes around the room. Hopping up, I step over the mess I've made and make my way over to the door.

"Sounds like someone is being murdered in here," Miller says in greeting when I swing open the door. He's covered in sweat after hitting up the gym and even all sweaty and gross, he still manages to look amazing and hot. If he's not at the rink, he's either in the gym or hanging with Tyler, his new best friend ... and son. I'm still in shock that Miller is Tyler's dad but at the same time, I'm not surprised at all.

"Just my pride being butchered," I tell him. He looks quizzically at me. "I'm trying to put Tyler's bike together but..." I shrug my shoulders and step aside so he can see the mess, aka distance, I've made.

"Would you like help?"

"I can't ask you to do that."

"You're not asking, I'm offering. Let me go shower and I'll be back over to help."

"Thanks," I tell him, "and as a thank you, I'll provide beer and pizza."

"Luckily for you, it's cheat day so I'll say yes to pizza, but I'll pass on the beer."

"That's right, no alcohol mid-season."

"You know me too well." He winks and that lil' eye movement causes my insides to turn to mush and my cheeks to heat. "Back in five." With that, he walks over to his apartment and heads inside to shower.

Closing the door, I place an order for pizza. While I wait, I try to work out how to put the handlebars together. I've just put the grips on when there's a knock at the door. Jumping up, I walk over with the completed handlebars in my hand, "I did it," I singsong when I open the door.

"Go you," he says, offering me his hand for a high five.

Clapping his hand, I smile brightly at him and step aside, letting him in. His scent envelops me, I close my eyes and breathe in deeply. When I open my eyes again, Miller is staring at me. His gaze is almost heated but the moment, or whatever the hell that was, is interrupted when there's another knock at the door.

Opening it again, the pizza delivery guy is there. Paying for the pizza, I take the box and head back inside. Placing the box down on the counter, I open the fridge and grab two waters. "You can have a beer," Miller says, taking a seat at the island.

"If I'm going to put the bike together, I need to have an alcohol-free head but as soon as it's together, I'll be having a celebratory vino."

"Solid plan," he affirms.

"So, food or bike first?" I ask.

I'm pretty sure I know what his answer will be and, no surprise, I guessed right when he emphatically states, "Food, I'm starved."

"You're always hungry."

"Well, when you work out as much as I do, I need to fuel this machine." Reaching out, he opens the box and his eyes widen when he sees the pizza. "Is that vegetarian with Cajun chicken?"

"Yep, it's the best."

"I thought I was the only one to like that. Back home, there's this place Mom and I always go to and they do the best vegetarian with tandoori chicken." He kisses his fingers in a "chef's kiss" kind of way.

"The Pizza Place on Fifth?" I ask and he nods in agreement. "We always had pizza from there too, Selene always teased me for my topping choice."

"She'd tease me too and then try to sneak a piece when she'd think I wasn't looking."

We both laugh and then dive into the pizza. Once we've eaten and cleared away the box, we get to work. And by we, I mean, I sit on the sofa and watch Miller put the bike together.

"You made that look so easy," I tell him when he returns from stashing the bike at his place until the weekend. With the bike all put together and hidden, I start gathering the tools to put them back into the toolbox I have.

"I just followed the instructions," he nonchalantly says.

"They were in Finnish to me."

"Finnish? Not Greek?"

"Nope." I shrug. "Finnish."

"I've never been to Finland so I don't actually know anything about the Finnish language."

"*Well, I haven't either, to tell you the truth, but I would love to go one of these days.*"

"*I'd love to, as well. I hear the northern lights from Finnish Lapland are pretty amazing.*"

"*I thought it was Tromsø in Norway that has the best view of them?*"

"*Well, we will just have to go to both places and compare.*"

Looking over at him, I imagine traveling the world with him. Making love under the northern lights, but then I shake that thought off because it will never happen. Needing to focus on the task at hand and not getting down and dirty with Miller, I realize the plier thingy is missing from my kit.

"*Where are you, plier thingy?*" *I mumble to myself and then I spy it under the sofa.*

Miller and I both reach over to get the tool at the same time and his hand ends up on top of mine.

We both freeze.

Our eyes flick to his hand on mine and then we stare at one another. My tongue darts out and I slide it over my bottom lip. His gaze focuses on the movement and moves back to my eyes. Silently we stare at one another and, like moths to a flame, our heads begin to slowly move toward one another. Our lips are millimeters apart when the door to the apartment swings open, interrupting the moment. Pulling apart quickly, I jump up and focus on Tyler and Cassandra entering.

My cheeks are heated and from the look Cassandra is giving me, she knows something happened, well, almost happened, but I shake my head. I can't discuss or acknowledge what almost happened because, right now, my heart is racing in a way like never before when it comes to Miller and my crush.

. . .

That special knock snaps me back to the present and it has my heart racing, but before I can get up, Tyler comes racing down the hallway. "Me get it," he shouts. Sliding across the floor in his socks ala Tom Cruise in *Risky Business* style, I sit here and watch as he pulls open the door.

From where I'm sitting I see Tyler's little face light up because there in the doorway is T-Rex, aka Miller. Before Tyler can say anything, T-Rex starts singing "Happy Birthday" and when he steps aside, behind him is a new bike. It's green—dinosaur green—and hanging off the handlebars is a dinosaur helmet.

"A biiiiiike," Tyler excitedly squeals. "T-Rex got me a bike."

"Actually," I say, standing up to meet them in the doorway. "I got you a bike, T-Rex just delivered it for me."

"You're the best, Mom," Tyler singsongs.

He turns and gives me a hug before he races out into the hall, climbs onto his new bike, clips on his helmet, and begins to do laps in the hallway. "Can we go to the park?" he asks as he zooms back down the hallway.

"What about your party?" I remind him, just as T-Rex suggests, "We can go tomorrow."

"Yesssssss," Tyler fists pumps the air. "This is the best birthday ever."

He gets back to riding up and down the hallway, joy all over his now five-year-old face. T-Rex shuffles into Miller's apartment to change and I find myself grinning. I can't believe Miller dressed up as a dinosaur to deliver Tyler's bike. He really is great with Tyler and it makes my feelings for him grow the more time he spends with Tyler.

Standing here, I watch Tyler ride around without a care in the world and, suddenly, I miss my sister.

"You okay?" Miller asks from beside me. I hadn't even

realized he'd come back out. When I look up, he's in cargos and a green Henley that makes his eyes pop.

"Yeah, just thinking about Selene. She always loved birthdays."

"Yeah, 'cause they were all about her," Miller notes with a chuckle.

"Very true," I add, "and she'd get presents."

I find myself smiling because birthdays were always so special to my sister, and I make a mental note to always make them special for Tyler. I can honor his bio mom this way because I know if she was here, she'd go all out for him.

"Come on, Buddy," I call out, "We need to start getting ready for your party."

"Do you need a hand?" Miller offers.

"You've already done enough." I nod toward the bike. "You deserve some Miller time, just come down when the party starts."

It looks like Miller wants to argue but the elevator doors open and Mom and Dad step out, their arms laden with gifts for the birthday boy. When Tyler sees them, he jumps off his bike and races over to greet them. "Nanna. Poppy," he excitedly shouts their names.

"Happy birthday, sweetheart." Mom crouches down and pulls him into her arms, hugging him tightly.

From beside me, Miller takes my hand in his and squeezes. An electrical current jolts between us. My gaze drops to our hands and then back to his face. We stand here and mutely stare at one another. The clearing of a throat has Miller letting go of my hand and we both look up to see my dad standing there. His expression is unreadable but at the same time, he's giving off total Dad vibes. Miller says hello to my parents and then he quickly tells me he'll see us later, before he heads back into his apartment.

"Wentworth lives across the hall?" Dad sternly asks.

"Yeah, small world." From the look on Dad's face, he isn't impressed. Then I state, "I'm glad you guys are here, you can help me set up, we got a lil' waylaid by Tyler and his new bike."

"T-Rex delivered my bike," he informs Dad.

"No way," he exclaims. "I'm sorry to say, it's just Nanna and I delivering this." He holds up one of the many gift bags and gifts in his arms.

"Pressssentssss," Tyler squeals with excitement, once again reminding me of my sister.

We head inside and after Tyler has opened all of the presents from Mom and Dad, we gather everything for the party and head down to the pool to set up.

28

EVIE

THE PARTY HAS WRAPPED up and I think it was a hit. The last of the leftover food has been put away. I think I over-catered, but it's always better to be overprepared than underprepared. The birthday boy was spoiled and you could not wipe the grin of his face.

The kids—hockey players included—all had a blast, swimming and frolicking around the pool. The games were a hit and Tyler's T-Rex cake was the best cake I have ever seen. Miller really outdid himself with that one. Even as the host, I had fun, but entertaining ten five-year-olds and a team of hockey players is tiring.

I'm still in disbelief at how much the guys on the team spoiled Tyler, especially Miller. He went over and above for his little best friend. Seeing the joy on Tyler's face was priceless and this will be a birthday he will remember forever ... even with the intrusion of Klaus Van der Kündt.

When he waltzed into the pool area as if he owned the place, my heart stopped. I was sitting on a lounger and my eyes followed him as he walked over to Dad. His gait had a swagger that pissed me off. Old age has done him no favors and as I watched him with Dad, all I could think about was Sel's letter and the lines *"You were right that I was running from Klaus"* and *"He is not Tyler's father."* Thank fuck *he's* not Tyler's father. I don't know how I would cope if I had to hide *that* secret. It's hard enough hiding what I'm hiding as it is, especially with the bond between Miller and Tyler growing by the day.

Whenever Miller is around—which is quite a lot—I hyperfocus on the two of them together. They really do act like father and son. How I never saw it before I will never know.

It's like their souls are calling to one another and as the secret gatekeeper, I'm keeping father and son apart. As much as I want to keep Sel's secret, I also want him to know he's Tyler's father because he's amazing with him. But I promised my sister I would keep who Tyler is a secret, and I won't betray her like that. Yes she's dead but even in death people deserve to have their secrets kept. I do wish I could talk to someone about this. I'm not sure if I can do this forever, but I promised. Therefore, this secret is mine and mine alone to bear.

Mom and Dad offered to take Tyler back to their hotel, but I told them he can go tomorrow. I wanted him tonight, even though he was asleep before his head hit the pillow. Just knowing he's under the same roof as me and safe is a sensation I can't explain. I sometimes wonder if I'm overprotective of him, but then again, with what I know about Klaus, I need to be extremely cautious when it comes to him.

Now that everything is done, it's time to wine down with the girls. Kennedy, Cassandra, and I are sitting in the living room, having one last drink before we call it a night.

"#1 Crush" by Garbage comes on and my head begins to bop along with the beat.

"I love this song," Cassandra states before doing an exaggerated "UHHHH UHHHHH," like Shirley does when the songs starts. Followed by a really, really off-key, "I would die for you..."

"Our ears are dying," I tease, earning myself a bird flip.

"Who's your number one crush?" Kennedy asks.

At the same time, Cass and I both shout, "Jason Statham."

"Jinx," I shout before I lift my glass and tilt it toward her in a silent toast due to our same taste in celebrity hotties.

"No." Kennedy waggles her finger side to side. "I wanna know who your real life, not fantasy, never going to happen crush is because, no offense, ladies, if Jason Statham was to walk through there." She points to my front door. "I would stab a bitch to be first in line." Shaking my head, I chuckle at her because I would do exactly the same thing. "Stabbing aside, spill the deets, Eves."

She looks pointedly at me and not wanting to answer, I take a sip ... a large sip.

"We're waiting," Cassandra singsongs.

"I can't tell you who my number one crush is, because, well, he and I will never be."

"Pleeeeeeeeease," Kennedy begs, then she adds, "but I'm pretty sure I already know who you're referring to."

"As if you do, no one knows and his name is a secret,"—along with many other secrets that my vault of a brain has locked away—"and I will take his name to the grave."

Then she utters two words that shock me, "Miller Wentworth."

My eyes widen. My mouth drops opens. "How ... how did you guess?"

"Please," she scoffs, "blind Freddie can see that you two have unrequited feelings for each other."

"What she said," Cassandra agrees with a nod.

"He does not," I refute, "besides, I'm too old for him."

"As if," she sasses in a very Cher from *Clueless* kind of way. "If I can date a man who is fifteen years older than me, you can date someone younger."

"Ummm, back the truck up, when did you start dating an older man? And more to the point, how are we only hearing about this now? And even more pointedly, who is your mystery older man?"

"Shit," she hisses. "Please forget I said anything. We, ummm, shit." She looks at me with fear in her eyes. "You can't say anything guys." Her gaze flicks between Cassandra and me. "Promise me? Please?" She's begging now and seeing the fear on her face, I feel bad that I teased her.

"I promise," we both affirm at the same time.

"One question before we forget, are ... are you in trouble?"

"No." She vehemently shakes her head. A grin appears on her face and I know she's telling the truth. "I'm not in trouble. It's just, complicated, and we decided to not say anything for now."

"If he's embarrassed to be with you, then he's not worth it," Cassandra states and I find myself nodding in agreement.

Again, she shakes her head. "It's nothing like that, it's just, well, we just can't for now but I promise you, he treats me perfectly perfect." She gets a loved-up look on her face, and I have a feeling my friend has fallen hard for her mystery man ... even if I'm positive I know who said man is. Then she shocks me when she adds, "He's sweet in the street and a freak in the sheets." She waggles her eyebrows at us and then the three of us cackle like hyenas.

"Okay, well, when you're ready to share the deets, I'm—"

"We're," Cassandra interrupts.

"Sorry, we're," I emphasize that word, "all ears."

"I appreciate that, now getting back to you and Miller." I knew this was coming, but I also kind of hoped she'd forget all about it. "Spill?"

And so I do, I tell her everything from Miller dating Selene and my longtime secret crush on him. I do leave out our kiss and dry hump at her funeral because that's not something I'm proud of. I also leave out the baby daddy part. I know I can tell these girls anything and it'll be locked away under girl code, but I need to respect Sel's wishes. Thankfully, conversation turns to the final season of *The Summer I Turned Pretty*. We all agree that Belly should be with Conrad and we hope the show sticks to the books, even though rumor has it that it'll be different than the books.

Later that night, I lie in bed unable to sleep because I keep thinking about the girls and what they said about Miller liking me too. That would be a dream come true if we got together but with the secrets I have, I just can't go there.

MY LIPS ARE LOCKED to Evie's as I press her into the side of the lockers, slipping my thigh between hers. She moans into my mouth as she grinds herself against my leg. "More," she whimpers into my mouth.

"You want my cock, baby?"

"Please," she begs.

"I love when you beg for my cock. Make yourself come on my leg and then I'll give you my cock."

My words spur her on and she rapidly rides my thigh. Her juices drip down my leg, swiping my finger through the liquid, I bring it to her lips. With her eyes locked on mine, she wraps her delectable lips around my digit and sucks. A few more swivels of her hips and she comes with a guttural moan, the sound echoing around the locker room. Before she has a chance to catch her breath, I slide my hands underneath her ass and lift her up, spearing her down on my shaft.

"Yesssssss," she mewls as I begin to thrust my hips rapidly into her.

BANG BANG BANG

Her head bangs against the lockers as I pound into her. Over and over my shaft spears into her, each thrust pushing each of us closer to the edge.

BANG BANG BANG

The banging gets louder and louder and I'm ready to explode when a husky, "Miller," echoes in my ears, causing me to come. My eyes fly open as warm cum sprays my chest and chin. I'm shirtless on the sofa in my living room, with my sweats pushed down and my hand jerking my dick. One shoe is on and I'm confused as to what's happening right now.

"Yo, Miller," the deep voice calls out, followed by another **BANG BANG BANG** on my door.

"Coming," I yell out, then I chuckle to myself because I literally just came. Pulling the blanket off the back of my couch, I wipe up my hand, chest, and chin before tossing it down on the armchair. Grabbing my shirt, I pull it over my head, stuff my dick back into my sweats, and walk over to the door. Opening it, I find Kallen and JJ standing there.

"You oversleep?" JJ asks, barging into my apartment.

"Yeah, sorry. Give me five to get ready." Without waiting for them to reply, I race into my room. We aren't heading out and I don't need to get ready, but I need a moment. That was the third time this week I've had a wet dream about Evie.

Ever since Lexi said what she said the other week, I've been unable to stop thinking about Evie. There's been a few almost kisses here and there, but each time we've been interrupted. Is that the universe's way of telling me this is a bad idea? I don't want to ruin what we have because then I wouldn't be able to hang out with Tyler, and I freakin' love that kid. I've not really spent much time with kids before, but when I hang out with Tyler, I love it. Maybe I should invite him over to hang with the guys and me today? Before I can think on that anymore, from the other room, Kallen shouts, "The fuck?"

Racing out into the living room, I stop mid-stride when I see he's sitting on the armchair with the blanket I just used to wipe up. He's staring at the wet spot on the blanket, and I see the moment he realizes what's on the soft material in his hand. "Is that cum?" He tosses the offending item onto the floor just as JJ starts to cackle in a way only JJ can. "Not funny, asshole."

"It kinda is because when Miller and I roomed at college, it was me who used his jizz-covered towel."

"Why can't he jerk off in the shower, like normal people?"

"Excuse me," I tell them, walking farther into the room. "This is my apartment and I will jerk off in my own house wherever I want"—then I look to JJ—"and for your information, back in college, I told you to stop using my towel."

"I never used it after that," he huffs, crossing his arms.

"Then my point was made."

"And your point now is you don't want us coming over anymore?"

"No, I don't have a point now. I just woke up from a highly erotic dream and well, your banging coincided with my banging and that"—I point to the blanket on the floor—"is the remnants of my dream."

"Question." JJ raises his hand, as if we're in elementary school, "Why are you sleeping on the couch? It's not like you have anyone to be in the doghouse with."

"No clue," I offer, shaking my head. "I must have come out here in my sleep."

"You sure did." JJ chuckles like a fifteen-year-old boy.

"You do that often?" Kallen asks.

"Not that I'm aware of."

"Never while we roomed," JJ says.

"Let's put my nocturnal habits away and get on with the reason you guys are here."

"Not until you deal with that jizz-covered thing."

"Fine." Walking over to the offending blanket, I grab it off the carpet and pop it straight into the washing machine. When I return, Kallen and JJ have the Wii set up and it's game time.

We spend the day playing Wii and talking about the upcoming season and our predictions. JJ mentions that Lexi is excited to be working with Evie, and I have to agree. I'm happy to have her on board as well.

Several times I go to ask the guys what I should do about Evie, but each time I chicken out. Plus, guys don't really talk about their feelings for chicks and whatnot, so I leave it be.

Climbing into bed later that night, I decide to leave things with Evie as it is. I don't want to rock the boat since we have to work together ... However, I do have another schmexy dream about her, but this time I bend her over the treatment room table and fuck her from behind. I will never look at that table the same way again but, thankfully, I have no plans to end up as a patient of hers so I have nothing to worry about.

30

EVIE

HOLDING TIGHTLY on to Tyler's hand, we walk down the street to the corner store because someone—me—forgot to get toilet paper last week. After having to use a tissue just now—eeeeew—I cannot wait until tomorrow when I do the weekly groceries to get more.

Since it's still early, ish, I decide we can get an ice cream while we grab the toilet paper, what a combo. With our ice creams and toilet paper in hand, we step out onto the busy street and we come face-to-face with the last person I expected to see, Klaus Van der Kündt.

"Evie," he says my name and the sound of his voice sends chills down my spine.

"Mr. Van der Kündt, hi."

"Please, call me Klaus," he says, and again a chill runs over me.

"What are you doing in New York?"

"I'm here following up a lead on your sister."

"Ohhh," is all I can manage to reply because I can't let

him know he was who she was running from, or that I know he was sleeping with my sister.

"That's all you have to say about your sister's murder, ohh?"

"Well, what else am I supposed to say?"

"Don't you want to know who murdered her? Or why?"

"Of course I do, but it happened near home and she's never been to New York."

"And how do you know?"

"Well, I don't know for sure, but New York was never a place she liked. She'd more likely hit up California."

"Where you just so happened to be living." He pauses for effect and watches me intently. "You don't happen to be keeping secrets from your father and me, are you?" I feel his gaze deep in my soul and not in the way I feel Miller's when he looks at me.

"I—" I'm interrupted by Tyler when he tugs on my hand. "I need to pee, Mommy."

Klaus drops his gaze to Tyler and now he's staring at him in a way that's creepier than when he was staring at me. "You never did tell me who his parents were."

"You don't know them, I met them in California."

"So you said, but why are his adoption records sealed? What are you hiding from me?"

"You ... you looked into my adoption of Tyler?" He nods. "Why?"

"Just curious."

"Moooooommy, I need to go now."

"Okay, Buddy." I tell him. Looking back to Klaus, I smile. "I ... I need to go, it was good to see you, Mr. Van...I mean Klaus." Before he can say anything else, I tug on Tyler's hand and walk away from him and head toward home.

As Tyler and I walk along the busy street, I play over the encounter just now with Klaus. He really is a creep, especially since he's been looking into Tyler's adoption. I wasn't even aware the records had been sealed but, then again, Selene went to great lengths to keep his paternity a secret. Maybe I need to talk to Dad about this. But that would mean betraying her and what she asked of me. This was her one last wish before she died and this is something I need to deal with on my own. But Klaus looking into Tyler isn't sitting right with me. Why the sudden interest? Maybe I need to reach out to Mr. Burrows and see if he has any suggestions.

Apart from me, he's the only other person who knows Tyler's parentage. While I trust him, I don't want to bring anything down on him should Klaus decide to take things further, and I wouldn't put it past him.

My body is shaking as Tyler and I walk up the stairs to the building. Tyler lets go of my hand and runs ahead of me. The doorman, Declan, opens the door and welcomes Tyler home with a high five and a head nod to me. "Evening, Ms. Salvatore. Did that gentleman find you?"

"K-K-Klaus was here?" I ask.

"Yes, but he wasn't on your approved visitor list and when we told him so, he wasn't too happy."

"I'm sorry about that, but I appreciate you following protocol."

"He may be friends with your father but unless they're on the list, no one gets past me."

Relief floods me that this is such a secure building. "Please do not ever let that man in."

He nods. "Is everything okay?"

Now it's my turn to nod. "I'm fine," I tell him, but we both know I'm anything but. I'm shaking like a leaf.

"Come on, Mom," Tyler sings out, poking his head out of the waiting elevator.

"Good night, Declan."

"Good night, Ms. and Master Salvatore."

Racing across the lobby, I meet Tyler in the elevator and he presses the button for our floor. The car starts moving but it stops along the way and when the doors open, standing there all sweaty and godlike from a workout is Miller.

"Miller," Tyler excitedly shouts, "I got ice cream." He lifts his ice cream up to show Miller and that's when I notice his hand is covered in melted ice cream. "Want a lick?"

"Tyler, you can't ask someone that," I reprimand my son.

"It's fine," Miller says. Then he crouches down to get on Tyler's level, something I notice he does quite often when talking to Tyler. "Your mom's right, you can't just offer people a lick of your ice cream, but for the record, that's my favorite ice cream. So next time you go get one, come get me and I can have one too."

"Cool," Tyler excitedly replies.

Miller stands up and when he looks at me, his eyes widen. "You okay, Eves?"

Nodding, I smile over at him but we both know, I'm not. "I'm—"

"Don't even think about telling me you're fine." I open my mouth to protest, but he raises his hand halting me. "Here's what's going to happen, I'm going to go home and shower. Then once you know who is asleep, you're going to tell me what's got you so freaked out."

"I'd like that," I tell him and from the shocked look on his face, I think he was expecting me to blow him off. To be honest, I'm surprised I agreed so easily but talking to someone about Klaus is just what I need ... even if I will have to skirt the truth about a few things.

The elevator reaches our floor and being the gentleman he is, he stretches out his arm, holding the door open, allowing Tyler and I to step out first. Like Miller, I hold our apartment door open for Tyler and before it closes, Miller says from across the hall, "See you soon." He winks and then enters his apartment, leaving me flustered and slightly excited for what's to come later this evening.

31

MILLER

JUMPING INTO THE SHOWER, a cold one, I wash myself quickly and pull on a pair of sweats and a Crushers hoodie. Slipping my feet into my slides, I grab my phone and head across the hall to see what had Evie spooked in the elevator just now.

She's one of the strongest people I know, but seeing her visibly shaking left me wanting to murder whoever made her so scared. Raising my hand to knock, I take a deep breath because nerves are taking flight, just like they do on game day.

KNOCK KNOCK KNOCK

After rapping my knuckles on the wood, I wait, and when the door swings open, Evie's eyes well with tears as soon as she sees me. Without saying a word, I step into her apartment and pull her into my arms. She wraps hers around my waist, rests her head on my chest, and she breaks down. Her body shakes as she lets it all out.

Scooping her up in my arms, bridal style, I kick the door

closed and walk over to her sofa. Sitting down, I hold her in my lap and let her cry it out.

I'm not sure how long we sit here with her silently crying, but I could sit here forever with her in my arms. She fits perfectly into my body, it's as if we're two interconnecting pieces of a puzzle, finally connecting into place.

"Sorry," she murmurs, breaking the silence.

"You have nothing to be sorry about, Eves. I'm just glad I could be here for you. And I mean that, you can tell me anything and I'll keep it in the vault."

She lifts her head and even with tear-stained cheeks, she's still the most beautiful person I have ever seen in my life. "I can't tell you everything but I can tell you, someone scared me tonight."

"Someone? Who?" I ask, my blood boiling at the thought of anyone harming Evie.

She shakes her head, "I ... I can't tell you who, but he scared me and he was asking about Tyler and—"

"Why was he asking about Tyler? Is it to do with his father? You never mention Tyler's dad."

"It's complicated," she says. I can tell she wants to say more, but she's scared because, once again, her body is shaking. Taking her hand in mine, I lace our fingers together and rest them in her lap.

"Will he harm you and Tyler?"

"I ... I don't know, but he's—"

"Married? Someone powerful?"

"Both," she murmurs.

"You hooked up with a married guy?" She shakes her head. "So he's married and powerful. He's not Tyler's dad, but he's invested in Tyler. Why?"

"I'm not Tyler's mother—"

"You kidnapped him?"

"No, you dick, I adopted him—"

"What do you mean?" I interrupt because I'm a lil' confused right now. "Is … is Tyler not yours?"

"Legally he is but, umm, no, I didn't give birth to him."

"What?"

"His biological mother is, was, a dear friend of mine. When she died, she left him to me because she had no other family she could turn to."

"And Tyler doesn't know you're not his mom-mom?"

She shakes her head. "No, he doesn't, but one day I'll tell him all about his mom. She…" She pauses and swallows deeply. "She was an amazing mom and fam—friend. I would do anything for her."

"Wow, that's, I had no idea."

"No one does. It's all so complicated but I would do anything for him. I promised his mother I would look after him and love him and keep him safe."

"And the father?"

"Again, complicated. I only recently learned who he is, and I'm dealing with that."

"You know you're pretty amazing, right?"

"I don't know about that."

"Eves, you're raising another person's child as if they're your own. That's pretty amazing. Not many people would do that for a friend."

"She was the best and she just made a bad choice. I thought everything was going to be okay but now, now I'm scared. I promised her I would keep him safe, and I will do everything in my power to keep that promise to her."

"Can your dad help? You know, use his mafia connections and whatnot."

"You make him out to be like Tony Soprano or something." I eye her because Daniel Salvatore is a mafia guy, therefore, he *is* like Tony Soprano. "But no, I can't go to Dad, he's—" She shakes her head. "Just no."

It surprises me that she won't go to her dad. Yes, he's a mafia guy but he would do anything for his daughters, and his grandson, but then I guess maybe he won't help because Tyler isn't a Salvatore by blood.

"Then tell me what I can do, Eves."

"This," she murmurs and snuggles back into my embrace. "Just hold me."

"That I can do." Without thinking, I lean forward and press a kiss to the top of her head. She lifts hers up and gazes into my eyes—my soul even. I feel her stare deep within. Like on game day, those nervous butterflies are taking flight.

Our heads are so close that our breaths mingle together. Reaching out, I cup her cheek and rub the pad of my finger along her jawline. I don't know who moves first but one minute we're staring at one another and the next, her lips are pressed against mine and we're kissing.

With our lips locked, Evie shuffles around on my lap and straddles me, our lips never once breaking apart. Threading my fingers into her hair, I gently tug on the strands, eliciting a meek gasp, which allows me to push my tongue deeper into her mouth. She gyrates her hips and it reminds me of my dream when she was doing this to my leg in the locker room. Sliding my hands down her sides, I slip them under her top and grip her hips. My skin sizzles against hers, I hold her to me and thrust my hips up into her. Gripping the bottom of her top, I lift it up and tear it over her head. Tossing it to the side, we breathlessly pant and stare at one another. My gaze roams over her chest, she's wearing a lace bra that looks fucking stunning.

Leaning forward, I press my face between her tits, sucking and biting her skin. Nipping over her breast, I gently bite down on her nipple through the lace. Her head drops back and she presses her pussy farther onto my rock-hard cock.

Making out with Evie is so much better than in my dreams. She's all woman. Even if she was a million pounds, she'd still be sexy because it's what's on the inside that counts, and Evie Salvatore is the best person I know. She's raising another woman's child as her own and after what she told me tonight, she would literally die for him. You can't get any more special than that.

Licking up her neck and across her jaw, I cover her mouth once again and push my tongue into her mouth. Reaching behind her, I unclasp her bra but before I can get it off, from down the hall a small voice calls out, "Mommy, I had an accident."

Evie rests her forehead against mine and laughs. Pulling back, she shakes her head. "Tyler and his bladder." I look at her inquisitively, "Him needing to pee interrupted me earlier, and now me with you."

She reaches behind her back, reclasps her bra and rises off of me. Immediately I miss her pressed against me but I know she needs to go deal with Tyler. "You look after him and I'll see myself out but, Eves, we will be revisiting this"—I flick my finger back and forth between us—"because kissing you is my new favorite hobby."

She leans forward and kisses me quickly. Breaking the kiss, she pulls back and stares at me but when Tyler calls out again, she steps away to deal with Tyler and his wet sheets.

Readjusting myself, I stand up and let myself out. With a smile on my face, I head back to my place. I finally kissed Evie and it was everything a second first kiss should be, and I can't wait to kiss her again.

32

EVIE

IT'S BEEN three days since Miller and I kissed, and it's been three days of radio silence from him. I'm beginning to wonder if maybe I dreamed kissing him, but my thoughts are interrupted when, from the locker room, I hear a guttural, "Fuuuuuck. Fuck. Fuuuuuck."

Heading to the entry of the treatment room, my eyes widen when I see Miller is being carried by Colton and JJ. His face is scrunched in pain but due to his protective equipment I can't see where he's injured. "What happened?"

"My knee went one way and I went the other," Miller hisses through clenched teeth.

Stepping to the side, I let them into the room. "Get him up on the table," I tell them. Colton and JJ do as I ask. Both of them apologizing to Miller when he hisses and grunts. "Colton, can you go find Doc please?"

"On it," Colton confirms and races out of the room.

"Okay, Miller, we're gonna have to remove your gear." He nods. "Let's get your skates off to start."

"Mmmhmpf," he agrees, his face scrunched up.

"Lie back," I tell him but he defiantly shakes his head and stays upright as JJ and I start removing his skates. Once they're off, we start on his leg pads. I know I have his injured side when he nearly jumps off the table when I lift his leg up. I carefully take the injured leg in my hand and with the pad finally removed, I get an unobstructed look at it. His knee is already starting to swell. Racing over to the fridge, I pull out some ice packs. "We'll start with—"

"RICE," Miller interrupts, "Rest, Ice, Compression, and Elevation. This isn't my first rodeo with a MCL injury."

Nodding, I gently place the packs on his knee, one underneath and one over the top. He hisses when I bend the top one to get full coverage of his knee. "Sorry," I whisper.

Reaching up, I take his hand and give it a reassuring squeeze.

"That helps," he mutters, and I don't know if he's referring to the ice or me holding his hand.

"Okay, Miller, tell me what happened," Doc Michels says as he comes into the room. He grabs a pillow and while he listens to Miller explain what happened, he slides the pillow under to elevate his knee and then reapplies the ice.

"...it's similar to what happened in college when I did my MCL."

"You've had an injury like this before?" Miller nods. "Excellent," Doc gleefully voices. "Well, not good that you're hurt but excellent in that we can treat you as per our new plan and, hopefully, it'll be a quicker recovery than the first time around." He looks down at Miller. "You don't mind being a part of our program, do you?"

"If it gets me back on the ice sooner, then you can do whatever you want to me, Doc."

"Excellent," Doc repeats, reminding me of Monty Burns from *The Simpsons*.

An hour later, Miller and Doc head off to the hospital for an MRI but before they leave, Doc asks me to map out a treatment plan for Miller.

As much as I hate seeing Miller in pain, this is what I live for, and I'm the best at what I do and cannot wait to aid in his recovery.

"Knock, knock," I sing out, pushing the door to Miller's apartment open.

"Hey," he says from the sofa when I walk in.

"How you doing?"

"Been better."

"You're lucky, it's only a Grade 2 tear, which means that if you follow the plan we've set out, you'll be back on the ice in four to six weeks."

"I'll miss the start of the season."

"Which is better than the whole season," I remind him. "You need anything?"

"A kiss might help."

"I must have missed that being a part of your treatment plan."

"Are you, a medical professional, going to withhold my medication?"

"Considering this is an off-the-books treatment you're wanting to try, I guess I could be persuaded."

"I can keep a secret."

Shaking my head, I stare down at him. "I don't want to hide this, whatever this is."

"This"—he flicks his finger between us—"is us figuring things out and, for the record, I'm happy to not hide it too. We don't need to label it for now, but I know I've been fighting my feelings for you for a while now."

"You have?" He nods. "Well, since we're sharing, I've-AlwaysHadACrushOnYou."

"I'm sorry, I don't speak rushed, can you repeat what you just said in English?"

"I said, I've always had a crush on you."

"Define always?"

"Since you were, ummm, dating my sister."

"Is that so?" I nod. "Well, I always thought you were hot too, now come here and give Daddy a kiss."

Shaking my head, I cross my arms in a "no deal" way. "Never, and I mean never, refer to yourself as Daddy again. That is one kink I will never get into."

"What kinks *are* you into?"

"Well, I've always wanted to play dirty nurse."

"I volunteer as tribute," he eagerly offers.

"Noted, but I think we need to let you rest a bit first, and I kinda want our first time to just be us. No playing, if you get my drift."

"You're already thinking about sex? I thought it was the male who is usually the fiend but, then again, I've never dated an older woman before. However, I did think that the older they got, the less enthusiastic they were when it came to sex."

"Hey, seven years doesn't make me a grandma and, I will have you know, I've never had anyone complain ab—"

"Ahhh uh." He raises his hand, halting me. "You will never mention previous partners around me. The past is the past. All we focus on is you and me. Now, can I have my kiss? Please?"

"Such a demanding patient," I tease but giving him

what he wants, I lean down and press my lips to Miller's. Just like the other night when he kissed me, my lips tingle and my whole body comes alive. If I feel like this after a kiss, what's it going to be like when we finally sleep together?

...Three weeks later

"YOU'RE ALL CLEAR," Doc says and those three words are music to my ears.

"You mean it?" I ask, just to be sure.

"One-hundred-percent."

"But it's only been three and a half weeks. When I was in college it was almost six before I was cleared to play."

"Because, back in college, you didn't have me on your case. And not to toot my own horn, I'm pretty good at what I do, and I have an amazing team backing me."

"That you do." My eyes drift over to Evie, who is sitting at the desk in the back. She's biting on her bottom lip and it has me thinking of the other night ...

...Hopping out of the shower, I grab my towel and dry off. I've just returned from the pool. Doc suggested water therapy and, I have to say, it was a game changer. When they first

suggested it, I thought they were full of shit, but I'm man enough to admit it pucking—damn you, Chelsea—worked. Apparently, by utilizing the buoyancy and viscosity of the water, it helps patients to engage in exercises that are less impactful on injured areas. This leads to a faster and more effective rehabilitation process.

Wrapping my towel around my waist, I step into my room and stop mid-step when I look up and see Evie standing in the doorway to my room ... in the sexiest nurses dress I have ever seen. The white dress, if you can call it that, barely holds in her tits. The hemline just covers her panties, and her legs are encased in sheer white stockings with garters holding them up, and on her feet, a pair of sky-high, white fuck-me heels.

She's seductively leaning against the doorframe, biting on her bottom lip. "It's time for your medicine," she seductively purrs, running the tip of her finger down her chest and over the top of her spilling tits.

"Yes, yes, it is." I nod in agreement.

"On the bed," she commands and her authoritative tone has my dick perking up because apart from some kisses, a finger bang, and a lot of dry-humping, Evie and I haven't ventured into the bedroom yet. This is a completely new side of her and I have to say, I approve.

Following her directions, I make my way over to the bed. Dropping down, I take a seat on the edge and wait for my next order.

My heart is racing and my dick, well, he's popped up to say hello and because I only have a towel around my waist, there's no hiding how hard I am.

Evie pushes off the doorframe and floats into my bedroom. She may be dressed in white like an angel but, I assure you, she's a devil in disguise. My eyes roam over her from head to toe. "Fuck, Eves, you are, fuck, I have no words."

"That'll be fifty cents," she states, coming to a stop in front of me.

"Babe, I'll cut you a check because I'm not going to curb what I want to say when you're dressed like that."

"You like this, do you?" I nod my head. "Well," she purrs, "if you like this, then you're gonna love what's underneath."

Leaning down, she rests her hands on my thighs and my gaze drops to her chest. "My eyes are up here, Miller." Lifting my gaze to her face, I lick my lips as I stare at the devil before me. Bending forward, she presses her lips to mine and I forget everything. All I can focus on is her lips on mine and her intoxicating smell.

All too soon, she breaks the kiss and takes a step back. With her eyes locked on mine, she lifts her hand to the zipper at the front of her dress and, ever so slowly, she tugs it down. As the material separates, it reveals a sexy as sin body encased in a sheer lace bra and panties with attached garters. When the zipper pops free, she slides the dress down her arms, dropping it to the floor. Standing before me is the sexiest woman I have ever seen. Garters have never really been anything I've found appealing before but right now, best fucking invention ever.

"Fuck, Eves, you sure know how to bring a man to his knees."

"Actually, it's me who will be dropping to my knees. You, good sir, are just going to sit there while I administer your medication ... orally."

Dropping to her knees, she loosens my towel and it falls down to the bed. My cock springs free. I don't think I've ever been this hard before. Licking her lips, she reaches out and grips my shaft in her fist, squeezing it. A hiss passes through my lips, but the sensations whirring in my body are anything *but painful. Eves lifts her gaze to mine and winks. With her eyes locked on mine, she leans forward, lowers her head, sticks her tongue out, and swirls it over the tip before swallowing my shaft. Her lips slide down my dick and she gives it a suck before licking back up. In and out, up and down, she licks and sucks my cock as if it's a melting popsicle.*

Reaching down, she cups my balls and presses on that spot at the base of my cock and, without warning, I come down her throat. She drinks down everything I have and when I've released everything my body has to release, my cock pops out of her mouth.

"Good boy," she coos. Hearing that has my dick once again twitching back to life. This woman is going to be the death of me with the things her mouth can do.

"That's great news, Doc," Coach Maxwell says, slapping me on the back. I hadn't even realized he'd come into the room; I was too busy reminiscing about my time in Blowtown.

"Fantastic news." I nod in agreement. "So, can I hit the ice now?"

"Considering practice for the day is over, no," Coach Maxwell growls. "You can start back on the ice tomorrow, but if there's any twinge and pain in your knee, you tell someone. We need you in tip-top shape if we're going to beat the Dragons this coming weekend."

"Yes, Coach," I tell him. Then I look back to Doc. "Thanks again, Doc, I really appreciate all that you did."

"You did all the hard work, we just guided you."

Climbing off the table, I leave Coach Maxwell, Coach McQueen, who just walked in and Doc to chat. Making my way over to Eves at the desk in the back, I lean my ass on the edge and stare down at her. "What time are you finishing?"

"Five-ish, I just have to get this report for Doc finished.

Then I need to pick up some groceries, grab Tyler from Cassandra's, and then—"

"Why don't I do the groceries and pick Tyler up for you?"

"You don't mind?" she asks.

"Not at all, just give Cass a head's up. And if it sweetens the deal, I'll organize dinner as well."

"Who are you and what have you done with my boyfriend?"

"Say that again," I tell her.

She looks seductively up at me and whispers, "Boyfriend."

"I love hearing you call me that."

"I like calling you that, now scoot so I can get out of here. My boyfriend is cooking me dinner tonight, and I don't want to keep him waiting."

"Baby, I'd wait forever for you."

Leaning down, I place a quick kiss on her lips and leave her to get back to her report. Grabbing my gear, I head out to do my chores. But first, I head to Cass's to pick up Tyler so I can have some guy time with the lil' slugger.

34
EVIE

SITTING HERE, I watch Miller walk out of the treatment room, and I can't believe this is my life. I have an amazing job, a fantastic son, and Miller-freaking-Wentworth is my boyfriend. Never in my wildest dreams did I ever think *that* would ever happen. Not only is he my dead sister's ex but he's also the biological father of my son, who is actually my nephew. Sometimes I think I'm living in a soap opera—the mafia daughter raising her dead sister's son and she just so happens to hook up with her dead sister's son's biological father, who she's secretly lusted over for many many years. Yeah, that's totally soap opera worthy but in my case, I'm gonna get the happily ever after.

So many times, I've wanted to confess all to him, especially since he and I are officially a couple. However, if I want to get my HEA with Miller, this secret has to stay that, a secret. Revealing it would tear us apart, therefore, I will take it to my grave.

Miller and I have only been official for a few weeks but I've fallen hard and fast for this man. It's crazy to even be tossing the "L" word around, but I think I love him. He treats me like a princess and he's amazing with Tyler. And I know Tyler loves him too, the other night when I was tucking him in, he asked me if Miller could be his dad. That was a knife to the heart because technically, well no, biologically, he is. When I watch the two of them together, it's like watching father and son. They have a bond like no other and me keeping this secret will preserve that bond. At the end of the day, I will do anything for Tyler and Miller.

Pushing thoughts of Miller and my secret to the side, I get back to work. Popping my earbuds in, I click play on my playlist and get to it. Before I know it, all my reports are completed and the items on my to-do list have been checked off and a new one has been written.

I'm officially done for the day and it feels good to be up-to-date. Closing the lid on my laptop, I lean back in my chair and stretch out my muscles. Being hunched over at a desk is not my favorite thing to do, but it's a necessary evil. Looking at the clock, I realize I still have an hour till Miller said he'd be back, so I decide to get a quick workout in.

Grabbing my bag, I switch off the lights in the office and treatment room and head toward the gym. Best thing about my work attire is that it's easy to slip from work to gym. Pulling off my shirt, it leaves me in yoga pants and a crop top. Pulling my dark locks up into a messy bun, I connect my phone to the speakers in here and jump onto the rowing machine—I love the rower. It gives you a full body workout, all while you're warming up.

Fifteen minutes later, my warm-up is complete and a light sheen of sweat covers my body. Wiping my face, I head over to the mats and I drop down to start on my first set of push-ups. After punching out three sets of twenty, I roll onto my back and start on my sit-ups. After completing the last set, I collapse back to the mat, close my eyes, and breathe in deeply. I hate sit-ups but like paperwork, they're a necessary evil.

When I open them again, I startle because Miller is standing above me. "Hi, beautiful," he says, the timbre of his voice vibrates all over me.

"Hey, stud."

"That was very Sandy from *Grease* of you."

"Are you even old enough to know that movie?"

"Mom and I used to pick an old movie to watch every weekend and that one just so happens to be a favorite of hers. Me personally, I love *Stand by Me* and *The Goonies*."

"Goonies never say die," we both say at the same time.

"You're early," I tell him, lifting myself up. Leaning on my elbows, I gaze up at the man before me.

"I actually think I'm right on time." His eyes roam over me and my skin heats at the intensity of his stare. "I think you might need a hand washing your back."

"Is that so?" He nods. "Where's Tyler?"

"He's sleeping over at McQueen's."

"So it's just us?" He nods. "Till morning?" Again, he nods. "Well, since you're here, I was thinking you might wanna help me stretch..."

"Stretch what?"

"My glutes." Dropping to my back, I move my legs so my feet touch, creating a diamond with my legs. If it wasn't for my pants, I'd be wide open for his viewing and fucking pleasure.

"I've never seen this glute exercise before."

"It's one for you and only you."

"Is that right?"

"Mmmhmpf. But it works best if you remove your clothes."

Without acknowledging me, he grips the neck of his tee and pulls it off in that one-handed sexy way guys do. He drops it to the mat beside me before hooking his fingers into the band of his sweatpants and, in one fell swoop, he removes both his sweats and briefs. Leaving him standing above me gloriously naked.

"Like what you see, baby?"

"Very much," I agree, licking my lips.

"Now that I'm clothes free, how do I assist you? Show me what you want me to do to you."

With my eyes locked on his, I trace my finger down my neck and into my cleavage. Circling my nipples over the material of my crop top, I caress my mounds. Moving my hand down farther, I trace around the edge of my belly button before snaking my hand under the band of my pants.

"Uhhh uh," Miller calls out, shaking his head. "I wanna see, lose the pants."

Without saying anything, I push my pants and panties down to my ankles. Because of my sneakers, I can't kick them off but that doesn't matter, all that matters is the look on Miller's face right now. Moving back into my diamond position, I lie back and get back to the task at hand. Slipping my finger into my slit, I moan when I brush over my clit.

"Spread those lips and show me how wet you are," he commands.

Lifting my other hand, I spread myself open and with my eyes locked on his, I watch him watch me as I run my finger up and down my slit.

"Push it in and show me how wet you are."

Doing as I'm told, I press my finger inside and pull it out, a squelching sound echoes in the gym. I'm wetter than I've ever been before and I should be embarrassed, but I'm not. It only turns me on more. Lifting my hand up, I show him. Stepping forward, he grips my wrist, brings my fingers to his lips, and sucks my juices off.

"You have the sweetest tasting nectar; I think I need to drink it from the source."

"Do it," I pant like the wanton hussy I've become.

Stepping down to my feet, he drops to his knees and like a tiger stalking its prey—me, I'm the prey—he crawls forward. Starting at my ankle, with his eyes locked on mine, he places soft kisses up my calf, over my knee, and along my thigh. He nibbles the inside of my leg, ever so close to where I want him, but he never makes that final move. "Please," I beg and no sooner does the word pass through my lips, and he sticks his tongue out. Licking me from taint to clit. His tongue slides through my slit like a hot knife through butter. Immediately, every nerve ending in my body comes alive. When he bites down on my clit and sucks, I nearly come there and then.

"Yes," I mewl, pressing myself into his face.

With my pants around my ankles, I'm restricted with my movement and Miller knows this. Sliding his hands under my ass, he lifts me up and dives in. He licks and sucks and fucks me with his face and tongue. His tongue spears in and out of me. His nose tickles my clit. When he inserts a finger into my ass, it sets off the most exquisite orgasm in the history of orgasms. I feel like I'm floating as he pulls every inch of my release from my soul.

My body goes lax and he removes his finger and face from between my thighs. Resting on his haunches, he stares at me as I come back to Earth. "Wow," I hiss.

"Think you can handle more?"

I honestly don't know but from the look on Miller's face, I don't really have a choice ... and I'm okay with that.

35
MILLER

SEEING Evie lying on the mat in the gym, flushed from her orgasm, is one of the sexiest things I've ever seen. It's up there with sexy dirty nurse Evie. Her brown eyes have turned a deep chocolate color and I'm mesmerized by them. My cock is rock fucking hard and I need to be inside her, but I don't want to push her. Her orgasm just now was pretty intense. Her body stiffened in a way I've never seen a body stiffen when a woman comes, but then she let out a sound that will play in my mind forever and I knew she was okay.

"Think you can handle more?" She nods and thank fuck because I need to be inside her, now.

Not letting her change her mind, I cover her body with mine, and with my eyes locked on her, I line my dick up at her soaked entrance and push inside. Her pussy hugs my cock as if it was made for it. With our eyes fused on one another, I thrust in and out of her, our pelvises grinding together.

"Kiss me," she demands.

Leaning down, I cover her mouth with mine and plunge my tongue into her mouth in sync with my cock sliding into her pussy. She wraps her arms around my neck and we fall into a rhythm. Kissing down her neck, I nip across her collarbone and gently bite her nipple through her crop top. Needing to see her tits, I push the material up, exposing her breasts. Taking her nipple into my mouth, I suck. Unintelligible words slip through her lips and I chuckle against her skin.

"Don't laugh at me," she warns.

"Never at you," I tell her. Slipping my hand between us, I press down on her clit and massage the tight bundle of nerves.

"Yesssssss," she hisses. "I'm close."

"Come for me, baby," I urge her.

"I'll come when I want to cooooooome." She's mid-beratement when I pinch her clit between my thumb and forefinger. Her walls clench down, squeezing my cock and just before I come, I realize I'm not wearing a condom so I quickly pull out. Gripping my shaft, I pump my dick and cover her in my cum. Ropes of creamy liquid paint her stomach and crop top.

Sitting here with my hand on my dick, I stare at the woman beneath me in amazement. I've never felt this way about anyone before, and I realize I never want another woman.

She's it for me.

"I love you." Those three words slip out of my mouth before I have a chance to hold them back.

Her eyes widen at my words. It's too soon to be throwing the "L" word around but then she utters, "I love you too, Miller."

"You ... you love me too?"

"I do, Miller. So, so much. I've always loved you and never in my wildest dreams did I think I'd get a chance with you." She laughs. "It's funny, you've always been on my mind and ever since I realized we were working for the same team and living in the same building, it felt like fate was trying to tell us something."

"Baby, I've got you on my mind too and, now that you're mine, I ain't gonna let you go."

She beckons me forward with her finger and as I kiss her again, my dick hardens between us. With our lips locked and love surrounding us, I fuck her again on the floor in the gym. After messing her up, we grab a shower, separately, because if I saw her naked and wet, we'd never get out of here. "I have to confess something," I tell Evie as we grab our things, ready to head home.

"What?" she hesitantly asks.

"I've thought about us doing this…"

"Doing what?"

"Fucking here in the locker room."

"You imagined fucking me in the gym?"

"Well, it was out here but same-same. Actually, I've imagined fucking you in lots of different places."

"Like where?"

"Ummm, well, there's the windows in my apartment—"

"We could make that one a reality because it would totally be hot if you ask me."

"Duly noted," I tell her.

"Where else?"

"In the pool at our place. In the gym—"

"Well, we *have* done it in the gym," she reminds me with a waggle of her eyebrows

"Yes, but I imagined we were on the weight bench and you rode me cowgirl."

"Hmmmpf, maybe we should give that a try."

"Really?"

"Not right now but sure, one day."

"Ummm, well, okay then. I'm starting to think you like fucking in public."

"Do not," she hisses.

"Do too, but for the record, I like fucking you in general. So public, private, wherever, as long as I'm with you, I'm down to fuck."

"Duly noted," she repeats my phrase and before I fuck her here again, we head out. Hand in hand, Evie and I exit the stadium. We get our Uber to drop us off around the corner so we can grab a bite to eat. We seem to have worked up quite the appetite in the gym.

When we step out on the street, I once again take Evie's hand in mine and we head home. As we approach the building, I see a lone figure standing on the curb. When we get closer, I recognize who it is, Klaus Van der Cunt is waiting for us.

Seeing him irks me, just like it always does. I hate that cunt and even all these years later, that hate is just as hateful.

"What's he doing here?" I murmur and when Evie looks up, I feel her body stiffen beside me. And not in the way I felt her stiffen just a few hours ago.

"Nothing good, that's for sure," she replies.

He turns our way and when he notices us holding hands, his face sours. "I see you and your sister like to share." His words piss me off but they also confuse me.

"Klaus, what are you doing here?" she asks him, her voice squeaky. She's scared of him and it has me wondering why. Selene was always touchy feely with him, but Evie's reaction is the complete opposite.

"Where's your son?" He places emphasis on the word

son, and his implication that Evie is a bad mom pisses me off.

"At a sleepover," she tells him, but personally I wish she hadn't said anything. Where Tyler is at is none of his concern.

He nods. "I see. Evie, I was wondering if we can have a chat? It's about Selene."

"Okay," she whispers.

"Is there somewhere private we can go?" he asks, his eyes are on me and I don't like the way he's looking at me.

"Whatever you need to say, you can say in front of Miller. We don't have any secrets."

"Very well then." A sinister look washes over him, and when he speaks next, there's malice in his tone. "Your sister and I were in a sexual relationship before she left, and well, I have reason to believe your son," he places emphasis on that word, "is my son."

What the fuck? I did not see *that* coming, but my fears that what he is saying is true are abated when Evie confidently informs him, "I assure you, Klaus, Tyler is not your son."

"And I don't believe a word that comes out of your lying whore mouth. Tyler is—"

"That's enough," I growl. "You don't get to insult my girlfriend after spilling lies about her sister."

He turns his attention to me. "I assure you, Mr. Wentworth, I only tell the truth." He leers at Evie. "Don't I?"

Her mouth opens and closes. Then she says a sentence that crushes me, "It's true, Miller."

"Tyler is his?" I hiss.

"No." She vehemently shakes her head. "Tyler is NOT his, but Sel was sleeping with him before she left."

"We were in love," he states, but I don't believe him.

And the look on Evie's face confirms that Sel was *not* in love with the cunt.

"She ... she was cheating on me?"

"I'm so sorry, Miller. I ... I didn't want to tarnish her memory so I never told you."

"When did you know?"

"Not until after she left. She ... she visited me in California and she told me *he's* why she left, but she didn't tell me anything else."

"Where's my son?" Van der Cunt shouts at us.

"He's not your son," Evie hisses at him and from the adamant tone she's using, I believe her.

"You need to leave," I tell him. "You're not welcome here."

"I will prove he's mine and when I do, he will be coming with me."

Evie pulls away from me and she explodes, "Over my dead fucking body will you take my son. I will kill you before you get your hands on him. Now, as Miller said, fuck off and leave us the hell alone."

Without another word, he climbs into the Escalade idling at the curb. The tires screech as his driver pulls out into traffic. When I look back to Evie, she's visibly trembling. "You okay?" I ask her.

She utters a meek, "Yes," but then she shakes her head. "That man scares me." She lifts her gaze to mine, "I'm ... I'm sorry I never told you about Selene and him."

"You have nothing to be sorry about." I pause. "So, you said he was why she left," She nods her head. "Can you tell me more?"

"I will but not here."

"Okay," I tell her. Before we head inside, I pull her into my arms and press a kiss to her forehead. "It's all going to be okay. I will not let him hurt you or Tyler."

She nods against my chest, but I'm not confident she believes me. Today has not gone how I predicted but at the same time, I wouldn't change a thing. Yeah, it sucks to discover my high school girlfriend cheated on me, but Evie loves me and that's all that matters. Everything with Selene is in the past and now that there are no more secrets between us, we have the future to look forward to.

36
EVIE

THE ELEVATOR RIDE UP is quiet between Miller and me, but it isn't uncomfortable. Each of us are in our own heads, processing. At the same time, I'm racking my brain as to what I can tell him without betraying Selene. My biggest dilemma, should I confess the truth to him? It's not like she can get mad at me for spilling the truth but, at the end of the day, I don't think I can betray her. It's all so confusing and when we reach our floor, I'm still not sure as to what I'm going to tell Miller.

Stepping into my apartment, I head into the kitchen and I grab a glass of water. Chugging it back, I close my eyes. When I reopen them, they're brimming with tears. Slamming the glass down in frustration, the glass shatters and slices my hand. "Fuck," I hiss.

Standing here, I just stare at my hand as blood drips all over the counter. "This feels like déjà vu," Miller says from beside me.

"Not quite because now the first aid kit is above the fridge, and it won't follow with me breaking down." *Maybe.*

He reaches across the island and pulls a tissue out of the box. Then he takes my cut hand in his and presses the tissue to my wound. Stemming the blood flow, he brings my hand up to his lips and presses a kiss to my wrist. "Hold this," he tells me.

Nodding, I hold the blood-soaked tissue to my cut as Miller grabs the first aid kit down. He opens the kit, grabs a bandage and the antiseptic liquid. Placing them on the counter next to me, he takes my hand in his, removes the tissue, and pours the antiseptic over my wound. I scrunch my face up at the sting, but Miller gently blows and the pain eases. Picking up the bandage, he opens it and covers the small cut. "Why is it the small cuts always bleed the most?"

"I don't know, I'll ask Siri."

Pulling his phone out, he does exactly that and a few seconds later, Siri informs us, "The smallest cuts bleed the most because they often involve tiny, superficial blood vessels near the skin's surface. These vessels are easily broken and while the bleeding is usually not severe, it can appear more prominent due to the close proximity to the skin."

"Hang on a minute, aren't you a doctor, shouldn't you know that?"

"Shock," I tell him. "I was in shock from the blood loss and I couldn't brain."

"Yes, such massive blood loss for your massive cut," he teases me.

"Thank you for saving me from bleeding out." Looking at him, I reach up and cup his cheek in my palms. "I love you to infinity."

"I love you to infinity too, but why do I feel like this is a final I love you of sorts?"

"Never." I enforce my promise by shaking my head but,

deep down, I know if he ever finds out what I'm hiding, there will be no more infinity I love yous, that's for sure.

"You sure you're okay? You look a little pale."

"Yes. No. I don't know, but shouldn't I be the one asking you that? You just discovered you were cheated on."

"That's in the past, but Selene and I were never meant to be. And now that I know she was cheating on me with him, so many things make sense. It's funny," he chuckles, "it doesn't hurt that she ran rather than talking to me. She may not have been in love with me, but I thought we were friends. I think the fact she couldn't talk to me hurts the most."

"She ran from all of us," I remind him.

"You know, I saw her just after she left."

"You did?" I ask but I know he did because, well, Tyler is proof of them seeing one another.

"Yeah, she showed up at my dorm around Thanksgiving, I think it was. We umm, spent the night together, and then the next day she was gone, again." Hurt is etched all over his face, and I hate Selene for hurting him. Miller is the sweetest, kindest guy around. How she could cheat on him, I will never know. Especially with Klaus. He's not even silver fox good-looking, he's just a plain old dude.

"I'm sorry she hurt you," I tell him.

"As I said, it's in the past and if she hadn't run off, you and I never would have happened, so I can't find myself being mad. Does it suck to find out what you thought was a great relationship wasn't? Yeah, it does, but as I said, a lot of things make sense now. I just wish it wasn't with an old guy ... or an asshole." He pauses. "But why does he think Tyler is his? I mean, when I saw Selene she wasn't pregnant. Well, not that I knew of."

"I don't know why he thinks Tyler is his."

"Could Sel have had a baby?"

His question doesn't shock me because it's pretty logical and I hate I'm about to lie to his face. "I guess she could have had his baby."

"But you don't think that's the case?"

Vigorously I shake my head. "God, no, she feared him. There's no way she would have gone back to him."

"But then why is he focusing on Tyler?"

"He discovered I adopted him—"

"How?"

"I don't know how but I'm one-billion-percent sure he isn't Tyler's father. And as I've said previously, I made a promise to look after him and I will uphold that promise."

"You're pretty amazing, Eves. Not many people in their twenties—"

"Thirties," I interrupt him. "I'm thirty-two."

"Okay, not many single people in their thirties would take on a child for a friend."

"She was my family but regardless of this, I'm not like most people."

"You certainly are not." His voice is laced with admiration and while I love he thinks that, if he knew the secret I am harboring regarding him and Tyler, he wouldn't think I'm so amazing. Needing to deflect away from Tyler, I get back to Selene and what he discovered tonight. "Now, do you want to know what I know about Sel and *him*?"

He shakes his head. "Nah, it's in the past. Nothing will change if I know the specifics, so I'm good."

"You really are something, Mr. Wentworth."

"Something good, right?"

"Something very good," I affirm.

A silence falls between us but it's not awkward. That's one thing I love about being with Miller, we don't need to fill every minute with words. Right now, I think each of us is processing. We each have a lot to unpack but it's broken when Miller says, "You know what I do want to do?"

"What's that?"

He pulls me into his arms, sliding his around my waist while I drape mine over his shoulders so I stare into his eyes, his gorgeous brown eyes. "I wanna watch *The Goonies* with you, and then I want to fuck you against the windows there." He flicks his head toward the windows. "Then, I'm gonna take you to bed and make love to you. But before we fall asleep in each other's arms, I'm going to worship every inch of your body. And in the morning, because Tyler isn't here, I'm going to feast on your pussy for breakfast."

"I like the sound of that."

Miller brings up the movie, while I make some popcorn and then we snuggle on the sofa and watch *The Goonies*. I fall asleep during the movie but I stir when Miller places me into my bed. He climbs in behind me and we spoon.

"I love you to infinity," I sleepily mumble.

"Back at ya, baby."

The last thing I remember is Miller kissing my shoulder before I drift off to sleep. We don't get to have sex against the windows and my body isn't devoured from head to toe, but this is nice too. Any moment in Miller's arms is nice and I will never take them for granted.

37

MILLER

SITTING ON THE BUS, I can't wait to get home. We've been traveling for a series of away games and as much as I love hockey, I hate not having my own bed, but most of all, I miss Evie and Tyler.

Ever since our run-in with Van der Cunt the other month, Evie's and my relationship has only gotten stronger and my bond with Tyler, it now feels unbreakable. Never did I think a five-year-old kid with an obsession for dinosaurs would be my best friend.

At the end of a grueling day, I love nothing more than coming home to hang with Tyler and Evie. The three of us have fallen into a routine, and I love it. Being a dad of sorts wasn't on my radar, but Tyler is an amazing kid. If I ever have a kid, I want him to be as cool as Tyler.

The bus pulls into the parking lot and when I look up, I smile when I see my family waiting for me. We aren't offi-cially family but one of these days, we officially will be. Evie will have my last name and like she adopted Tyler, I'll adopt him too, and then we will give him a brother or sister, maybe one of each, and we'll live happily ever after.

"Miller," Tyler calls out my name when I step off the bus.

"Tyler," I shout out as he races toward me, launching himself into my arms. "How you doing, Buddy? Did you look after Mommy for me while I was away?" He nods, grinning brightly. "That's my man."

We walk over to Eves and I pull her into my arms, giving her a kiss. Tyler lets out an, "Eeeeew," drawing out and exaggerating the word.

"One of these days," I tell him when I remove my lips from Evie's, "you'll find a girl to kiss, and you won't find it so eeeeew."

Lacing my fingers with Evie's, we grab my bag from under the bus and then we climb into her car and head home. Traffic is a total bitch—when is it not in New York—and it takes over an hour to get from the stadium to home.

Pulling into Evie's allocated spot, we climb out and head up to our floor. I've pretty much moved into Evie's place, but I don't want to presume I'm automatically welcome. When Evie guides me to her door, I'm given my answer.

Stepping into her apartment, I drop my bag and press a kiss to her temple. "I wanna take you both out for dinner."

"McDonald's?" Tyler suggests.

I shake my head. "I was thinking something a little flashier than that." Letting go of Evie's hand, I drop down to his level. "I want you to go and shower, and then I want you to put on your fanciest outfit because I'm going to spoil you both tonight."

"Okay," Tyler excitedly shouts. Turning around, he races off to get ready.

"What are you up to?" Evie asks when I stand back up.

"Nothing, I just want to spoil my two favorite people."

"You don't need to do that."

"I know, but I want to."

"Well, I'm not going to say no to seeing you all dressed up." She steps over to me and runs her fingertip over my pecs. "I have to admit, I love seeing you in your suit after your games." She leans into my ear and whispers, "It gets me so hot that I have to relieve the pressure between my thighs. I come so hard to the vision of you in your suit."

"Shit, babe, you can't say things like that when we're about to go out in public."

"So, I'm guessing that you really don't want to hear that I got a wax yesterday and they waxed ev-rey-where." She slides her hands down my chest and she grips my dick, giving it a squeeze. "I can't wait to have you for dessert when we get home." With one final squeeze, she steps away from me and walks backward, beckoning me to her with her finger. "You coming?"

Swallowing deeply, I shake my head. "As much as it pains me to say no, I know if I go into that shower with you, we will not be making it to dinner, and with the things I want to do to you, we don't want to scare Tyler."

"Your loss," she teases. She spins around and before she disappears down the hallway, she looks over her shoulder. "See you soon, Stud."

Picking up my bag, I head over to my place to get ready for the evening ahead. I had to jerk off in the shower, twice, just to relieve the pressure. My cock has been rock-hard ever since I saw Evie when the bus pulled in. Then when she told me about her waxing appointment, fuck, I was nearly done for. Had Tyler not been in her apartment, I would have had her pressed up against the windows, and I would have fucked her hard and fast.

Adjusting my tie, I grab my wallet, keys, and phone and

head back over to Evie's. Letting myself in, I smile when I see Tyler is in a suit and he's struggling with his tie. "Want a hand?" He looks up and nods.

Walking into the living area, I sit on the sofa and Tyler comes over. He stops between my legs and I help him with his tie. I've just finished the perfect half Windsor knot when he asks me a question that knocks me on my ass. "Can you be my dad?"

"I, umm, have you spoken to your mom about this?" He shakes his head. "I think you need to check with your mom first, but I would love to be your dad."

"Hi," a soft voice says from the other side of the room.

When I look toward the voice, my dick once again hardens in my pants. Standing there, with tears in her eyes, is the most beautiful woman I've ever seen. It doesn't matter if she's in sweats around the house, her uniform at work, or dolled up to the nines, she's a smoke show. My preference is her naked and riding me but we can't be naked and fucking every minute of the day, which is a travesty if you ask me.

Tonight, Evie is wearing an emerald-green halter dress that hugs her curves, showcases her tits, and accentuates her legs. Her hair hangs in loose waves around her shoulders. Her makeup is light and perfect. "You look—"

"Pretty," Tyler interrupts.

"More than pretty," I tell him. "Eves, you're exquisite."

"You look pretty good yourself, Mr. Wentworth, and you, Master Salvatore, look very handsome."

"Dad did my tie," he tells Evie, and her eyes widen just like mine.

"You're calling him Dad?" she questions.

"Yep, Cate has a dad and I really want one too."

"You do, do you?"

"Yepp." He nods affirmatively. "I asked Miller to be my dad just before."

"And Miller said it was okay to call him Dad?"

"He said I had to ask you and I'm sorry I didn't, but I want Miller to be my dad. Can he, Mom? Can he be my dad?"

"I ... ummm, well, if he wants to be, I guess he can."

Tyler looks up at me. "Will you be my dad?"

"I'd be honored to, Tyler."

With a fist pump, Tyler hisses, "Yessssss."

"Guess tonight is a celebration," Evie says to me.

"Guess it is."

Dinner two nights ago with Evie and Tyler was perfect. Hearing Tyler call me Dad did something to me and, ever since, I haven't been able to stop smiling. "Get your head in the game, Wentworth," Coach shouts at me.

It's the end of the first period and we're down, 0-1. The Gems scored in the last twenty seconds of the period when I missed a pass from JJ because I was too busy looking at Tyler in the crowd with my mom. She flew in for a visit since yesterday was my birthday, and she wanted to meet my new family, since I'm officially a dad now. I know it's too soon to even think about proposing, but I want it all with Evie and Tyler. I may only be twenty-five years old but when you know, you know.

The break is over and we retake the ice for the second period. "You good?" JJ asks me as we skate across the ice.

"I'm better than good, man," I tell him. And I mean it. My mom is in the crowd. Tyler is calling me Dad and my girlfriend is sitting on the bench with Doc, doing what she loves. Life is fan-fuckin-tastic right now and if we win this game, it will be fan-fuckin-tabolous.

"Then play fucking better." With that, he skates off and we wait for the puck to drop.

After my pep talk from both Coach Maxwell and JJ, I play a magical game and two periods later, we come away with the win, 3-1. Two of the three goal scored by yours truly.

After the usual on-ice hoo-ha of a win, we head back to the locker rooms to change for the press conference. After the conference, I head out to find my family and when I do, my heart fills with joy. Mom, Tyler, and Eves are standing in a huddle laughing. The three of them don't have a care in the world. As I stand here watching my three most favorite people in the world, I realize I have everything I have ever wanted. I'm not going to take a minute for granted with them because life is too short not to live in the moment.

Usually, I'd head to Squires with the team to celebrate but with Mom in town, I decide to skip the shenanigans to head home with Mom, Evie, and Tyler. Ohh how times have changed, but I do not regret my decision at all.

Tyler convinced Mom to have a sleepover. Right now, the two of them are sound asleep in the middle of my living room, in the blanket fort we all built together. It was supposed to be for the three of us but, luckily for me—sorry Mom—there wasn't enough room for my six-foot-two frame so Tyler kicked me out.

Speaking of, Tyler is currently snoring his head off, as is Mom. And I can't wait to tease her about it tomorrow. Like always, she will refute the fact and say, "A lady doesn't snore." I'm tempted to record her snoring, but I'm not that much of an asshole.

Knowing Tyler will be safe here with Mom, I sneak out and pad across the hall to Evie's. Letting myself in, I smile when I find her curled up on the sofa with her Kindle and a glass of wine.

"So this is what you've been doing while I've been building a blanket fort?"

She looks up and smiles when she hears my voice. In the dim lighting, she looks like an angel. How did I get so lucky to snag a girl like her? "Hey, it's not my fault Tyler ditched me for you and your mom."

"If it makes you feel better, he ditched me too."

"How so?" she asks, tapping the cushion next to her. Dropping down beside her, I shuffle close so our legs are touching.

"The fort wasn't big enough for the three of us, so I was evicted."

"Ohhh, poor baby." She taps my cheek condescendingly. "Welcome to the reject club."

"We can be rejects together."

"Rejects forever." She taps her chest twice and then does a peace sign at me.

"You're such a dork but as long as we're together, I don't care where we are."

"Ditto," she replies and that one word reply means the world to me. I love that she feels the same way I do. If I lost hockey tomorrow, it would suck, but losing her and Tyler, that would be devastating. "So, what are you reading?"

"It's spicy, you won't like it," she teases.

"Spicy, hey?" I waggle my eyebrows at her.

Shaking her head, she laughs before closing her Kindle cover and placing it on the coffee table. "Actually, if you must know, I'm reading Brittney Spear's biography, *The Woman in Me*. She's really a remarkable woman, she's been through so much in her life. I really feel for her."

"Then you must be like her because you too are a remarkable woman."

"I don't know about that," she coyly replies.

"Babe, you're raising another person's child as if he's your own. That in itself is pretty remarkable." She just shrugs. "Don't underestimate yourself, Eves."

"Let's agree to disagree." She takes a sip of her wine and I decide to leave it be. I know she hates being praised so I guess I'll just have to praise her in another way. "So, I have an idea..."

38

EVIE

"SO, I HAVE AN IDEA…" Miller says and I can tell from the heated look in his gaze, it's something sexual. It must be the wine talking, but I'm going to do whatever he suggests.

"Go on," I prompt, desire building within, even without him telling me what his idea is.

"Well, a few months ago, I had this dream."

"And what happened in this dream?"

He begins to trace circles on my bare thigh, a shiver racks through my body. My nipples pebble and, like a heat-seeking missile, Miller's eyes drop to them. "Eyes up here, buddy."

"Sorry—"

"No, you're not," I playfully reply.

"Yeah, you're right." He chuckles. "So, getting back to my dream. I, well, we, you and I were in my apartment and we were getting it on … against the windows."

Again I nod, liking where this is going. "Carry on."

"Well, you were in that sexy as fuck swimsuit of yours,

and you had one leg bent while you leaned against the glass provocatively. Standing there all sexy like, you gave me come-hither eyes and beckoned me forward with your finger."

Leaning forward, I place my glass down on the coffee table and—with a swing to my hips—I prance over to the window, turn, and lift my leg into position. Leaning back against the glass, I stick out my chest and stare intently at Miller sitting on my sofa. With my eyes locked on his, I bite my bottom lip, tilt my head back, and run my finger across my upper chest. "Like this?" I seductively purr.

"Fuck me, Eves," he breathlessly expresses, nodding his head. "With the moonlight shining behind you, you look like a fucking goddess. And I have to say, this is the best fucking porno I've ever watched."

His words and the growing erection in his sweats are a massive confidence boost. My heart is racing right now and I cannot wait to see what happens next. "Okay, so what happens next in this dream of yours?"

"Well, I stand up and walk over to you." Giving him what I hope is come-hither eyes, I internally sigh with relief when he stands up. Ever so slowly, like sloth slow, he steps over to me. "Once I was in front of you, I do this." He gently glides his palm down my sides and back up again. "Like in my dream, your nipples pebble but you also whimpered at my touch."

"Well, touch me in a way that makes me whimper."

He nods in acknowledgement and, this time, when he slides his hand down my sides, on the upward motion, he slips his hands under my cami and up to my breasts. His palms cup my mounds, gently squeezing and tugging on my nipples. I manage to do one better than a whimper, I hiss and moan at the sensations pouring through my body. It's like my tits have a lifeline to my vagina and with each tug and pull, it lights me up down there. "Like that?" I murmur.

"So much better than in my dream."

"What's next?"

"I ... I lean forward and suck your nipple through your bikini top."

"Will a silk cami work?"

"I don't give a fuck what you're wearing, I just want you."

"Then suck," I command.

Leaning forward, he sucks on the taut peek, pressing against my cami. Since his hand is underneath, he guides my nipple to his mouth and not only does he suck me through the material, but he also gently nips at the tip. Another moan slips out and I mewl a seductive, "Yes."

Without continuing his story, he moves his other hand from my breast and down between my legs. He cups my pussy and presses the pad of his palm into my clit.

"Please," I pant, my body is ready to combust and we're both still fully clothed. Who knew seductive story time could be so hot.

"Tell me what you want?"

"When did it become a live action dream?"

"About fifteen minutes ago when we started this."

"I love your dreams," I tell him. He's running the pad of his finger up and down my slit. My panties are soaked and another illicit moan slips out. "I need more," I tell him.

"Well, how about you finish the story for us?"

"Okay, well, I, umm, I can't think with you doing that."

"What, this?" he asks. He slips his hand up the leg of my pajama shorts, pushes my panties to the side, and runs his finger up and down my slit, circling my clit when he reaches the top. His lips are wrapped around my nipple and I don't know where to focus.

Pleasure is coming at me from every direction. I don't know what's up and what's down.

"Come for me, Eves," he orders. "Soak my hand and fingers so your pussy is slick and ready for my dick."

His dirty words are my undoing and with a sound like a wild feral animal would make, I come all over his fingers and hand. My body quakes and quivers as I come back to Earth after it skyrockets into an orgasmic orbit.

Removing his hand from my pants, he brings his fingers to his mouth and licks them clean with his gaze fused to mine. Once every last drop has been cleaned off, he grips the hem of my cami and lifts it over my head. Dropping it to the carpet, he drops to his knees and pulls my bottoms and panties down together. Kicking them to the side, I lean against the glass, staring down at him. His gaze is locked on to my bare pussy. Before I know what's happening, he throws one of my legs over his shoulder and presses his face into my mound, piercing his tongue in and out of me aggressively. He feasts on my pussy like a starved man and brings me to climax, again; this time in an embarrassingly short period of time, but this man has a very talented tongue.

"What was that?" I breathlessly pant when he lowers my leg back down.

"I wanted to drink from the source and, yeah, it tastes so much better direct."

"I ... I don't even know what to say to that."

"You don't need to say anything but just know, I'm so ready to fuck you now."

"I ... okay," What else am I supposed to say to that?

With his eyes locked on mine, he slowly removes his clothes. Starting with his shirt, he pulls it over his head and drops it to the carpet. Then he removes his pants and briefs. Once he's as naked as me, he reaches down and squeezes his shaft, giving it a few tugs.

My eyes roam over his naked form and even though I just came, twice, I'm ready to go again. "How do you want me?"

39
MILLER

HOW DO YOU WANT ME? Best five words I have ever heard.

"Well, up until now, this has been my dream, how about you direct the finale?"

"After two amazing orgasms I can't think straight."

"Amazing, huh?"

"You don't need me praising you, you already have a big enough—"

"Dick," I offer.

"Not the body part I was going to refer to, but I think the noises I let loose and the mess I made on your hands and face speak for how amazing round one and one point five were. Now for round two." She leans back against the glass, lifting her leg back into position and, once again, looking like a fucking goddess. A naked goddess waiting for me to devour her. "How do you want me?"

"That there is a good start."

"How about this then?" She lifts her hand and traces

her fingertips down the valley of her breasts to her belly button and back up again.

"I think you can do better than that," I growl.

Reaching down, I grip my cock and stroke myself. She watches what I'm doing, biting her bottom lip. Taking a cue from me, she traces her finger down again but this time she keeps going. Swirling her finger over her clit, she dips down farther and pushes it inside herself. Thinking she's going to keep pleasuring herself, she shocks me when she removes her finger and brings it to her mouth. She paints her lips with her arousal and beckons me to her.

Eating up the distance between us in two strides, I grip her cheeks in my palms. She's expecting me to kiss her, but I shock her by licking along her lips, savoring her flavor before I bite and suck on her bottom lip. Evie moans and it turns into something animalistic when I plunge my tongue into her mouth.

Covering my hands on her cheeks, she presses her chest into mine and kisses me back.

"I need you," she pants.

"You've got me," I reply.

"Please," she begs, and who am I to deny her?

Taking a step back, I grip my dick and gingerly stroke my shaft. It's harder than steel right now and I'm ready to slide inside Evie. The tip glistens with precum. Her eyes are locked on my dick and from the heat reflecting in her eyes, she's ready for orgasm number two.

Stepping to her, I place my hands under her ass and lift her up. Her legs wrap around my waist and I press her back into the glass, hoping like hell I don't fuck us through it, causing us to fall to our death. As much as death by fucking would be amazing, I don't want anyone to see a naked Evie except for me. And I'm pretty sure Jaxson, my agent, would murder me for being naked in public, I'm not Stefan after all.

Lifting her up higher, she reaches between us and guides my dick to her entrance, and then I lower her down. Her lips spread and she sucks my cock into her, the head easily sliding inside. She groans something unintelligible as I begin to thrust in and out of her.

"Fuuuuuck," I hiss. "Your pussy is made for my dick, Eves."

"Oh my God," she pants.

"Name's Miller, not God."

"Shut up," she snaps before she lets out a moan, letting me know I hit that magical spot deep within her. "Miller, please," she begs. I'm not sure what she's begging for, but I lean forward and cover her mouth with mine. My tongue plunges in and out of her mouth in sync with what's happening below.

Her walls tighten around me and I know she's close.

"Touch your clit, Eves," I command. "Bring yourself to the brink so I can see you fall apart as my dick slams into you."

She slips her hand between us and no sooner does she brush her finger over the tight bundle of nerves, her pussy clamps down and she screams my name as she crashes over the edge. Seeing her fall apart has me coming seconds behind her.

Leaning my forehead against hers, I mumble, "That was a million times better than in my dreams and every time with you is better than the last."

Stepping back from the window, I carry Evie down the hall and into her en suite. Placing her down on the edge of the vanity, I grab a washcloth and clean between her legs and my dick. Picking her up again, I carry her over to her bed. One handed, I push the sheets back and gently lower her down. She shimmies over and taps the mattress next to her. Climbing in beside her, I pull the duvet over us and we snuggle, blissfully drifting off to sleep with the woman of my dreams in my arms.

The other night with Evie was the best fucking night of my life. The things that woman let me do to her and the things she did to me will forever be etched in my mind. In my soul even. I knew I loved her before that night but now, I don't think love is a strong enough word for how I feel.

"She's good for you," Mom says just before I pull up at the terminal. "You've met the one, haven't you?"

"I think so," I confirm.

"And you don't care she has a child with another man?" I wonder if I should tell her Tyler isn't biologically hers, but I quickly quash that thought. It's not my secret to tell so I'll keep it to myself for now.

"No, I don't," I honestly tell her. "He's awesome." And I mean that one-hundred-and-fifty percent. They're a package deal and I'm happy with that. He brings a joy to my life I didn't know was missing. Evie is not just my partner, she's my equal. Yes, we've only been together for a short period of time but when you know, you know.

"He really is a great kid." She pauses and then smiles. "You know, he reminds me so much of you when you were his age."

"I think it's because he's been hanging around me too long. I will admit, sometimes I feel like he looks like me, but then I blink and I don't see it anymore."

"Maybe that's your mind telling you you really are happy to have him in your life."

"You might be right, Mom."

"I'm so proud of you, Miller."

"Thanks, Mom, but I could not have done this or gotten this far without you, or Dad."

"I wish he was still here to see you living out your dreams."

"He's with me every time I take the ice, Mom. Sometimes I can feel him guiding me to make the moves that I do."

"He always was your number one supporter so I'm not surprised, even from the grave, he's still supporting and guiding you."

Pulling up at the terminal, I put the car in park and we climb out. Grabbing Mom's case from the trunk, I pop it on the sidewalk and then I pull her in for a hug. "Love you, Mom."

"Love you too, baby boy, and before you say it, I know you're not a baby but you will always be my baby boy."

"You know me too well."

We pull apart, say our goodbyes, and I stay here, watching as she walks into the terminal. When I see the security guard walking toward me, I quickly climb back into my car and head home ... to my girlfriend, and her son.

40

EVIE

THE LAST FEW weeks with Miller have been perfectly perfect. He's slipped into our lives seamlessly. We've become a family, and I love ending my day with my two favorite people.

The guys have the weekend off and I cannot wait to do nothing for a few days with Miller and Tyler, after I collect him from school this afternoon.

Signing Tyler out, the two of us head to the park for an ice cream and just as the sun starts to set, we head off for home. Tyler is trying to negotiate takeout for dinner but I want to cook for us. Miller will be the deciding vote but I already know he's going to side with Tyler, like he always does. Those two love ganging up on me but I have to admit, I don't mind because seeing the two of them bond like that is heartwarming.

We're just around the corner from home when a black Escalade pulls up beside us and Klaus Van der Kündt steps out. He marches over to us, his gaze is locked on Tyler, and I instinctively push him behind me in a protective manner.

When he sees what I do, he growls low in his throat. "Mr. Van der Kündt, what are you doing back in New York?"

"I've come to get my son," he hisses vehemently.

"I wasn't aware you had one." I'm impressed with how confident I sound because on the inside, I'm shaking like a leaf. He's always scared me and now, under his intense stare, I'm quaking in my boots.

"Don't play coy, Ms. Salvatore, it doesn't suit you. Now, hand over my son."

"I beg your pardon?"

"I'll take my son that you've been hiding from me. He's the rightful heir to the Van der Kündt fortune." *Shit. Shit. Shit.* I don't know how I'm going to protect us. He's well, him, and I'm just a five-foot-eleven woman and Tyler is a five-year-old boy. One thing I do know, I will protect Tyler with my life and he will *not* be taking my son from me.

"I wasn't aware you were dying ... or that you had a son," I tell him.

"Don't fucking test me, Ms. Salvatore."

From behind me, Tyler pokes his head around my leg and holds his little hand out, palm up. "You saids a bad word, that'll be a quarter." If I wasn't standing before a man I perceive as the devil incarnate, I might laugh but from the look of disdain on his face, this is no time to be laughing. Gently, I protectively tuck Tyler behind me again.

"I'll fucking swear if I want to fucking swear." From behind me, I feel Tyler's body begin to shake with fear. He presses himself into me and on instinct, I reach behind me and protectively rest my hand on his head. I might be scared shitless right now, but Tyler needs me to be strong. "Kid," he growls, "get the fuck into my car."

"I don't go with peoples I don't know," he meekly says from behind me and I'm so proud of him for refusing to get into the car. He must be just as scared as me but, at the same time, he's not giving in to the man before us.

"Just fucki—"

"What's going on here?" Miller shouts, running toward us.

When I look up, relief slams into me when I see Miller is here. He seems just as angry as Van der Cunt when he steps in front of me, putting himself between me and extremely angry and volatile Mr. Van der Kündt.

No one says anything.

The air surrounding us is thick with animosity and fear. Outright anger pours from the man accusing me of hiding his son from him. "I'm here for my son," Klaus arrogantly states.

Miller turns back to me and in doing so, he's using his body to shield Tyler and me from Mr. Van der Kündt. Lifting his hands, he places them on my upper arms, squeezing in a reassuring way. His touch instantly calms me, but I'm still tightly strung and on edge.

"Are you okay?" My head moves up and down, indicating I'm okay but we both know, I'm anything but. "He didn't hurt you, did he?" His words are laced with fear. Easing that fear, I shake my head, unable to voice my fears right now.

"Give me my fucking son," Mr. Van der Kündt growls through clenched teeth, taking a step toward us.

Seeing him move sparks my inner momma bear and I defiantly step around Miller and glare at the asshole. "Tyler is not yours, Mr. Van der Kündt." He grunts his disapproval and I know, no matter what I say, he's not going to believe me.

"I have proof Selene had a child. *My* child." He looks to Miller. "And I know he's mine because she wasn't fucking you because she promised me she'd stopped."

From behind me, Miller hisses, "Sorry to break it to you, asshole, but she was screwing us both right up until she left."

For the first time since he held me up, he actually looks like he may be incorrect regarding Tyler, but then he shakes his head. "Why else would his adoption records be sealed? Why did she run? None of it makes sense unless she was taking what was rightfully mine. And now, I'm here—"

"My sister wasn't who any of us thought she was," I interrupt. "Yes, you're correct that she was pregnant." I see Miller stiffen at the revelation, and I hope he doesn't connect the dots. "And yes she had a child." My eyes drift to Tyler, who is now grasping onto Miller's leg. "But I assure you, Mr. Van der Kündt, Tyler is not yours." I stop and raise my hand. "And before you ask, no, I do not know who the father is. My sister did not divulge that information and it was not on his original birth certificate."

"Where's the proof of that? How do I know you aren't deceiving me?"

"I'm not a vindictive person like that, sir. I only know what Selene and the lawyer who handled the adoption told me."

"But she was preg—"

"When was the last time you were with her sexually?" I question and I hope to hell Selene didn't lie about the last time she saw him.

"May," he hisses. "The day of prom to be exact." He leers at Miller in a condescending way.

"Tyler was born in August, therefore, he cannot be yours because if you and her were together in May, nine months later is—"

"February," Miller interjects after a brief silence, and I hope he doesn't keep calculating, otherwise, I'll be having another difficult conversation this evening and this one is enough.

"How do we know you haven't just changed this child's birth date?"

"Do I look like I know how to do that?"

"Your father would," he emphatically states.

"Do you really think my dad would do that? You and I both know he hadn't seen Selene since she left. He, like you, searched high and low for her. Do you really think he would do that if he knew where she was all that time?" That stumps him. "Exactly," I triumphantly state. "I know you want a son, but my son is not yours to take."

He stands on the sidewalk, seething as he processes everything I just said. Without another word, he climbs into the back of the Escalade, slamming the door behind him. The sound of the door shutting causes my body to relax but it doesn't fully relax until his car is out of sight. When it turns the corner at the end of the street, I let out the breath I didn't know I was holding.

Spinning around, I drop down and pull Tyler into my arms. "You okay, Buddy?"

"I don't like him," he whimpers in my shoulder.

"I don't like him either, but I promise I won't let him hurt you."

"And neither will I," Miller says, joining our group hug.

The three of us hold each other on the sidewalk, drawing strength from one another. Miller is the first to break away and I immediately miss his embrace. "How about we head inside? I'll order us dinner and then we can—"

"Go for a swim?" Tyler eagerly suggests, his little body now buzzing with excitement and not fear.

"Orrrrrrr we can go for a swim and have burgers by the pool," I offer as an alternative.

Tyler's eyes widen and the biggest smile appears on his face. "You mean it?" Nodding, I find myself grinning back at him. "Yes." He fists pumps the air.

Thirty minutes later, Miller and Tyler are in the pool playing Marco Polo and I'm sitting on what's become *our* loungers watching them frolic about. Seeing the two of them having fun together warms my heart and after our run-in with Mr. Van der Kündt earlier, I wonder if I should just tell Miller the truth about him and Tyler. I know I swore to keep things regarding Tyler a secret, but maybe it's time to confess. Secrets never do anyone any good, and it's not like Selene can get mad at me. Right? But at the same time, Miller could take Tyler from me. He is his biological father after all. I feel like no matter what I do, I'm screwed and not in the fun way. Maybe it's best to just keep this secret after all.

41

MILLER

WHEN I ROUNDED the corner earlier this afternoon and saw Eves and Tyler with Van der Cunt, I was curious. When I heard him shout, "I'll fucking swear if I want to fucking swear. Now, kid, get into my fucking car," anger started to bubble within. My heartbeat sped up and I quickened my step to reach them.

Relief flooded Evie's face when she saw me and her reaction calmed my raging inner beast, slightly. That rage however reared back up again with the accusations Van der Cunt was throwing around like confetti.

The most shocking thing to come from his mouth was that Selene had a kid. What the fuck? I thought he was lying at first, but then Evie confirmed her sister did have a child and Tyler is really her nephew. I remember Evie saying a couple of weeks back that Van der Cunt thinks Tyler is his and now he has so-called proof. However, Evie put him in his place when she started spouting about dates and the last time he was with her, making it impossible for him to be the father.

Quickly I count in my head and I don't think Tyler could be mine. Then again, math isn't my finest subject, but Evie wouldn't keep something like that from me, would she?

I'm positive he isn't mine because I've always used protection. Well, up until Evie I did, but I clearly remember Selene always having protection on hand and she was anal about making sure she took her pill daily or got her shot when she switched it over. Her always having protection was something I found attractive because, back then, I was too young to be a dad.

Evie has been quiet for most of the evening, but I don't really blame her. Van der Cunt is always a draining son of a bitch whenever he's around. And right now, she's probably thinking about her sister and all that she's missing out on with Tyler.

It's funny, now I know Selene is Tyler's bio mom, I can see it clear as day. I also can't stop thinking about what Mom said too. Tyler has a lot of my mannerisms and then I start to wonder again if he is mine. I hate myself for questioning if Evie is keeping such a monumental secret from me, but what lingers just under the surface is doubt. Making me question, is Tyler mine?

42

EVIE

LAST NIGHT WAS the worst night's sleep I've ever had. Whenever I closed my eyes, I dreamed every conceivable scenario of what would happen when Miller finds out. Let me tell you, none of my dream scenarios worked out in my favor.

"You look like shit," Lexi says, placing a large coffee down in front of me. "Did Miller keep you up all night making all your wildest dreams come true?"

At the mention of dreams coming true, my eyes well with tears and, the next thing I know, I'm sitting at the desk in the treatment room crying my eyes out.

"Why are you crying?" Lexi asks, rounding the desk and sitting on the edge.

"It's," I blubber, "I've made such a mess of things and now ... now..." I can't continue because I know when the truth comes out, Miller is going to leave me. Then he'll take me to court to get custody of Tyler, and I'll have nothing except my job. Then I'll have to quit it too because Miller is on the team and he's more important than I am.

Lex pulls me into a hug and when her arms wrap around me in a comforting manner, it causes me to cry harder because it's just like a Miller hug.

I'm not sure how long I cling to Lexi but the sound of the team shuffling into the locker room after their morning practice causes me to look up. She sees fear on my face and Lexi being Lexi, she manages to smuggle me undetected out of the treatment room and into the tunnels. Taking my hand, she drags me into the stadium and we take a seat, rink side.

"Okay, spill," she says, breaking the silence once I've stopped crying.

Looking at her, I consider not saying anything, but I know I need to talk to someone. So I decide "what the hell" and tell her everything. This secret has become too hard to keep and another person's perspective might help me make the right decision. "Okay, so what I'm about to tell you is crazy."

"Crazier than your dad being a mafia dude, who lent money to my boyfriend's father, and he now can't repay that money? Well, I've seen *The Godfather*. I know what's coming for him."

"Well, that just adds another facet to my already far-fetched story."

"Do I need to get popcorn?"

"Tequila might be better."

"Ohh, wow, okay, well, let's start story time."

"Maybe after I tell you, we can sneak out for an afternoon of cocktails, and you can help me come up with an action plan that doesn't involve everything imploding."

"You had me at cocktails." She chuckles and, somehow, hearing that eases the pressure building on my chest right now. "But if you really want help, maybe we should grab the girls."

"I ... I, I don't know if I want everyone to know but, then again, it's all going to come out so it might be nice to have people on my side."

"Did you kill someone?" she hesitantly asks and I guess —coming from a mafia family—I can see why she'd think that, but Dad has done everything in his power to keep Sel and I away from that side of his life. He just didn't count on his youngest daughter having an affair with one of his colleagues, setting off a chain reaction of shit hitting the fan.

"Okay, so, you went to school with Selene, right?" She nods. "Well, Selene was having an affair with an older man." I decide to leave the who out because I don't trust that Mr. Van der Kündt wouldn't hurt anyone who knows this secret. "It turned to shit and that's why she ran." Then I give her the CliffsNotes version of everything.

"Holy shit, this is very *Days of Our Lives*-esque."

"I know, right? But this is real life and I have so much to lose if this is all revealed. At the same time, I hate keeping Tyler from his dad, but with Mr. Van der Kündt waiting in the wings—thinking Tyler is his—maybe it's time to reveal it all."

"Do you really think Mr. Van der Kündt would try anything? I mean, he knows your dad pretty well. Wouldn't that fuck up the alliance the five families have?"

"I'm not really a part of that side of things but, I mean, anything is possible, right?"

She nods and then asks something that stumps me, "You don't think he had anything to do with Selene's death, do you? I mean, from what you said, he's pissed she left and took his supposed son, who isn't his son."

My eyes widen at her question. When I think about everything I know, and how I feel about Mr. Van der Kündt, it's entirely possible he's involved in her death. Yes, the authorities say her crash was an accident, but Dad said he knows when something has been covered up and he of all people would know how to cover that up.

"Holy fuck, Lex, you might be on to something there."

"Then if that's the case, I really think you need to go to your dad, and you need to tell Miller the truth."

Then my worst fear materializes when from behind me, I hear a deep voice say, "Tell me the truth about what?"

43

MILLER

"TELL ME THE TRUTH ABOUT WHAT?" I ask as JJ and I walk up to the girls in the stands.

"Miller," Evie breathlessly says my name, fear written all over her face. "I, ummm, shit." She's stammering and nervous and that in turn makes me nervous.

"We should go," Lexi says, standing up. She leans down to Evie and whispers, "Tell him, and I'll be here if you need me."

She nods at her friend but doesn't say anything. Lexi walks past me and smiles, but it does nothing to ease the wariness building within me right now.

Walking down the last few steps, I lean against the plexiglass and cross my arms, waiting for Evie to tell me what's going on. "Eves?" I ask when the silence becomes deafening.

She inhales deeply and when she lifts her gaze to mine, I can't read her expression. "Please know that I did what I did because she asked me to."

"Oooookay," I draw the word out. *Who is she?*

"So, as you know, Selene had a baby and that baby is Tyler. I legally adopted him when paperwork from a lawyer turned up with her relinquishing parental rights. There was no letter explaining anything and, even though I didn't know who Tyler's father was, I signed the papers because he's my nephew and my sister needed my help. A few months back..." She pauses and takes a deep breath. "A few months back, I got another letter from the lawyer, turns out, Sel did leave a letter explaining everything but they misplaced it. I ... I finally got all the answers but she, once again, swore me to secrecy."

"You know who Tyler's dad is?"

She drops her head and stares at the floor. Quietly she utters, "Yeah, I do."

When she lifts her head and looks at me, I know. Without her voicing it, I know who his dad is. "I'm his dad," I murmur. It's not a question, it's a statement.

She nods her head and confirms with a meek, "Yes, Miller, you're his dad."

Hearing those words out loud causes an anger like I've never felt before to course through me. Spinning around, I slam my fist into the plexiglass, wincing at the pain from the hit. "Why didn't you tell me?" I growl at her.

"Because I made a promise."

"You fucking lied to me," I sneer at her. Then for extra emphasis, I add, "You. Lied." I pause between each word.

"I didn't lie per se, I just omitted the truth."

"Aka lied." Running my hands through my hair in anger, I pull at the strands because hurting my hair and not my fist is a more sensible thing to do. But the bite of pain at my scalp does nothing to ease the hurt at discovering I'm a dad.

"Miller," Evie breathlessly says my name, "I'm sorry I kept that from you."

"Tyler is my son," I state again. It's weird saying it out loud, but at the same time that statement flows out of my mouth with ease. "What the fuck, Eves?" But before I let her say anything, I turn my back on her and walk away.

So many emotions are flowing through me right now, but the one that sticks out the most is hurt. Hurt radiates within, and then I get pissed because I suspected I might have been his dad on several occasions. Hell, even my mom's had her suspicion but no, I did nothing. What kind of dad does that make me?

Walking into the locker room, I walk up to the first row of lockers and I slam my fist into the metal. Over and over again, my knuckles collide with the locker, wincing in pain with each strike of my knuckles into the metal. The more I hit it, the angrier I become.

"Miller, stop!" Evie shouts from behind me.

"Leave me alone, Evie," I hiss, but Evie being Evie, she ignores me and invades my space. She slides herself between me and the locker and takes my hand in hers. She looks over my knuckles and scrunches her face up at the damage I've done to the skin.

Like always when she touches me, my body comes alive. My blood simmers for her. My heart beats for her. Every breath I take is for her, and for Tyler ... my son.

Ever so gently, she runs her fingers over my split knuckles. Apart from it hurting like a bitch, I know I haven't broken anything. For a brief second, I focus on her touch, but then I remember what I just discovered and any feelings I was starting to feel evaporate.

Wrenching my hand from her grasp, I take a step back and glare at her. "Why? Just tell me that."

She inhales deeply and closes her eyes. Silence envelops us.

"Selene made me promise not to tell anyone about Tyler's parentage and, until now, I haven't told a soul."

"You couldn't tell me? Did you not trust that I'd keep her secret too?"

"I promised her!" she shouts at me.

"You chose to keep a dead woman's secret over telling me the truth. Over telling the man you supposedly love that he has a son. You know what fucks me off the most in all of this? You chose to keep a secret for a dead woman who, from everything I've discovered recently, is a lying fucking bitch. And to make matters worse, feeling such hatred for a dead woman makes me feel like a shit human being. Did you consider me in any of this? Did ... did you maybe consider that I'd want to get to know my son?"

"You have gotten to know him."

"As a friend!" I shout. "I'm his dad, Eves. Do you know how I feel right now? I've missed out on so much in his life."

"I only recently found out myself," she reiterates, trying to defend her actions. I don't know what pisses me off more —her defending herself or her keeping it from me.

"I don't fucking care if you'd known from day one. As soon as you and I became more, you should have told me." I pause. "You know who else has a right to know? Tyler. Did you think about him in any of this?" Not letting her get a word in, I continue, "No, you didn't. You only thought about what was easy for you."

"It's not like that, Miller. Please, just ... please, don't take him from me. He's all I have left of my sister."

"Do you really think that little of me? Do you really think I would be vindictive like that? Clearly, you don't know me at all and, clearly, I don't know you at all."

"You do," she cries. "Nobody knows me like you do. I love everything about us, Miller. We are a family. Tyler loves you and I know you love him too."

"Of course I do, how can I not? That kid is fucking amazing, considering all the lies that have surrounded him."

"Not once have I lied to him, Miller. Not once."

"So you only lied to me then, huh?"

"I didn't li—"

"Stop fucking saying that, because you did. There's been several conversations and moments when you could have told me the truth, but you didn't. You took the coward's way out."

"I'm sorry," she cries. "Please," she begs, "please forgive me."

"I don't know if I will ever be able to forgive you for this, Evie."

Without waiting for her to say anything, I grab my bag from my cubby and walk out of the locker room. The last thing I hear is Evie sobbing, but fuck her. She lied and kept my son from me, and I don't think I can forgive her for that.

44

EVIE

WATCHING Miller walk away is the hardest thing I've ever had to do. For months now, I've hated the fact I was lying to Miller but at the same time, I don't because I was following my sister's wishes. Then I think of Tyler and a sob breaks free.

Falling to the floor, I curl into a ball in the middle of the locker room and fall apart. Eventually, I cry myself to sleep, only to be woken by a hand on my shoulder. Opening my eyes, I look up into the concerned eyes of Cassandra.

"What's happened?" she asks, confusion all over her face.

Swallowing deeply, I sigh. "I fucked up and ..." I shuffle into a sitting position and then I meekly whisper, "I lost Miller."

Just as I finish my confession, from behind Cassandra a little head pops into my line of vision, and my eyes well with tears at seeing his little face. "Mommy, what's wrong?"

Hearing his little voice breaks the dam and tears begin to streak down my face. He steps around Cassandra and throws himself into my arms and hugs me. "It's okay, Mommy." His voice and words break my heart further because nothing is going to be okay.

Wrapping my arms around him, I hold on tightly to him and sob harder. Finally, the tears stop but I'm still clinging tightly on to Tyler.

"Tyler, Buddy," Cassandra says, "can you do me a favor?" She crouches down to our level. "Can you get Mommy a bottle of water, please?"

He nods his little head, crawls off my lap, and races over to the fridge to get my drink. As soon as he's out of earshot, Cassandra pounces. "Evie, babe, what happened?"

I repeat what I said when she first walked in, "I fucked up and lost Miller because I kept something from him that's pretty big."

"It can't be that bad," she offers.

"I kept that he's," I head nod toward Tyler, "his Dad."

Her eyes widen and her mouth drops open. "Ohh," she manages to squeak out.

"Yeah, ohh."

"What do you say, we head back to your place? We'll order pizza and over a bottle of wine and greasy carbs, you can tell me everything. Then we can come up with a game plan to fix this mess you find yourself in."

Nodding, I smile at my nanny just as Tyler returns with my water. "Thanks, Buddy," I tell him, ruffling his hair. "Ready to go home?"

He nods, smiling brightly at me. Pushing aside every-thing, I focus on Tyler. He doesn't need to be drawn into my mess, even though he's the center of said mess. I don't know how to deal with the repercussions of my secrets, plural, being revealed, but one thing I do know, I need to make sure Tyler is safe and loved.

Together, Cassandra, Tyler, and I head home, stopping

to grab pizza and the wine along the way. Cassandra grabs two bottles because, and I quote, "When your boyfriend is the father of the son you adopted because your dead sister swore you to secrecy is revealed, it calls for two bottles" ... but I don't think there's enough wine in the world to deal with this revelation.

Tyler is asleep and tucked up in bed and it's finally story time.

"Holy shit," Cassandra rasps when I finish telling her everything. While I was bathing Tyler, Cass called in reinforcements. Just as I returned from tucking Tyler in, Kennedy arrived with another bottle of wine and a carton of cookie dough ice cream.

Kennedy replies with a, "That's, umm, yeah, wow."

"I told you it was massive."

"It's like *Days of Our Lives* and *The Sopranos* had a baby," Kennedy says, causing me to snort my wine.

"We can call it *Mafia Lives*," Cassandra unhelpfully adds.

"How did I not know you were from a mafia family?" Kennedy asks, once the two of them stop cackling over their fake soap opera.

"That's what you're focusing on right now?" I ask, shoving another spoonful of ice cream into my mouth. FYI, cookie dough ice cream goes extremely well with red wine.

"For starters I am," Kennedy confirms before taking a sip of her wine. "So, have you ever seen anyone end up with the fishes?"

"Yeah, have you?" Cassandra eagerly asks.

"What?" I hiss, "No, I have not. And my dad isn't—"

"No. No. No." Cassandra raises her hand, halting me. "Your dad totally has done that. You aren't the head of a mafia family and not have blood on your hands, but since you're defending Papa Salvatore, I'm going to say *you* haven't."

"You would be correct but I have a feeling if I tell him this story, Mr. Van der Kündt might be sleeping with the fishes, as you put it."

"Sounds like he needs to be sleeping with the fishes," Kennedy states matter-of-factly. "'Cause, excuse my French, but he sounds like a cunt."

"Miller calls him Van der Cunt," I tell them with a sad, pathetic laugh.

"Fitting"—she nods in confirmation—"but if you ask me, it officially should be pronounced Cunt. I don't care that the lil' dots over the u change the pronunciation. From here on out, he will officially be known as Van der Cunt. Now Van der Cunt aside, how are you going to win back the baby daddy?"

"Do you think I have a chance to win him back?"

They both nod their heads.

"We do, Eves," Kennedy affirms for the two of them. "That man loves you and Tyler fiercely. He has a right to be angry and I'm sorry for saying that, but he does. You kept something pretty monumental from him. He needs time to process."

"I guess you're right, I just hate that I hurt him. You should have seen his knuckles after he punched the locker. He's lucky he didn't damage his hand."

"Again, I think he's entitled to that."

"So, how do I fix this?"

Kennedy looks to Cassandra and she leans forward. Reaching over, she squeezes my knees. "For now, give him space to process. Both of the Salvatore sisters have torn his heart to pieces, but the difference now is you're still here to face the music."

"I really hurt him, guys, and I hate myself for that."

"Hating yourself isn't going to help."

"Cass is right," Kennedy agrees, I'm starting to feel like these two are ganging up on me but, at the same time, it's nice to have them on my team. "You need to push how you feel aside and you need to focus on Miller and Tyler. They're the two with the most to lose here but, at the same time, the three of you have everything to gain. So, for now, you give him space to process. Let him yell and punch, not you; he does that and we will need your dad to help him sleep with the fishes. Once he's let it all out, you talk and then you fuck. Then you fuck some more and finally, you live happily ever after."

Nodding, I smile. "I hope you're right." Giving him space will be hard but if it means we get our happily ever after as a family, then space is what I'll give him.

...one week later

"WENTWORTH," Doc Michels calls from the doorway to his office. "My office when you get a chance, I have a question about your recovery."

"Be there in a sec," I call out. I've just returned from the showers and this is the last thing I want to do. I can't wait to get out of here. Today has been a shit show and training with a hangover sucks donkey dick.

After leaving here the other day, I locked myself in my apartment and I drowned my sorrows in Jack, Jim, and José. I don't usually get black-out drunk during the season but in the last few days, I decided to party with my three friends. Hell, I even drank the cooking sherry I had in the pantry.

Today my hungover head was all over the place and because I wasn't paying attention and was off in la-la land, Coach punished me ... and the guys. I lost count as to how many bag skates we did. I came close to vomiting at one point and when that happened, I cursed Evie-fucking-Salvatore once again.

Pulling a clean tee over my head, I slip my feet into my slides and head over to Doc's office, but I stop mid-stride when I see Evie standing on the other side of the room. She looks just as broken as I feel and my first instinct is to make sure she's okay. Then I remember her lies and I don't give a shit about her. I hope she's suffering just as much as I am. "It's clear you two need to talk," Doc says, flicking his gaze between us.

"You told him?" I sneer at Evie.

"No, I did," Coach McQueen says from behind me. "And before you go off on the poor woman, might I remind you of *your* behavior this week? You need to deal with whatever the hell is going on between the two of you, and if you don't pull your finger out before the game tomorrow night, you'll be riding the bench."

"But—" I try to interrupt.

"Nope, no buts. The two of you are going to talk this shit out like mature adults and deal with what's going on between you two."

"Is this an intervention or some shit?"

"Call it what you will, but I will not have your kid drama mess with my team. Yes, it's shit she kept a secret from you, but she didn't keep the child from you. You already have a bond with him, don't fuck with that. Kids are resilient but a parent fucking them over because they're butthurt over something the other parent did, that's a shitty thing to do. You're better than that. You both are, now deal with this like mature adults."

Staring at the man I admire, I process his words and a lot of what he said is right. Evie did let me see Tyler, even after she discovered who I was. I can't fault her for keeping a secret her sister begged her to keep but, at the same time,

I'm hurt that she kept said secret from me. I would do anything to have my dad back, and knowing I missed out on the first five years of Tyler's life, it sucks.

"In the big scheme of things," Coach continues, "no one died, well, shit, sorry. Someone did die but she was doing what she thought was right for her child and, at the end of the day, isn't his welfare and happiness all that matters? Life is short, you don't know how long you have." He pauses, his eyes widening and then without another word, he turns on his heel, mumbling, "I ... I need to go." With that, he races out of the room, leaving me confused because one minute he's giving me a lecture, and the next, he's hightailing it out of the treatment room.

When I look up, Evie is smiling. "Why are you smiling?"

"Because I think I know what light bulb moment he just had."

"Care to share with the class?"

"It's not my secret to share."

"You and your fucking secrets. When will the secret keeping end?"

"Miller," she pleads, "this isn't my secret to share and regarding what I kept from you; it killed me to do so."

"I had a right to know, Evie. He's. My. Son."

"I know, but ..."

"But what?" I sneer at her.

"I promised Sel I wouldn't tell anyone and ... and I felt I owed that to my sister."

"Your sister was a bitch, much like her older sister."

"You knew she was a bitch before all of this. Hell, everyone knew she was a bitch, but we all still loved her 'cause that was Selene." She shakes her head, "It's no surprise that she's still fucking with us from the grave, but it's not only my fault. You fucked her and got her pregnant and on some level, deep down, you knew you had a connection with Tyler. The bond you two have isn't some miracle, it's because you're father and son. You. Knew," she throws at me and as I process what she just said, my hackles raise. Is she fucking kidding me right now, trying to pin some of this on me? Well, if she wants to be a bitch, two can play at that game so I'm gonna fuck with her. "I will never forgive you for this, Evie. From now on, we can speak through my lawyer."

Turning my back on her, I storm out of the room. I've only taken a few steps when she shoves me from behind, causing me to stumble. Spinning around to face her, I see a fuming Evie glaring at me.

"You will not threaten me like that and walk away."

"Or what?" I sneer, stepping into her space. Our faces are millimeters apart, our heated breaths mingle together.

"I'll take him and run."

"You wouldn't."

"Try me, Miller. I fucking dare you to try."

Before I know what I'm doing, I slide my hand behind her neck and slam my lips to hers. She pushes on my chest, trying to get away, but her fighting me turns me on in a way like I've never been turned on before. Holding on to her tighter, I kiss her harder. Sliding my other hand around her side, I squeeze her ass and pull her into me. Grinding my pelvis into hers, she begins to kiss me back. She moans into my mouth and then she's sucking on my lips. Shocking me, she bites my lip, hard, and draws blood.

Pulling back, I stare at her with wide eyes. Her lip is covered with my blood. Lifting my hand, I reach up and smear it down her chin. Gripping her hips, I walk her backward and press her into the side of the lockers, caging her in with my body. Both of us are breathlessly panting. Hate and arousal envelops us as we continue to stare at one another.

At the same time, we each lean forward. Our lips collide together in a hungry, angry kiss. Our teeth clash as we messily kiss one another.

With our lips fused together, I push down her leggings and panties as she frees my dick from my sweats. Lifting her up effortlessly, my dick slides into her hot, wet channel. We both moan at the intrusion. Wrapping her legs around me, I begin to piston my hips. My dick slides in and out as I fuck her hard against the side of the lockers.

With my eyes glued to hers, I stare at her and slam in and out of her. My anger from before pours back into me, causing me to fuck her harder.

Voices can be heard on the other side of the locker room, causing me to stop mid-thrust. Sliding my hands under her ass, I turn and walk into the treatment room, kicking the door closed behind me. Stalking over to the treatment table, I pull her off of me and place her down on her feet. Placing my hands on her shoulders, I spin her around and push on her lower back, bending her over the side of the table. Gripping her hips, I hold her still as I slam into her from behind, I start to fuck her again.

Digging my fingers into her skin, I increase my speed and rut into her harder than I ever have before. She moans and I sneer, "Shut your mouth or I'll stop."

She lowers her head down, covering her mouth so I keep going.

Reaching around, I slide my hand between her thighs and pinch her clit. "Fuuuuuuuuck," she mewls into her arm. "I'm, I'm..." But I don't want her to come yet. Pulling out, she snaps her head toward me and glares at me over her shoulder.

Standing up, she shuffles around to face me and I see anger reflecting back at me. "What the fuck, Miller?" she angrily hisses.

"Not so good being deprived of something you want, is it?"

"It's not the same thing, Miller."

"No, nothing will ever compare to being kept from your son."

"I'm sorry," she cries, shaking her head. "I ... I felt like no matter what I did, it was going to be the wrong thing. If I told you, I'd be betraying Selene and one of the last things she ever asked of me. At the same time, not telling you was eating at me because you and Tyler have such a special bond. And then there was me and you, I love you with everything I have. I have always loved you, but at the same time, I was dying inside for lying. And as selfish as it sounds, I didn't want to lose you ... or him. And ... and now, you're going to take him from me."

"I'm not," I tell her, shaking my head. "I just said that in anger, and I'm sorry I did that."

"It's okay," she laments. "I deserve it because I know what I did was shit and I really am sorry."

Silence fills the room and as I take a moment to process it all, I know we need to talk, calmly. This, whatever we were doing just now, isn't the answer. "I think we need to talk about this. Clear the air and all that."

"I'd like that too," she agrees, nodding, "but, umm, do you think you can put your dick away? It's distracting, and I don't need any distractions when we have this conversation."

"I never thought I'd hear a girl asking for me to put my dick away." She shakes her head. "But for the record, I'd like to finish what we started just now because fucking you makes me feel good, and I can't remember the last time I felt good. So, wha—" Her phone rings, stopping me from finishing that sentence, and I know she needs to get it because it's Cass's tone.

Reaching into her bag, she pulls it out and swipes to answer. Bringing her phone to her ear, she says, "Hey, Cass." She listens to Cass and then her face pales. Whatever Cass has told her, it's not good news. "I'll ... I'll be right there," she states and then hangs up. Looking over at me, she utters two words that shake me to my core. "Tyler's gone."

46
EVIE

WHILE I WAS GETTING hate fucked by Miller, our son was being kidnapped by some psycho asshole.

When Cass realized Tyler was gone, she called me immediately. She offered to call the police, but I told her to wait until Miller and I got there. We quickly raced to my car and thirty minutes later, we were racing into my apartment. Cass was sitting at the island, tears streaking down her cheeks.

"I'm so sorry," she cries, jumping up to meet us in the entryway. "We ... we were in the pool area and one minute he was there and then, then he was gone."

"Why weren't you watching him?" Miller growls at her.

"I was, I turned my back to get the sunscreen and when I looked up, he was gone."

There's a knock on the apartment door and when I open it, I see Declan from downstairs standing there. "Evening, Ms. Salvatore, I pulled the footage from the lobby and garages around the time Master Salvatore went missing, and I found this." He hands me the iPad in his hands and I press play. Staring at the screen, I watch as a man steps out of the elevator into the underground garages with his head down. He has Tyler haphazardly thrown over his shoulder. His little body hangs limply upside down. It doesn't look like he's struggling or moving. Covering my mouth, I gasp at the footage before me. Tears well in my eyes as I watch the man open the back door to a car, throwing Tyler inside, before he slams the door shut. He climbs into the front passenger seat and the car peels out of the underground parking lot.

"This is all my fault," I cry as I stare at the screen before me. "Had I just told everyone from the beginning who Tyler's parents were, none of this would have happened." Covering my face with my hands, I break down and sob. "I really am a shit human being and if any harm comes to my son, I will not be held accountable for what I do when I get my hands on him."

"Do you know who this man is?" Declan asks, but I shake my head. I don't want him or the police knowing that Klaus Van der Kündt has my son but when I look back up at Declan, I get the feeling he knows I'm lying. The only person I want dealing with this is my dad.

"I ... I'll get my dad on it," I voice.

"Your dad?" Miller voices, his tone shocked that I would want my dad involved in this. I try not to be involved in that side of the family but Klaus is Dad's friend, well was, not sure they'll still be friends after this. Their friendship aside, Dad can do things the police can't and since Dad knows Klaus quite well, he will hopefully have insider information that will help us get Tyler back.

"There's no one else I would trust with this."

"Are you sure?" Miller asks.

"Positive. Dad will do anything for his family."

"I'll send the footage to Mr. Salvatore now," Declan says and as his words register, my gaze snaps toward

Declan. His eyes are wide when he realizes what he just said. "You ... you work for my dad?" He nods. "How long have you been following me?" I question.

"Since you moved to New York." *What the hell, Dad?* "Ms. Salvatore, he's had eyes on you ever since your sister was murdered."

"How did I not know?"

"Because we're good at what we do," he nonchalantly replies. It doesn't come across as cocky, it's just a fact, but considering he's an employee of my father's, I know he'll be the best of the best. My dad only hires people who excel in their field. He didn't rise to his position from having shit people surrounding him ... well, he has one shitty person, but after this, he'll be swimming with the fishes.

"But..." Shaking my head, I'm at a loss for words. "Can you please wait for me to call him? He ... he doesn't know everything, well anything really, and I want it to come from me."

"Very well," he affirms. "In the meantime, I'll start tracking the car and hopefully by the time your father has been informed, we will have a location on Mr. Van der Kündt and your son." So he did know I was lying about recognizing who took Tyler. But after learning who he's employed by, I'm not surprised.

Declan heads out and I turn to Miller, but before I can say anything he says, "Are you sure about using your dad and not the police?"

"I'm sure." I nod. "Dad knows him and that will hopefully help." Grabbing my phone out of my handbag, I bring up Dad's number and hit call.

"Evie, sweetheart, I was just thinking about you," he says when he answers.

"Dad," I whisper.

"What's wrong?"

"I ... I need your help, Dad." As soon as I utter those words, the tears start to fall and then I'm sobbing into the phone.

"What's wrong, baby?"

"I ... shit," I blubber, beginning to cry harder. Dad is yelling for me to tell him what's going on, but finding the words to articulate what's happened and what I've been keeping from everyone is impossible.

Miller snatches my phone from me. "Sir, Van der Cunt kidnapped Tyler and we need your help getting my son back."

The two of them chat and then Miller thrusts the phone back at me, not uttering a word. "Dad," I squeak out.

"I'm here, baby, now, in your own words, tell me everything and don't think any little tidbit isn't important."

Nodding, I swallow back the lump in my throat. I drop down onto the sofa, bring my knees up to my chest, and I tell him everything about Selene and Tyler and Miller and most of all, how Mr. Van der Kündt is not who he thinks he is. When I finish, I add, "I ... I messed up and ... and he took him and I, we, need your help."

"You didn't mess up, baby, but I promise you, he's a dead man," Dad growls. "Your mother and I will be there by morning. For now, tell Declan everything you know."

"You're not mad?" I hesitantly ask him.

"Why would I be mad?"

"Because I kept this a secret. If I had just been honest from the beginning, Selene would still be alive"—I look over at Miller—"and Tyler would be safe."

"Sweetheart, I'm not mad and I'm not surprised you did that for your sister. You have the biggest heart and you were doing what you thought was best. As did she. The person we need to be pissed at is my soon-to-be dead friend. No one hurts my family and lives to tell the tale.

Now, get some sleep, Mom and I will be there in the morning."

Hanging up from Dad, I give the CliffsNotes version to Cass and Miller on what's going to happen. Cass breaks down again, apologizing for losing him on her watch. Miller and I both try to placate her but I know how she feels because my secrets led to this.

After calming her down, I tuck her into my bed and she's asleep before I've shut the door behind me. The poor thing is exhausted from crying so hard.

Walking back into the living room, I stop and stare at Miller.

"Come here," he says, opening his arms.

Walking over to him, I wrap mine around him and cry into his chest. When I have no more tears left to cry, we decide that with nothing to do until morning, we may as well head to bed and get some sleep. Not that I'll be getting any. I will never sleep until Tyler is safe home with me.

Sadly, Miller says goodnight and heads toward the door, he's not staying here. I'd love nothing more than to lie in his arms but even though we talked things through earlier, sort of, he's still hurt. Lying on the sofa, I curl into a ball and cry for my missing little boy, but most of all I cry for hurting the one person I love most in this world.

47
MILLER

WAKING THE NEXT MORNING, I let out a frustrated sigh when I realize everything that happened yesterday was real and it wasn't a dream.

Tyler IS my son.

Evie lied about MY son.

Klaus Van der Cunt TOOK my son because the fucking psycho thinks he's his kid.

Climbing out of bed, I jump into the shower and as the hot water beats down on me, I begin to cry as my emotions overwhelm me. I've just found out Tyler is my son and he's been taken from me. What if we never get him back? He will never know how much I love him, and I do. I've always loved him. It's like his soul called to me ... because we're related.

No longer am I filled with sadness, I'm back to being angry with Evie for keeping this secret from me.

Jumping out of the shower, I quickly dry off and dress in jeans and a Crushers tee. Slipping my feet into my slides, I grab my phone and head across the hall to Evie's place.

Opening the door, I step into her apartment and stop mid-stride when I see Evie's living room is filled with all of our friends—Cass, JJ and Lexi, Kallen and Chelsea, Jett and Margo, Colt, Coach McQueen, and his nanny, Kennedy. They're sitting pretty close together but I don't have time to focus on that, I want an update.

Looking around the room, I don't see her. "Where's Evie?" I growl.

All eyes flick to me but no one answers, then I hear the shower running in her bedroom and I know where she is. Marching down the hallway, I storm into her room and just as I enter the en suite, the shower turns off and she steps out. A shriek slips through her lips when she sees me standing there. "Shit, Miller, you scared me."

"Any news?" I hiss, ignoring her statement.

"Nothing," she timidly says. "Mom and Dad should be here soon."

My eyes want to wander over her wet, naked body and mine comes alive, just as it always does when Evie is naked and wet. But at the same time I want to wrap my hands around her neck and throttle her for keeping Tyler a secret from me. "Get fucking dressed," I sneer. Without waiting for an answer, I turn my back on her and walk back out to the living area.

All eyes are once again on me. "You good?" JJ asks.

"What do you think? My son, who I didn't know was my son, has been kidnapped by a fucking psycho because *she* kept his parentage from me."

"That's a bit harsh," Kennedy says, defending her friend.

"When your kid is kidnapped because someone lied, then we can talk, till then, I suggest you shut your fucking mouth."

"Watch your mouth, son," Coach McQueen interjects.

"We get you're upset, but turning on your friends is not going to bring Tyler back."

His words stop me and I know he's right. I look over at a crestfallen Kennedy, "Sorry." She nods and I follow it up with, "I just want him back." My eyes well with tears.

"We all want him back," Evie timidly voices from behind me. She squeezes my shoulder and I cover her hand with mine ... then I remember *she's* why he's gone, and I throw her hand off me.

"This is all your fault," I spit at Evie over my shoulder. Spinning to face her, I glare down at her. "Your fucking lies and secrets caused a madman to take my son. You better hope and pray he's returned safely without a hair out of place, otherwise, I will never forgive you, Evie. Never."

"Miller," JJ growls my name. "Enough. This is not her fault and you know it. The only person responsible for this is Van der Cunt."

"But—"

"Nope, no buts," he interrupts, placing himself between Evie and me. "You can go back to being an angry dickhead once Tyler is home and safe but for now, sit your ass down while we wait for Evie's mom and dad to get here. You and I both know that man will do anything for his family. He knows Van der Cunt better than anyone, and he will know what to do."

"He's right, Miller," the woman, who in the light of day I cannot stand to look at, agrees with my friend. I thought I was mad yesterday, but waking this morning and Tyler still being gone made all the anger come back tenfold.

"Shut it, Evie, I don't want to hear a thing you have to say." Shaking my head, I run my hands through my hair and tug at the strands in frustration. "I can't be here." Without another word, I storm out of Eveie's apartment, slamming the door behind me.

Entering the stairwell, I take the stairs, two at a time, to the pool deck. Stepping out into the sunshine, I tilt my head back and let the morning sun beat down on me. Walking over to *our* lounger, I sit on the end and drop my head into my hands. I don't know how long I sit like this but it isn't until a body stops before me that I lift my head again. When I do, I smile when I see my mom standing there. "Mom." The word swooshes out and I stand up, wrapping my arms around her. When she hugs me back, the floodgates open and, once again, I find myself crying like a little bitch.

"Ohhh, baby, I'm so sorry," she coos in that mom-like way that somehow soothes my pain a little.

"How are you here?" I ask, pulling away.

She wipes at my tear-stained cheeks, takes my hand in hers, and pulls me back into a seated position. "Mrs. Salvatore came over and told me everything," she sadly smiles at me. "I knew he was yours. I just knew it."

"But he's gone."

"He'll be back," she confidently states. I wish I had her confidence because right now, all I feel is despair and hopelessness.

48
EVIE

STANDING HERE, I watch Miller storm out of my apartment and for the second time in twenty-four hours, the man I love stated facts that are true. And like the first time I heard them voiced aloud, they cut like a bitch. My body goes numb and my heart, once again, shatters.

Tyler is gone.

Miller is gone, and it's all because of the secrets I kept.

This mess *is* all my fault.

If everyone knew Miller was Tyler's dad then he'd be safe at home with me, us, right now. And Miller would be here with me and not on the other side of that door hating me. Falling to my knees in the middle of my living room, I let out an inhuman wail and fall to pieces.

Tears streak down my cheeks.

Snot leaks from my nose and my body shakes as I grieve losing everyone I have ever loved.

I can feel people hovering around me but I don't look up. Right now, all I want is to be alone, but I know every single person here will argue I shouldn't be alone. So I just stay here in a ball on the floor, and I cry. I didn't know a human could cry so much, surely my body would have run out of tears by now.

I've cried so hard my body is exhausted. I can't even lift my head, but that is taken out of my control when someone slides their arms under me and picks me up. At first, I think it's Miller and then I inhale, but it's not his smell—fresh ice and mint—and I start to sniffle again. They carry me into my bedroom and gently place me down onto my bed. Rolling away from them, I pull my legs up and I hug myself. Not wanting to be a complete bitch, I mumble a meek, "Thank you."

"We're here if you need anything," JJ states. I should have known it was him. He and Miller are so much alike in temperament, but he's not Miller and he's the one I want right now ... but I will never have him again.

Staring at the wall, I think over all the times I could have told Miller everything, and I hate myself for keeping secrets. They never stay secret; I should have just told him. It's not like Selene could get mad at me and, at the end of the day, she wanted what's best for Tyler. Tyler. I think of my little boy and how scared he must be right now. I hope Van der Cunt is looking after him. Lying here, I feel helpless but most of all, I feel like a failure. My sister asked me to do one thing, protect Tyler, and I couldn't even do that.

I'm exhausted from crying so much and drift off to sleep, but I'm woken when a hand touches my shoulder. Looking over my shoulder, I smile for the first time since I discovered Tyler was missing when I see my mom and dad standing next to my bed.

Pushing myself up, I shuffle to my knees and pull them both into a hug. My eyes well with tears and I tearfully whimper, "Mom. Dad ... I ... I'm so sorry I didn't say anything. This is all my fault."

"Ohhh, honey," Mom coos, cupping my cheek in that motherly way. "There is only one person responsible for this and that's Klaus." She shakes her head, "I cannot believe what he's done. He took advantage of my baby and now, now, he has my grandson."

"He'll be dead by sunset," Dad hisses. When I look over at him, I see nothing but anger on his face.

"You should add me to the kill list too because this is all my fault."

"The only person to blame here is Klaus," Dad sneers his name and I don't think I've ever seen Dad so angry in my life. "After you called me last night, I had an associate of mine look into my so-called friend. Let's just say, none of us knew him like we thought we did and after my discoveries, my gut is telling me he's the one responsible for Selene's death."

"What?" Mom and I both gasp the word at the same time.

"That's not important right now. We need to focus on getting Tyler back, but I promise you, he's going to pay for everything he's done. No one messes with my family and gets away with it." He pauses. "I failed Selene, I will not fail my grandson too."

"Anything?" I ask after I reenter the living room, my hair still wet from my shower.

"Not yet, sweetheart," Mom says, handing me a cup of coffee and a plate with a chocolate croissant.

"Did Martha send these?" I ask.

Mom shakes her head. "No, they're from the bakery

down the street. Rick and Kennedy went and got food for everyone, and I asked them to get you your favorite. I know it's not Martha's, but..." She shrugs her shoulders.

"Thanks, Mom."

Taking the plate and mug from her, I walk over to the sofa and drop down onto the cushion, careful not to spill a drop of my coffee. I always say that an adult spilling coffee is the equivalent to a kid spilling their favorite drink, aka sacrilege. Bringing my cup to my lips, I take a sip. The boldness of the coffee warms my body and a small smile appears on my face. My smile widens when I take a bite of my croissant.

"That'd be right, my son is missing and you're sitting here drinking coffee and eating pastries," Miller sneers from the kitchen.

Turning my head, I see him standing there, anger etched into his face. There are deep black circles under his eyes and he looks terrible. "Miller," I whisper. "I—"

"Save it," he growls. "It really doesn't surprise me that you're sitting here like a fucking princess while my son is out there with a fucking madman. How Selene thought *you* were the right person to look after him, I will never know. I will never forgive you—"

"You might wanna think very hard about what you say next to my daughter," Dad growls from the hallway.

"Sir, with all due respect," Miller shouts, "you don't know anything. Did you know your daughter here has hidden the truth about everything when it comes to Selene and Tyler and Van der Cunt?"

"I'm aware," Dad confirms, "and are you aware that she's had to bear this burden all on her own? Think about when Selene died, she had to grieve her sister's death while raising her sister's son. She's had to look into a mini version of Selene every fucking day, and not once did she put herself first. She has done everything for my grandson. You should be thanking her for—"

"Getting him kidnapped by a madman? If she had just told everyone the truth, Tyler would still be here. It's because of her fucking lies." Then he sneers a "bitch," under his breath.

"Miller Dominic Wentworth," his mom scolds, "you will apologize to Evie now. She is hurting, just like you. Klaus is who you need to be directing your anger at, not each other. Every single person in this room would give their life for that little boy."

"You don't know that," he snipes.

"I do," she throws back at her son. "Because that's what being a parent means, having faith in those who surround you. Now, sit your ass back down and let the adults come up with a plan to get Tyler out safely, so he can come home to his mom and dad because Klaus is clearly delusional when it comes to that little boy."

"She's right," my dad interjects. "I don't think any amount of evidence would have prevented this from happening because when Klaus gets an idea in his head, he runs with it. It's no secret he's wanted a son to take over his empire because he refuses to hand over the Van der Kündt reins to Annika. We all know he's a misogynistic dick, and this has opened my eyes to what Klaus is really like. When I find him, Annika will get her shot because no one messes with my family and walks away. No one."

The room falls silent as we process Dad's words. The silence is broken when Dad's phone rings. "Talk to me, Declan."

Placing my mug down, I stare intently at Dad. He's not saying anything, he just nods his head and utters a stern, "Uhhh ha," over and over. Finally, he hangs up.

"That was Declan—"

"No shit," Miller hisses, earning himself a famous Daniel Salvatore glare.

"As I was saying, that was Declan, they've located Klaus. Dani is with him but from what Declan can ascertain, she's pissed at her husband for kidnapping Tyler. He seems to think, like us, she's finally seeing her husband for who he is."

"Then what are we waiting for, let's go," I declare, standing up.

"Not so fast, missy," Dad says in his "I mean business" tone. "You," he points to me, "and you," he points to Miller, "are both staying here. And—"

"Like fuck," Miller yells, as I beg, "Daaaad, please."

He shakes his head. "No," he emphatically states with a raised hand. "You're both too emotional and too close to the situation."

"As are you," I throw at him.

"The difference is, I can compartmentalize my feelings. This isn't the first time I've dealt with a kidnapping." He looks over at Mom and the look on his face softens. Back when Mom was pregnant with me, a drug kingpin kidnapped Mom. He wanted Dad's turf in Chicago and thought taking Mom was the way to get what he wanted. He didn't count on Dad's alliance with the Chicago Five and, well, he and his crew were never heard of again. Mom was safely returned. Dad became her hero, but I'm pretty sure he already was. My mom loves my dad fiercely, and he loves her and his family with everything he has.

"You can't do this one on your own, Dad," I remind him. Flopping back down to the sofa, I cross my arms and glare at my dad, but once Daniel Salvatore has made up his mind, that's it. There's no changing it. The only person who could manipulate him was Selene and if she couldn't, she just went ahead and did what she wanted anyway, conse-quences be damned.

"I know, it's why I've called two of the other families to New York. The other is watching back home and we all agree, this infringement cannot go unpunished. Klaus is one of the five and he will be dealt with in due time, but first, we need to get my grandson back." He looks steadfastly between Miller and me. "You two are going to sit your asses back down and let me handle this. I need to brief the others, and then I will go and get your son back."

Without saying anything else, Dad walks out into the hall to make his calls.

"This is bullshit," Miller huffs, dropping down onto the sofa next to me. His leg touches mine and it's the first time we've made physical contact since Tyler was taken. My leg buzzes from the contact and on instinct, I reach out and rest my hand on his thigh.

"Dad will get him back," I reiterate.

He covers my hand and squeezes. Turning my head to look at him, he begins to lean in and I think he's going to kiss me but he leans down to my ear, "I'm not sitting around twiddling my thumbs while Tyler is out there."

"What do you propose?"

"We say we're going for a walk and to call us when they have news. Instead, we'll be downstairs in JJ's car and when your dad heads off, we follow him."

My head begins to bob up and down in agreement. "Okay," I whisper, "let's go get our boy."

49

MILLER

SITTING in the front seat of JJ's car, I'm just as nervous as when I wait for the puck to drop on game day. When I asked JJ for his keys, he demanded to know why. The lie started to roll off my tongue but before I'd finished, he gave me the "do I look like a fool?" look. So I told him what Evie and I were planning to do. After deliberating for a few seconds, he agreed to hand them over as long as he could come. Then Lexi demanded to come too, and well, here we are on our stakeout. The four of us are in JJ's car, impatiently waiting for Mr. Salvatore to make his move.

"There he is," Lexi shrieks from the back seat.

Looking across the street, I watch as Mr. Salvatore, Declan, and another man race over to the black SUV idling at the curb. They all climb in and when it pulls away from the curb, I wait for a car to pass and then I pull out and follow them.

"How do you know to do this?" JJ asks as we make a left.

"I've watched enough *NCIS* and *Law and Order* to know how to tail someone."

"I call bullshit," JJ sniggers, "because as much as I've watched *ER* and *Grey's Anatomy*, there's no way I can perform a tracheal-thingy-magiggy."

"I can," Evie states, "and the technical term is a tracheotomy."

"Show off," I mumble and from the corner of my eye, I see her smile. Seeing that lip lift causes something inside of me to come alive again because, for the last day, I haven't seen anything but fear and regret on her face. I'm starting to come to the realization this isn't her fault, it's Van der Cunt's. I think I've been misplacing my anger because she was there and an easy target.

Mom made me see sense earlier when she scolded me in front of everyone. I know I was an ass, but I'm blaming it on the intensity of the situation. When we get Tyler back, I will apologize to Eves and hope like hell she'll forgive me.

"Ummm, guys," Lexi blurts from the back seat, "we've lapped this block three times now." Just as she says that, the car stops at the curb in front of a pawn shop. Declan climbs out and the car pulls back onto the road, parking on a side street, just down from where Declan hopped out.

"I'll go past them, pop a U-turn, and park on the other side of the street," I inform everyone.

We pull into our spot and watch Mr. Salvatore exit the car. Slamming his door, he then turns and walks across the street, toward us. "Down," I whisper-shout.

We all duck, but a few seconds later there's a tap on my window. When I lift my head, I smile at Mr. Salvatore standing beside my car. "Mr. Salvatore, fancy seeing you here."

"I thought you two were going for a walk."

"We did," I tell him. He raises his eyebrows at me. "Well, we walked to the car and then we kind of, umm, followed you."

"I know. We clocked you as soon as you pulled away from the curb." Again, he raises his eyebrows at me.

"So much for being an expert," JJ unhelpfully utters from the back.

"Luckily for you," Mr. Salvatore says, "while we were driving here, I decided that you two being here will be good. Tyler is going to be scared and seeing a familiar face will be just what he needs. He knows me, but I will be otherwise detained once we bust in there."

Evie turns to open her door. "Not so fast," he growls. "You two are not going into that building until Declan gives you the all clear."

"You can't go in alone," she pleads with her father.

"I'm not," he confidently states just as a white van pulls up, followed by two more. The back doors open and several men in black Kevlar file out.

"Holy shit," Lexi gasps, "who are they?"

"Reinforcements," Mr. Salvatore informs us. "Now, I mean it, stay here until Declan says it's safe to enter."

We all nod in agreement. Now that I'm seeing how everything is playing out, I agree staying here is the right thing to do. Without uttering another word, he turns on his heel and walks over to the group of men. It's like watching a scene in an action movie. One minute the street is full of Kevlar-clad men and the next, they disperse like lemmings and it's all go.

Sitting in the car, we wait and watch.

Seconds later, there's a loud bang as they kick down the doors on the abandoned warehouse next to the pawn shop. When I hear a gunshot, without thinking, I throw open my door and race across the street. Declan wraps his arms around me. "It's not safe."

"Let me go," I hiss through clenched teeth as I struggle trying get free. I'm a muscly guy but Declan is just as muscly. He's trained for this and he effortlessly holds me back. Then from the corner of my eye, I see a brown-haired angel run by. It takes a few seconds for my mind to catch up and then I realize, it's Evie. She races into the building without a backward glance, just as I shout, "Evie."

No surprises, she ignores me. She's on a mission and when Declan realizes Evie just slipped past him, he utters, "Fuck." He lets me go and together we race into the building.

My eyes dart around the dark building and I come to a stop when I see dead bodies scattered across the floor. In the middle of the room, Mr. Salvatore has Klaus on his knees with a gun pointed to his head.

"Where's my grandson?"

"I'll never tell," Klaus says with a laugh, earning himself a pistol-whip to the side of his head.

Evie marches up to him, "Where's my son?" she hisses before slapping him across the face. The sound echoes around the empty warehouse. *She really is like her sister.*

"You're a whore just like your sister was," Klaus sneers at her.

"Don't talk about my sister. You have no right."

He laughs and then he leers up at Evie, "I'm going to enjoy killing you ... just like I killed her."

"You ... you killed her?" Evie shakily questions.

"I did, the bitch hid my son from me. She needed to pay."

"He's not yours," Evie spits at him. "Miller is his father. We have the DNA tests to prove it."

"You're lying," he hisses.

"Why would I lie?" she asks him. "I know you want a son, but Tyler is not him. Please," she begs, "give me my son back."

Just as she says that, a small voice sings out, "Moooommy." All eyes look around, then we hear a little, "I'm up here."

All heads lift up toward the second floor where the voice came from and when I see his little head appear in my line of sight, my heart starts beating again.

"Tyler," Evie shouts, her voice filled with relief.

My gaze quickly looks over him and, from what I can see, he seems to be unharmed, thankfully. Movement in the corner of my eye has my head turning and just as I look to the asshole who took my son, the asshole in question elbows Mr. Salvatore in the ribs. He gasps from the impact, allowing Klaus to lunge for the gun in his hand. With another hit to the ribs, Mr. Salvatore doubles over, allowing Klaus to steal the gun from him.

In slow motion, I stand here and watch as he lifts his arms, raises the firearm, and with a sinister sneer on his face, he pulls the trigger.

50

EVIE

HEARING Tyler's little voice was music to my ears.

My head snapped in the direction I thought it came from, but I couldn't see him. Spinning in a circle, I glance around the dark building and then I hear him utter, "I'm up here."

Lifting my head, relief slams into me when I see him up on a landing with one of Dad's guys behind him. He waves at me excitedly and I quickly wave back. Turning around, I see a set of stairs and I take off toward them. I've only taken a few steps when there's a loud bang and suddenly my body is falling, and with a crash, I land on the dirty dusty floor with a thud. My body bounces from the inertia and there's a burning sensation tearing through my abdomen.

Everything around me is muffled as I try to focus, but my vision is blurred. A shadow appears beside me but before it comes into focus, everything goes black.

My body hurts, but at the same time it feels numb and I feel like I'm floating. I can hear voices but everything is inaudible. Vaguely I make out the words, "missed vital organs," "recovery," and "blood loss," but none of that makes sense. I try to open my eyes but there's a weight holding them down. Then I feel a pressure on my hand and a whispered, "Please wake up, baby. Tyler and I need you."

"I'm here," I shout, but my voice just echoes in my head.

That's when I realize I'm unconscious, but why?

The last thing I remember is racing toward the stairs to reach Tyler, but then it's blank. A bright light flicks in my eyes and holy blindness, Batman. As quickly as the light appeared, it dims and when I refocus my vision, I see Selene.

"Am I dead?" I ask my dead sister. She shakes her head and smiles at me. "Where am I?"

"Not here and not there," she cryptically says.

"Ghost, or whatever you are, you are just as annoying as when you were alive you."

"Love you too, Sis, but you need to go back. They both need you."

Shaking my head, my eyes well with tears. "Miller doesn't want me because I kept your secrets."

"He loves you, Eves. He loves you like Dad loves Mom, and a love like that will survive this bump. Plus, Tyler wants the two of you to be happy together."

"How are you okay with me hooking up with your ex-boyfriend?"

"Because he was never my one true love, I wasn't destined for that."

"Yes—"

"No." She shakes her head. "I was a horrible human being. I cheated on my boyfriend with a married man. The only good thing I did in my life was have Tyler and leave him with you. You're a great mom, Eves, and you will be an even better wife. Now go, go back to your boys."

"I don't want to leave you," I tell her.

"I'll be fine. Seeing you and him happy is everything I need. I love you to infinity, Eves. Now, go."

With that, she disappears into the void. My eyes fly open and I immediately close my eyes again due to the brightness in the room. "Eves," Miller says, "stay with me, baby."

Blinking my eyes open, they adjust to the brightness and I manage to croak out, "I ... I'm here."

"Thank fuck," he emphatically states, pressing a kiss to my knuckles.

Our eyes lock and we silently stare at one another. As we gaze at one another, I realize we will be okay, and I find myself smiling that I didn't lose him after all. Opening my mouth, I go to speak but nothing comes out. "Throat. Dry," I croak.

Nodding, he lets go of my hand, stands up, and he fills up a cup of water for me. He pops a straw in and carefully brings it to my lips. Wrapping my lips around the straw, I take a sip. Followed by another and another. Never has a drink felt or tasted so good.

"Not too much or you'll be sick." He pulls the cup away and I glare at him. "Do you really want to vomit when you've just been shot?"

My brows scrunch in confusion, "I ... I got shot?"

"What do you remember?"

"I remember being at the warehouse and Tyler calling

out, and then nothing." Reaching over, I grab his arm. "Please tell me he's okay."

He nods and seeing his head bob up and down, relief slams into me. "He's with my mom and your mom getting ice cream."

"How ... how long have I been out?"

"Two days."

"Two days," I screech, wincing in pain at the ache in my throat from my sudden wail. "What the hell happened to me?"

"You were shot in the back by Van der Cunt when you tried to get to Tyler. The bullet went straight through and, miraculously, it didn't hit anything major. The doctors said your body went into shock and you'd wake up when you were ready."

Nodding, I let go of his hand because I'm not sure he wants me due to the lies I told and the secrets I kept. Yes, he seemed relieved when I woke up but relief and wanting me are two very different emotions. Shocking me, he grabs my hand again and laces our fingers together. Looking down at our clasped hands, I lift my gaze back to him. "I'm sorry for what I said to you when Tyler was missing."

"I'm sorry for keeping who you were from him."

"It's okay. I've had time to process while you were sleeping. Seeing how crazy Van der Cunt was, I can understand why you did what you did. And I can't fault you for keeping Selene's secrets."

"She came to me," I tell him.

"Huh?"

"When I was unconscious, she appeared and told me to go back to my boys."

"Well, I thank her for sending you home because I haven't had enough time with you."

"You still want me?"

"I will always want you, Eves. Almost losing you made me realize that life's too short to hold grudges. You and Tyler are my family, and families sometimes fight. Now, we put all of that behind us and we focus on the future."

"Are you sure? Because you said some pretty horrible things."

"I'm sure, and I'm so, so sorry for what I said. Can I blame it on fear?"

"Let's go with that, but I fucking hope nothing like that ever happens again."

"You and me both, but when you think about it, I'm a man. I will no doubt do something stupid down the road, and when I do, I hope you forgive me like I've forgiven you."

"Loving someone means forgiving them, so I love you and I forgive you."

"And I love you and I forgive you too, but if you ever get shot again, just don't."

"Duly noted," I tell him. "Now, do you think I can have a kiss? I hear kisses are good for gunshot wounds."

"Is that so?"

"Mmmhmpf." I nod. "After all, I am a doctor."

"Well, I guess I better follow medical advice."

He bends down and presses his lips to mine. As soon as I feel his against mine, everything feels right in the world. I'm on cloud nine right now because Tyler is safe and Miller is mine again.

...two months later

"HAPPY BIRTHDAY TO YOU," we all sing to Tyler as he and his friends stand around his cake.

Our little man turned six today and we're at his favorite place, the pool, for another pool party.

"Hip-hip hooray," we all cheer as he puffs out his little cheeks and blows out his candles.

"Don't forget to make a wish," JJ sings out.

"I wish for a baby brother," he tells everyone.

"They need to get married first," someone in the back calls out.

"What's married?" Tyler asks.

"Well," I tell him, crouching down to his height. "When two people love one another unconditionally, they want to share their love with their friends and live happily ever after."

"Like Nanna and Poppy?" he asks.

"Just like Nanna and Poppy." Then I think of my parents and get sad as I think that my dad never got to be a grandparent, but Mom makes up for his absence. She fell into the meemaw role like a duck to water.

Now that everyone knows who Tyler really is, they spoil him rotten. We've all decided, for now, we will let him believe Eves is his mom but when he's older, we will explain about Selene and who she really is. For now, his aunt Selene is in heaven with Pop Pop, watching over all of us.

With the cake cut and the kids all devouring it, I walk over to my girlfriend—I love saying that—and swipe my finger through the icing on her slice. "Hey," she scoffs.

"Sorry," I playfully tell her, as I suck on the tip of my finger. Her eyes dilate and she focuses on my finger in my mouth. Everything is highly sexualized with us at the moment, as we haven't had sex-sex since she was shot. There's been lots of oral but no official sex.

"More like sorry, not sorry."

"Same-same but regardless, you love me."

"Yes, yes I do."

The last two months since Tyler was kidnapped and Eves was shot have been crazy. The playoffs had just started when the shit hit the fan, the Crushers were at the top of the ladder. There was a chance I'd be winning the Cup with them in my first season but, like always, my family comes first and I chose to miss a few games to be with Tyler and Eves. After a week with them, she told me I was hovering—can you blame me? She demanded I start playing again. The team needed me more than they did and she assured me they would be fine.

Leaving them was hard but the team, who are my second family, rallied around and made it bearable, and we ended up winning the Cup. It was a career highlight. But I have to say, coming home each evening to Evie and Tyler, there's nothing like that.

We made our living arrangements official this past weekend with the three of us officially moving in together. We'd been spreading our time between the two apartments and when we got wind of an amazing apartment in the building becoming available, we swooped in and scooped it up.

I'd just secured a lucrative deal with *BodyArmor,* and with the endorsement monies, we decided to splurge and buy it.

Evie and I are now the proud owners of an apartment with unobstructed views of the city and the river, in the building we both fell in love with. We can watch the sunset every day from every room, and I cannot wait to christen each and every window in our townhouse in the sky. *WINK WINK*

"You're good at explaining things to him," she tells me after a brief silence. Then she laughs. "Remember when he asked where babies come from?"

"I never want to have to go through that again."

"Hey, I had to talk to him and Cate about penises and vaginas, you got off easy."

"Ugh, this parenting thing is tough."

"It is, but I wouldn't want to parent him with anyone else. You're a great dad, Miller."

"And you're a great mom," I tell her.

Placing her in front of me, I pull her back to my front and I slide my hands around her waist, resting them on her stomach. She covers my hands and leans back into me, and together we happily watch her dad in the pool with the kids, throwing them up into the air.

Mr. Salvatore as a grandfather is something I never thought I would see. When he's with the kids, there's no inkling that he's this big bad mafia guy. Speaking of mafia guys, Klaus Van der Cunt is now swimming with the fishes and his daughter, Annika, is the new head of the family. The first thing she did? Change the family name. She decided to take on her mother's maiden name of Gambino, so she can start over fresh. Seems Van der Cunt made a name for himself, and not in a good way. There's a lot of unrest within the Van—Gambino's now, but Mr. Salvatore is guiding Annika but she really doesn't need it. She's surprising everyone with how well she's doing, proving to her father that even though she's a woman in a man's world, she's just as tough and ruthless. If her dad wasn't such a misogynistic dick, he'd be proud of what his daughter is achieving.

Word on the street is anyone who was involved in Tyler's kidnapping has been "dealt with." According to Cass, it means they're now sleeping with the fishes.

Later that evening, I'm lying in bed gazing out the window, the city lights below illuminating the room, when a throat clears from beside me. Turning my head, my eyes bug out at the vision before me. Standing in the doorway to the en suite is an angel. Evie is dressed in a virginal white teddy. Her chocolate brown locks hang loosely around her shoulders. Her knee is bent and she's leaning against the doorframe in a pose that reminds me of when we fucked against the windows in her place last year.

"Fuck me," I pant.

"That's the plan," she seductively purrs.

"Are you sure?" She nods. "The doctor gave you the all

clear?" Again, she nods. "And by doctor, I mean *your* doctor, not *you* doctor."

"Dr. Aves gave me the all clear earlier this week."

"Fucking busy lives," I hiss. "Get over here," I command.

Pushing off the doorframe, she pads across the carpet and comes to a stop before me. Placing my hand on her leg, I gently run it up and under her teddy, squeezing her G-string-clad ass. "Your ass is delectable."

"As is yours, but I don't want you anywhere near my ass. We've had the conversation before. Asses are a one way passage and that's—"

"Not in ... even though you fucking love it when I press my finger there."

"Do not," she refutes, but we both know she loves it when I do. However, I'm man enough to admit, there's a difference between a finger and my dick, so I respect her wishes.

"Luckily for you, it's not your ass I want. It's been far too long since I've been balls deep inside of you."

"You have such a way with words."

"Why thank you," I tell her. "Why don't you lose the G-string but keep the teddy? It's sexy as fuck."

"And why would I do that?"

"Because I'm going to fuck you hard and fast. Then, I'm going to worship your body from head to toe, and then I'm going to make love to you."

"Glad to hear we're on the same page, but I propose an amendment."

"What would that be?"

"You need to get naked."

"Done."

Standing up, she takes a step back and watches as I push down my sweats, leaving me naked before her. With her eyes locked on mine, she hooks her fingers into the string of her thong and, ever so slowly, she peels the lace down her legs, kicking them to the side. She lifts the bottom of her teddy, baring herself to me. "You shaved?"

"I got a wax yesterday."

"You do love me," I tease her.

"I very much do love you, now, sit down on the edge of the bed so I can ride you hard and fast."

"Very well," I agree.

Dropping to the edge of the bed, I lean back on one arm and with the other, I stroke my cock. "Mine," she growls.

"Have at it then."

She steps toward me and straddles me; the head of my dick slides effortlessly through her slit. "Fuck, babe, you're soaked."

"Only for you," she tells me. "Now shut up and kiss me."

"Yes, ma'am," I tell her and before she can yell at me for calling her ma'am, I cover her mouth with mine and kiss her. Gripping her hips, I lift her up and line the head of my dick with her opening. Breaking the kiss, I stare deep into her eyes and watch her as I slam her down onto my shaft.

"Yes," she shouts as I seat her on me, our groins pressing together. Thankfully Tyler's room is at the other end of the apartment. I don't need to be explaining to him what I'm doing to his mommy.

She places her hands on my shoulders and she begins to ride me.

"I've missed this," I groan as she picks up her speed.

"Yes. Yes. Yes," she pants. Her eyes are closed and from the blissed out look on her face, I can tell she's in heaven right now.

"That's it," I voice, "ride me, baby. Fuck me harder."

"Yes," she mewls again and then she demands, "Suck my tits."

"Yes—"

"You call me ma'am one more time and I'm going to jump off, punch you in the dick, then I'll finish myself off, and leave you hanging."

"No need to be vicious ... ma'am." Before she can climb off of me, I stand up. Cupping her ass in my palms and, like clockwork, she wraps her legs around me as I make my way over to the windows. Pressing her back up against the glass, I lean down and suck on her tits through the lace of her teddy.

"Miller," she moans my name in that way that has my balls tingling and ready to explode.

"You need to come so I can come," I tell her.

"You know what to do," she reminds me.

Smirking against her tits, I slip my hand between us and press down on her clit. At the same time, I suck and gently bite down on her nipple. Her head drops back, her walls tighten around my dick, and then I feel it. She explodes, her juices pour out of her as her body locks and tenses as she comes, moaning my name. Feeling her fall apart has me coming too. Grunting, I empty myself deep inside of her.

"Fuck," she pants.

"That we did," I confirm.

Letting her down, I grip her cheeks in my palms and kiss her. Then I spin her around, her front to my back, and hold her to me. She takes my hands and, together, we rest them on her stomach as she presses her ass into my semi-hard dick. He twitches back to life and it amazes me how I can be ready to go again so soon after coming, but when it comes to Evie Salvatore and fucking her, just call me the Energizer Bunny because I can keep going and going and going.

"I love you to infinity," she murmurs.

"I love you to infinity too."

Smiling to myself, I get a vision of Evie and I standing here, her with a swollen stomach and my ring on her finger. Maybe Tyler will get his birthday wish sooner rather than later after all because I want to make that vision a reality.

52
EVIE

WALKING into the apartment after returning from the gym, I'm all sweaty and gross but when I see Miller and Tyler together in the living room, I stop and watch the two of them. They have such a good relationship, and I'm so glad my secrets didn't ruin that for them.

"What are you two up to?" I ask.

"Nothing," Tyler quickly says, looking sheepish.

"Smooth, dude, smooth," Miller teases him. "What Tyler was supposed to say is nothing for you to worry about. How was your workout?"

"Good, it feels great to be back in the gym."

"You aren't overdoing it?" he asks, concern laces his words.

"No, I'm not and stop babying me. I'm fine and for once when I say fine, I mean it. Life is good. I'm good."

"Well," he says, walking over to me, "it's about to get better because Tyler and I are taking you out."

"You are?"

"We are," Tyler excitedly squeals, jumping up and down on the spot.

"You two are up to something, aren't you?"

"No." Tyler giggles, before racing up the stairs to his room to do who knows what.

Miller pulls me into his arms. "What are you two concocting?" I ask again.

"It's guy stuff."

"I hate when you two gang up on me like that."

"You'd be bored so you're not missing much. Now, go shower. We leave in an hour. Dress nice."

"I always dress nice."

"Babe, you could be wearing a potato sack and I'd still think you're gorgeous, but for tonight, please dress—"

"Nice," I interrupt, earning myself a nod.

"If you're good, I'll join you in the shower." He waggles his eyebrows at me.

"If you want me to be ready within an hour, then I suggest you don't because after the other night, I'm feeling very, very frisky."

"Rain check?" he suggests.

"Tell me when and where and I'll be there ... naked and ready to rumble." Placing a quick kiss on his lips, I head up the stairs and into the master suite to change for my secret dinner date with my two favorite men.

Forty minutes later, I walk downstairs and when "Infinity" by Jaymes Young begins to play. I lift my head and my eyes widen as I take in the scene before me. The downstairs of our apartment has been turned into a romantic wonderland. Fairy lights dangle down in every window ... and that's a lot since all three sides of the lower level are windows. There are tea light candles, fairy light trees, and vases full of lights all over the place. Standing in the middle of the room, grinning like a carnival clown, with a bunch of white lilies is Tyler.

Walking down the last few steps, I make my way over to my son and crouch down to his height. "These are for you, Mommy." He hands me my flowers and presses a kiss to my cheek, just like Miller does. Tyler leans around me. "Did I do it right?"

From behind me, I hear Miller chuckle. "You were perfect."

Standing up, I spin around in the direction I heard Miller's voice come from and when I find him, my eyes widen once again and my mouth drops open. Down on bended knee is Miller. Like a moth drawn to the flame, I float, yes, I float over to him.

Glancing down at the man who has owned my heart since he was a teenager, I smile when I see, grasped in his fingers, is a diamond ring. And not just any diamond ring, he has Nonna Salvatore's ring. Covering my mouth, I drop down to my knees in front of him. "Evie Salvatore, you are the most amazing woman I have ever met. Your heart is as big as Doucheman's ego." I chuckle at that. "Your love has no end and everyone you come across is enthralled by you. And you're hot, so fucking hot." He pokes his head around me to Tyler. "Sorry, Buddy, I'll pop a quarter into the jar when this is done." Again, I chuckle. "You're the yin to my yang. The peanut butter to my jelly. I cannot imagine my life without you. I want to grow old and wrinkly with you, but most of all, I want to be able to puck you against the windows until I can no longer get it up. You're it for me, Evie Salvatore, and I want you to be my wife. My partner. You're already my everything, so wife is the next best thing. So, what do you say, will you marry me?"

My head bobs and the movement caused the tears

welling in my eyes to streak down my cheeks. "Yes, Miller, yes."

He slides Nonna Salvatore's ring onto my finger, then he grips my cheeks and kisses me. This kiss is the best kiss Miller and I have ever had. It's as if slipping that ring onto my finger was the missing piece of us.

A chorus of cheers erupt and when I turn, behind me I see all our friends and family standing there. "How?"

"We're sneaky," Tyler singsongs, grinning brightly. "Can I tell her what's next?" he excitedly asks Miller.

"There's more?"

"I hope I didn't overstep the boundary, but I was thinking we could also get married?"

"Now?" I question and he nods. "Really?" Again, he nods and then I find myself nodding. "Okay, let's do it. Let's get hitched."

53

MILLER

THANK FUCK she said yes and agreed to get married tonight, otherwise all my planning would have been for nothing. I know getting married so soon is crazy but when you know, you know. After what we've been through, I realized life is too short to wait, and I don't want to miss a minute without having Evie as my wife.

As soon as she agreed, her mom, Lexi, Chels, Margot, and Wren, who flew back just for this, whisk her upstairs to the spare bedroom where her mom has a dress hidden away. Sophie really stepped up helping me with all of this. She was monumental in getting everything organized, and I really hit the mother-in-law jackpot when it comes to her.

"You ready?" Mom asks, straightening my tie as I stand beneath the altar we had brought in.

"I am, so, so ready." Swallowing deeply, my eyes flick to the stairs, like they have every thirty seconds, looking for my wife-to-be.

"You're going to wear your eyes out if you keep looking at the stairs."

I laugh. "I know. I just want to be married."

"Your father would be so proud of you. You've grown into a wonderful young man. You're a fantastic dad and I have no doubt, you'll be an amazing husband too."

"I had great role models." She smiles, then I add, "I wish he was here."

"He is. He's always around for the special occasions because I can feel him in here." She presses on her chest. Pulling her in for a hug, she sniffles into my chest. "I love you, Miller."

"I love you too, Mom."

"It's showtime," Lexi sings out from the top of the stairs. Hearing those words causes nerves to course through my veins.

"You've got this, Miller," Mom assures, sensing my impending nerves. She gives me one last hug and then she takes her seat next to Evie's mom. I decided not to have a his side or her side because after this, we will all be one big happy family.

A little hand tugs on my hand and when I look down, I smile at my son. "What's up, Buddy?"

"I need to go pee pee."

"Your timing is impeccable."

Taking his hand, together we walk down the makeshift aisle, earning concerned looks from everyone currently taking their seats. "I'm not running, just a pee break."

A chorus of "phews" echoes around the room and I shake my head because nothing will stop me from marrying Evie today. Nothing.

Tyler quickly uses the toilet and then begins to wash his hands, singing the washy-washy song. Once his hands are all sparkly clean, he and I return to the top of the aisle and side by side, we wait for Evie to arrive.

"The Wedding March" begins to play and everyone

stands up. Taking a deep breath, I focus on the stairs and when I see her foot, I nearly come in my pants. Who knew a strappy sparkly heel could be so sexy? With each step she descends, more and more of her comes into view. If I thought I was going to pop at the sight of her foot, when I see the complete picture, it's game-fucking-over. I have no fucking clue what the style of dress she's wearing is called, but I do know it's perfect. It hugs her curves, highlights her tits, and makes her look like an angel. "Fuck me," I whisper, but my son's supersonic hearing hears and he outstretches his hand.

"Later," I murmur, my eyes locked on Evie and her dad.

After what feels like eleventy-billion light-years, Evie is finally standing before me. She turns her attention to Tyler. "You look dapper."

"That'll be a quarter," he says, causing everyone to laugh.

"Dapper isn't a swear word, it means handsome."

"Ohh," he sadly pouts, tucking his hand into his pocket.

Evie leans down and kisses him on the cheek. Then she turns her attention to me. Everything and everyone else in the room fades into the background and all I see is Evie. "You're breathtaking," I tell her as I take her hands in mine.

"You're not so bad yourself," she says with a wink. "Shall we?"

"Hell yes, we shall."

Stepping in front of the officiant, she begins.

The ceremony passes by in a blur. I manage to speak when needed and I thank the heavens I went with tradi-tional vows because words are hard right now. It's time for the rings and I turn to Tyler, who has been guarding them since I picked them up yesterday. Reaching into his pocket, he pulls them out and drops one. "Shit," he hisses.

Evie's and my eyes widen and I can't help it. I hold my

hand out and inform him, "That'll be a quarter." This causes everyone to laugh but then his little eyes fill with tears.

"I don't have one."

"You've got ten million of them," JJ says, earning himself a dig in the ribs from Lexi.

"Ohh, yeah," he says. He jumps off the altar and runs down the aisle. Then we hear the sound of a million coins hitting the floor, followed by a "Puck me."

"Hey," Chelsea pipes up, "he gets that from me."

Once again, everyone chuckles and then Tyler races back down the aisle and hands me a quarter before whispering, "I made a mess but I'll clean it later."

"Okay," I tell him, ruffling his hair. Then I look back at my almost wife. "Let's finish this."

Handing the rings to the officiant, she does her thing, and a few minutes later, she declares us husband and wife. Gripping my wife's—I love saying that—cheeks in my palms, I slam my lips to hers and kiss her. Pushing my tongue into her mouth, I give her the best kiss of her life before I dip her backward, causing her to squeal and giggle.

Today is the happiest day of my life, and I owe it all to the woman who just agreed to marry me—until death do us part—and my son. Never in my wildest dreams did I imagine that at the age of twenty-five would I have a six-year-old son or be married, but here I am and I could not be happier.

EPILOGUE - EVIE

"UGH," I groan, wiping my mouth on the wet washcloth Miller just handed me. "This morning sickness thing is bull-shit," I complain to my husband. It's nine o'clock in the evening and I'm still throwing up. Whoever called it morning sickness is a dick because I throw up at any time of the day.

"I'm sorry, baby," Miller says from next to me, rubbing my back.

"This is all your fault," I hiss at him.

"Babe, it takes two to tango."

"Yes, it does, but it only took one of your asshole sperms to find my egg and do this to me, ergo, your fault."

"Let's agree to disagree," he offers. "Now, what can I get you?"

"A bullet," I plead.

"Anything but that."

"I hate you." I snicker as I push myself upright.

"No, you don't. You love me and my super sperm."

Seriously, I swear I stopped the pill and the next time

we had sex, boom, I was pregnant. We didn't even get to have fun sexy times making this baby. Well, we did 'cause sex with Miller is always fun and sexy but, right now, the thought of his dick anywhere near me has me wanting to chop it off. Why women go back and do this multiple times, I will never know.

Scooping me up into his arms, he carries me into our bedroom and gently places me down on the mattress. Then he climbs in behind me and pulls me into him, spooning. This is my favorite way to go to sleep. Ever since we got married and he's home, this is how we drift off but now there's a new routine. Miller rests his hand on my still flat stomach and murmurs, "Goodnight, baby. Good night, baby momma."

And I always reply with a "Good night, Daddy," before I blissfully drift off to sleep ... until the next bout of any-time-of-the-fucking-day sickness decides to strike.

"Is Mommy okay?" I hear Tyler ask Miller as I reach the bottom of the stairs.

"Yeah, she's okay, she's just—"

"Pregnant," I interrupt. Padding across the room, I take a seat at the counter next to Tyler.

"Pregnant means there's a baby in your tummy, right?" I nod. "Does this mean I'm getting a baby brother?"

"It could be a girl," I remind him.

"Nope, no girls. Girls are gross."

"Hey, I'm a girl."

"No," he shakes his head, "you're my mom."

Looking over to Miller, I furrow my brow. "Should you or I break it to him that moms are girls and dads are boys?"

"I feel like that's your department, plus, I gotta run. I've got to get to the stadium."

"You're lucky you have a game to get to."

"Ohhh, yeah, or what?" He slides his hands around my waist and pulls me into his muscular chest.

"Well, I don't know, but something."

"Ohhh," he teases. "I'm quaking in my boots but, for what it's worth, you're a girl I love."

Spinning around to face him, I drape my arms over his shoulders. "Well, Miller Wentworth, you're my number one crush," I tell my gorgeous husband.

"Well, you, Evie Wentworth, are my number one period. Now shut up and give your baby daddy a kiss before I go to work."

Removing my hands from his shoulders, I grip my husband's cheeks and kiss him with everything I have. No longer do I pucking hate that I've always loved him. Now, I love him with everything I have, and I always will. I can't wait for this next adventure with my boys ... and hopefully a baby girl—sorry, Tyler—Mommy needs a little princess to even up things around here.

THE END!

Want to know more about Kennedy and Rick? You can read their story in the final pucking novel, I Pucking Hate To Want Your Love. **

BLURB

I swore I'd never give my heart to anyone again.
Then Kennedy Parsons walked into my life when I was barely holding it together.
She's beautiful, kind, and somehow connects with my kids when they need it most. But none of that matters—my heart still belongs to my late wife.
Or so I thought.
The more time we spend together, the deeper she gets under my skin—just like *she* did.
I think I pucking love her.
But I've already lost once… and I don't think I can survive losing again.
I'm so pucking screwed.

**preorder date is a placeholder date … it will release sooner

I Pucking Hate That I Love You
I Pucking Hate That You Love Me
A Pucking Good Christmas
It's Pucking Fake
I Pucking Hate To Love You
I Pucking Hate That I've Always Loved You
I Pucking Hate To Want Your Love

Available now on Amazon and in paperback from all online retailers or direct from the author.

ACKNOWLEDGMENTS

These things never get any easier and after 50 books, yep Miller and Evie were book number fifty, that's still the case. I always forget someone so this is a blanket thank you to everyone I have crossed paths with in the last nine years. Next year is my 10th year pubaversay and I feel like I need to do something special to celebrate so watch this space.

Now, on with the acknowledgements...

Sophie; Miller and Evie, in particular, would not exist if you didn't bully me into a mafia book. While this isn't super mafia-ry. It was fun to dabble and now I cannot wait to write Annika's story ... which **WILL** be a standalone mafia romance.

Karen Hrdlicka from **Barren Acres Editing**; thank you for everything that you do for me. Fifty books together and we're still talking THAT <— sorry not sorry, is an achievement in itself. Here's to fifty more.

Margaret; thank you for checking all my I's are dotted, my T's are crossed and there's no extra e's or s's.

Renae from **R.L. Cover Designs**; thank you for brining Miller and the rest of the pucking boys to life.

Kristie from **Vanilla Lily;** thank you for the alternate cover. As I said seven books ago, as soon as I saw the set, I had to have it.

Lainey from **DS Promotions** and **all of the bloggers** and **readers;** thank you for helping me share Miller and Evie with the world.

My beta babes **Bec, Lana, Marg, Soph** and **Rhi;** I

would be lost without you ladies. You give me advice when I second guess everything and you helped to bring this story to life. Thank you from the bottom of my heart.

Troy, my husband, my everything. You really are awesome at what you do and you are an even better husband and father. Love you long-time dude.

To my munchkins, **Piper** and **Kade**. You two are my greatest achievement and I'm so lucky to have you both in my life. Love you long-time guys and I look forward to the day when you are forty and can finally read my books.

And finally, **you, my reader**. This book is a different genre for me but I have to say, it was fun branching out. I hope you enjoyed Evie and Miller as much as I enjoyed writing them.

Cheers,
Dana XoXoX

PLAYLIST

Supremacy - Muse
How Did You Love - Shinedown
I Just Wanna Lice - Good Charlotte
What I've Done - Linking Park
Duality - Slipknot
Pain - Jimmy Eat World
Crawling - Linkin Park
Iris - Natalie Taylor
Uprising - Muse
Feel - Robbie Williams
Somebody Told Me - The Killers
Welcome to the Black Parade - My Chemical Romance
Somewhere I Belong - Linkin Park
Snuff (LIVE) - Corey Taylor
(Baby I've Got You) On My Mind - Powderfinger
Silence - Marshmallow, Khalid
Through Glass - Stone Sour
The Middle East Jimmy Eat World
Snuff - Slipknot
Treat You Better - Shawn Mendes

Best of You - Foo Fighters
Numb - Linkin Park
Savior - Rise Against
In Too Deep - Sum 41
#1 Crush - Garbage
It Ain't Me - Kygo, Selena Gomez
Infinity - Jaymes Young
I Miss You - blink-182
Scars - Papa Roach
Never Too Late - The Days Grace
Don't You (Forget About Me) - Simple Minds
In the End - Linkin Park
BURN IT DOWN - Linkin Park
Falling Down - Lil Peep, XXXTENTACION
Mockingbird - Eminem, Rhianna
Last Resort - Paper Roach
When You Walk in the Room - Paul Carrack
We Belong - Pat Benatar
Can't Fight This Feeling - REO Speedwagon

This playlist can be found on Spotify.

STAND ALONES

Antecedent

Doc Steel

Oops

Out of Nowhere

Deck...the Balls

Secrets and Sunrises

Fractured

The Christmas Ornament

Finding You

Before the Ashes

After the Ashes

Love Me Like You Do

Never Let Me Go

Seven Nights

Seven Kisses

Off the Books

Always in the Cards

Faking it with the Billionaire

Making it with the Billionaire

Love in the Club

Falling for a Knight

Daiquiri Dreams

PUCKING LOVE SERIES

I Pucking Hate That I Love You

A Pucking Good Christmas

I Pucking Hate That You Love Me

It's Pucking Fake

I Pucking Hate To Love You

A Not So Pucking Secret

I Pucking Hate That I've Always Loved You

I Pucking Hate To Want Your Love ... coming 2026

FALLING NOVELS

These men make it hard not to fall for them

Falling for Dr. Kelly

Falling for Dr. Knight

Falling for Agent Cox

Falling for Agent Cruz

Falling: The Complete Collection

LORDS OF CRESTWOOD PREP

Co-write with Tara Lee

Thatcher

Reign

Hendrix

Saint

ABOUT THE AUTHOR

DL Gallie is from Queensland, Australia, but she's lived in many different places all over the world, including the UK and Canada. She currently resides in Central Queensland with her husband and two munchkins. She and her husband have been together since she was sixteen, and  although they drive each other crazy at times, she couldn't imagine her life without him.

Shortly after her son was born, DL began reading again. With encouragement from her husband, she picked up the pen and started writing, and now the voices in her head won't shut up.

DL enjoys listening to music, drinking white wine in the summer, red wine in the winter, and beer all year round. She's also never been known to turn down a cocktail, especially a margarita.

FACEBOOK ~ INSTAGRAM ~ BOOKBUB

GOODREADS ~ WEBSITE

dana@dlgallieauthor.com

Sign up to my newsletter